Faith, Hope, and Baseball

A novel

Jim Meisner Jr

IMMORTAL
WORKS

Immortal Works LLC
1505 Glenrose Drive
Salt Lake City, Utah 84104
Tel: (385) 202-0116

© 2020 Jim Meisner, Jr.
www.faithhopeandbaseball.com

Cover Art by Ashley Literski
http://strangedevotion.wixsite.com/strangedesigns

ISBN 978-1-7349046-3-5 (Paperback)
ASIN B0893MWY2S (Kindle Edition)

To Victoria Grace; this is for you.

Chapter 1

The radio carried the announcer's excited voice through the near-empty room where Jason Yoder stood, half-listening as he flicked invisible dust from his new hat before carefully putting it on.

"Baseball in October. It can only mean one thing— the World Series. This year the team had a date with destiny..."

Jason made final adjustments to his new clothes as a shadow filled the doorway. He fingered the metal circle in his pocket for reassurance.

"Are you ready?"

"Ya," he replied, but his mind had wandered from the present to what seemed like two lifetimes ago when he had listened to the same announcer on the same radio. Jason was so different now, and yet so much around him remained unchanged.

He glanced about the neat and tidy room, considered the unique odors, and thought of an early fall afternoon.

He remembered the dry, dead leaves glowing red and orange, illuminated by the sun. He recalled the endless expanse of prairie where the air stirred and then paused to play in the cornstalks for a few hundred acres. It chased itself across an immaculate farmyard, twisted into a tiny spiral, and softly pushed against the dust, drifting down through the slats of the wagon.

His memories had taken him back to a place where the air was thick with the sweet smell of new hay, and the wind played across his face: Harvest time in central Iowa, where the same scene played out again and again, year after year.

⚾

JASON DRAGGED HIS MUSCULAR, sweaty forearm across his equally damp forehead and reached for another hay bale. His young, powerful hands wrestled the bale onto the hook. He whistled sharply and pulled the other end of the rope like a church bell ringer. That part of the job usually fell to a horse or mule, but Jason found it easier to pull the rope himself after attaching the hook. Besides, he had the strength of a draft horse, and he was only seventeen. He watched the bale quickly rise to the small door of the barn's loft. A pair of gloved hands pulled the bale in, and moments later lowered the hook again.

On a nearby hay bale, a battered, battery-operated radio quietly broadcast a baseball game.

"—A real disappointment," the announcer intoned as though reading the obituary of a stranger. "The whole season was just a real disappointment. We can't blame Manager Skip Anderson; he did the best he could with what he had. The season started strong, but—" The announcer paused, and Jason stole a glance at the radio.

He stood on a flatbed horse-drawn wagon surrounded by a few remaining heavy bales of hay. The rolled sleeves of his blue shirt exposed his massive muscles, and the straw hat on his head kept the early afternoon sun from his face. His hair and his hat were the same color as the bales he lifted.

After muscling another bale onto the hook, his gloved hands pulled the rope, sending the bale up. He whistled again, and the hands pulled the bale again, released the hook, and lowered it carefully. The backbreaking process repeated as it had all morning and into the afternoon, human cogs in a manual production line.

"Dallas Jackson steps to the plate," the announcer continued. "—Called strike... At twenty games out of first place, there's no tomorrow for the Cubbies. There's the pitch. Swing and a miss. Strike two. The Cubs end the season with the worst team batting average in history. The pitch— Jackson nails it..."

Jason stopped his work, his attention turning to the radio.

"A line-drive, deep, deep, over the right-field fence. Home run!"

Jason reacted with a small, happy smile, but his Amish composure returned immediately. It wouldn't do to get emotional about a baseball game. He stole a glance toward the loft and silently resumed his task.

The stack of bales grew smaller as the game progressed.

"Giants lead six-four. Jennings at the plate now, hitting .125 for the season, a career-low— The pitch, he swings, ground ball to short. Fielded cleanly, and he's out at first."

Jason responded by moving the bales still faster.

"Two down. Whitehall steps up for the Cubs. The old saying is 'wait 'til next year,' but in this case, there's no reason to wait. Most of the players on the bench today will still be here on opening day next year. So we're facing another year just like this one."

Jason was nearly finished, moving faster than he had all day for the final two bales.

"The windup. The pitch. Swing and a miss. Whitehall is oh-for-four today. There's the pitch— he swings, ground ball to first. Walters steps on the bag, and that's the end of the ballgame. And thankfully, mercifully, the end of the season. Today—most of the season for that matter—was some of the worst baseball I've witnessed in forty years of broadcasting—"

Jason turned off the radio and disappeared into the barn to put it away. Moments later, he returned to the wagon and whistled a final time, the note slightly sharper than before.

"We're done, Onkel," he said to the empty air.

A large, muscular man leaned out of the loft door. Like the boy, he too wore a blue shirt and straw hat. But unlike the smooth-skinned young man, the older man wore a long beard—his upper lip shaved, his chin covered by untrimmed hair, with strands of gray woven into the black. He fished a handkerchief from the pocket of his black trousers as he removed his hat. Wiping his hatband with the handkerchief, he breathed a weary breath.

"Ist das alles dann, Jason?" Issac spoke thickly in his native tongue.

"Ya, Onkel."

"Doo vill gaya?"

"Ya, Onkel."

"Blayp haim fra tsooppa."

"Ya, Onkel, I'll be home before supper." With the boundless energy of youth, Jason removed his work gloves as he dashed into the barn. He emerged seconds later with a baseball glove and ball.

"Jason?"

"Ya, Onkel?" he replied, looking up at his uncle.

"Iss dess day beesbaul?"

"It's just a game, Onkel. After June, I won't play anymore," he answered, looking around. "May I go now, please? You'll tell Maam?"

"Ya. Gaya, gaya," the uncle said with a dismissive wave of his weathered hand.

The breeze returned as Jason ran across the closely trimmed yard. He slipped his glove onto his right hand as he ran down the dusty driveway and threw the scuffed, off-white ball high into the air.

Judging the baseball's trajectory, he rushed to catch it as it reached its apex and slowly began to fall.

A PRISTINE NEW baseball rolled slowly in rough, sun-dried hands. Manager Skip Anderson stopped long enough to look at the words printed in black block letters: NATIONAL LEAGUE BASEBALL ASSOCIATION.

He picked at the first 'N' with his thumbnail for a moment. Still in uniform, Skip stood with Bench Coach Dave Watson in the Cubs dugout, looking out at the empty green field.

"They don't give two shakes about me, the team, the fans, the game, or even themselves," he said.

"They give two shakes about themselves," Dave corrected. "Three, four shakes about themselves."

Skip looked at the ball. ATIONAL LEAGUE BASEBALL ASSOCIATION. He started picking at the first 'O' in ASSOCIATION, ignoring the interruption.

"They wouldn't sacrifice to advance the runner, because it would affect their own numbers," he said, before pausing to admire his handiwork. "Why do I even bother to signal?"

He scattered infinitesimal flecks of black ink as he rolled the ball in his hands.

His mind wandered from the field before him to fields of the past. So many fields across the years. So many baseballs. Tens of thousands, easily. A hundred thousand? Had he touched a hundred thousand baseballs? Maybe more. He felt the red stitches with his fingernails.

He'd had a good career as a player in the minors. Worked his way up quickly. The unexpected phone call that moved him from AA to the Show. He couldn't forget the feeling of that day if he tried. The dirt, the grass, the clouds themselves seemed different in a major league stadium. The locker room, the travel, the food, the clothes— everything was different. Better. The best. The best of everything. It was living a dream, day after day, year after year. A teenage dream unfolding in the daily life of a man, ball after ball, one bat at a time. A life measured in box scores.

His hands could still feel the double to right field that won them the pennant, the tingle in his fingers that took them to the World Series. The series loss haunted the rest of his playing career, and then overshadowed his coaching.

Like the forgotten words to a familiar song, a series ring eluded him. Haunted him. He could feel the absence and unfulfilled potential like a phantom pain of a severed limb.

A decade in the major leagues. Then another five years. The injuries got to be too much, too often, and the recovery took longer and longer each time. After each injury, he had to settle for a new level of healthy, knowing the previous performance level was gone forever.

Eventually, there was nothing minor about a minor sprain, especially when he was hitting .133 in August. The injuries, the travel, and the daily grind took all the fun out of the game, so after sixteen years, he hung up his glove for the last time. He had the self-respect to hobble away with dignity, rather than be chased from the field, desperate to hang on.

Every September since that same feeling slowly came over him like shadows before sunset.

He enjoyed managing more than he had expected. It went beyond staying in the game or on the field. He actually enjoyed watching a young man improve. Helping a swing become as good as it could be. He'd chuckle to himself to see the swagger return to a player as he overcame a slump and hit his way back into contention, pulling his career back from the brink, one single at a time.

And yet, the minors weren't much fun the second time around. They were worse in many ways. But the return to the Show was as good as it was the first time. The responsibilities were much, much greater, and more demanding than he expected, more exhausting than he could have imagined— but he enjoyed being back in the Show so much more. Perhaps because he was older, mature and seasoned. Perhaps because he knew, at his age, he had so little to lose. Winning was different, too. It was as though a little of each of the men was part of him every time they won. Losing wasn't so bad, and winning was better as a coach. He really was lucky.

His career as a manager felt like a long trudge back from the minors, made slower by lingering injuries. As he got older, long-forgotten pains reappeared without warning. The wrenching pain in his right knee appearing halfway up a flight of stairs would instantly carry him back to that sunny Sunday afternoon when his spike caught the bag as he slid into second. Arthritis in his knee reminded him every morning before breakfast of who he used to be, and who he had become.

Despite the aches and pains as his body slowly betrayed him, he remained in excellent shape. His square shoulders still communicated power, and his overall demeanor demanded attention. He was the living embodiment of a born leader.

This past season seemed to take it out of him. He felt as though he'd aged twice as much in half the time. He enjoyed the game, but he hated—hated to his core—when the men disrespected the game. Not a man in the clubhouse knew the name Yosh Kawano, and their disrespectful apathy drove him crazy.

By the end of such a draining season, he began to question his own dedication. His edge was off, and he wasn't sure how he'd get it back. For the first time in his baseball career, he was beginning to think he didn't care if he got it back or not.

"I hate losing," Skip said through clenched teeth. "I hate it."

"I know."

"I hate it, and it's like they don't care. What's the point of playing if you're not playing to win with every pitch? Every swing of the bat? I don't understand what's going on out there," he said, gesturing at the field. "Or in their heads," he said, tapping the ball against his temple.

"I know," Dave said again for emphasis.

"I give 'em the take sign, and they swing away like it's batting practice."

"Batting practice," Dave agreed. "They're just young and excited."

Skip searched for answers as he surveyed the vast green expanse of grass in front of him. The iconic green ivy four hundred feet away was beginning its quick change to dark red, orange, and brown. He looked down at the ball again and absentmindedly tossed it into the afternoon air.

"I'd give my right hand for someone young and disciplined."

"I'd give your left one for someone young and good," Dave quipped. "Our old players aren't getting any younger, and the young ones aren't getting any better. But, next year's another season."

"Those are the best the minor league has to offer? What a disaster." Skip shook his head. "What's the point of expanding the roster? Did you see anyone in the past month that you can't live without?"

"Nope."

"Neither did I. What a train wreck."

"Maybe a couple of players."

"Maybe. I'll tell you, Dave, for the first time in twenty-five years, I'm not looking forward to coming back," Skip said, his fingernails working the stitches of the ball.

"Thinking of hanging up your cleats a final time?" Dave asked as they left the dugout and started slowly walking across the field.

"I'm just not looking forward to next year," Skip said, shaking his head.

"Good thing you'll have a month off to think about it," Dave replied. "Four weeks from now, you'll be planning for next season. You and Annie heading to L.A. again?"

"Not this year. She wants us to go visit the Amish."

"What do you mean, 'the Amish?'" Dave asked.

"The Amish. Black suits. Beards. You know, the Amish."

"What do you mean 'visit?'" Dave asked, clearly still not understanding. "Do you...you know, know Amish people?"

"No. We're going to the towns where they live and look at them."

"Sounds like lots of fun," Dave muttered. "Maybe when you come back, we can sit here and watch the grass grow. Where are these Amish?"

"Iowa."

"I'm sorry, it sounded like you said 'Iowa'?"

"I did."

"There are Amish in Iowa?"

"So they say." Skip nodded. "We're leaving tomorrow. Driving. Annie says it'll help me take my mind off the team for a while."

"That's a good idea. Relax. Look at some corn, some Amish people. Four weeks from now, you'll be screaming for Arizona, a cold beer, and a slice of Buddy's pizza."

Skip scratched at the gray in his short sideburns.

"Four weeks," he said. "Another five months, and we'll be back in Mesa again, watching this bunch and a new batch of rookies." He looked around at the expanse of grass. The grounds crew was working on the infield dirt, and the cleaning crew was scattered across the stands. He thought of opening day. Dozens and dozens of opening days. For the first time, he didn't look forward to the next one.

"A new set of no-talent bums," he muttered to himself. "I can hardly wait."

Angrily, he threw the ball into the air. It hung at its apex in the clear blue sky like a rawhide planet before rolling over and falling back to Earth.

A BASEBALL DROPPED into Jason's glove, signaling the final out to retire the side.

He jogged from his position at third base toward his team's bench, the dugout of Kalona High School. The fall ball season gave players the opportunity to hone their skills, and Jason enjoyed every minute of it.

Despite wearing the same uniform as his teammates, Jason stood out. Nearly six inches taller than his next largest teammate, his uniform was baggy, and his bowl cut hairstyle was clearly different under his ball cap.

Jason stowed his glove and selected a bat as Coach Pate looked on. Jason stole a glance toward two young people near the crowded bleachers.

Thirteen-year-old Adam had his fists thrust deep into the pockets of his black pants. Short for his age, but comporting himself with a silent dignity, he looked like a miniature Amish church elder. His sister, seventeen-year-old Faith, stood next to him, a wooden basket in her hands. From beneath his large straw hat, Adam imperceptibly nodded, and Faith smiled shyly when Jason winked at them. As usual, they didn't move from their normal positions as the game progressed.

In the bottom of the final inning with a tied score, Kalona needed a win to continue their steady march toward the state championship. Jason slipped his helmet on before moving to the on-deck circle. He absentmindedly took a few practice swings as he watched the batter before him strike out on three pitches.

The three pitches from the relief pitcher weren't much, but they were enough, Jason thought. Despite seeing the pitcher for the first time, he quickly, easily, saw what he was looking for. Jason took a few full-speed practice swings as he stepped to the plate while his teammates shouted encouragement.

"Let's go, Jason," Coach Pate called from the dugout. "Nice and easy. Take your time." Despite his outwardly calm demeanor and reassuring words, the tension showed on his tanned face.

The pitcher delivered a strike down the center of the plate as Jason turned to watch it slap into the catcher's mitt. Fastball.

"Strike one," the umpire yelled.

Jason took a few half swings and watched the pitcher go into his windup. He's throwing it again, he thought.

The pitcher fired the ball and Jason drilled a line drive down the first baseline.

Running to first, with the play in front of him, Jason saw the ball roll down the line. He tagged first base on a wide arc and continued on to second. After sliding into the bag well ahead of the fielder's throw, he snapped to his feet in a small cloud of dust and looked to third hungrily.

"That-a-boy, Jason," Coach Pate yelled across the field, clapping. "That-a-boy."

Distracted by Jason's slide, the second baseman briefly took his eye off the ball and bobbled the throw from right field. Jason dropped his head and took off for third, his arms pumping furiously.

The crowd roared its approval as Jason dashed toward the base. Rushing, the second baseman fumbled the throw. Jason slid into the bag face first, hands outstretched above the dirt, several feet ahead of the ball.

"Heads up base running, Jason, heads up," Coach Pate said, clapping again.

Chest heaving from exertion and covered in dirt, Jason's eyes followed the ball as it finally found its way back to the pitcher. He shifted his gaze to Coach Pate, who was already flashing signs, his hands and fingers dancing across his chest and cap.

Leaning forward, hands on his knees for a moment's rest, Jason watched the pitcher pause before his windup. As the pitcher's right foot planted in the dirt, Jason shifted his weight and was already four steps toward stealing home before the batter, Jason Miller, could turn and square his shoulders to bunt.

At the plate, Jacob executed the bunt perfectly, the deadened ball dropping onto the grass and dribbling toward the first baseline. The pitcher and first baseman charged forward as Jason poured on the speed. The first baseman fielded the ball barehanded and fired home.

Jason surged and threw his body forward.

The catcher swung his glove and ball through empty air as Jason slid under the tag, his hand brushing the plate.

"Safe!" cried the umpire.

A cloud of dust slowly settled around Jason, the umpire, and the catcher as the team rushed onto the field. Players crowded around and slapped Jason on the back with enthusiastic words of encouragement. He smiled sheepishly, embarrassed by the attention and the compliments.

Smiling and clapping, Adam and Faith waved to Jason, but he didn't see them. He was busy being swept off the field by his excited teammates.

PHIL PATE WAS ALSO a veteran baseball man. Like nearly all professional ballplayers, he'd been an extraordinary high school player. Drafted out of high school, he'd chosen instead to accept one of the many college scholarships he had been offered. College play came easy for him, too. He set a school record in triples before the end of his sophomore year.

He turned pro at the end of his junior year of college, playing a few months of rookie ball before moving up to single A. Distinguishing himself on the field and at the plate, he ended his first professional season in AA. While it wasn't the level he hoped for— every rookie begins spring training dreaming about playing in the World Series that October— he was happy with his performance.

As dedicated to academics as he was to athletics, he continued his education a few classes at a time during the winter months. His second year as a professional athlete began at the AAA level. With each rehabbing major leaguer he played with or against, he was reminded that he was tantalizing close to the Bigs. He felt he was always one more base hit a week away from being called up. The feeling continued throughout the year until he was called up in September. He spent 32 days living the major league life but had fewer than a dozen at-bats.

The next year found him beginning the season at AAA, but spending days at a time at the major league level. His talent, work ethic, and willingness to play any position made him popular with the club manager. He eventually took to carrying an overnight bag wherever he went, to make it easier to respond to the sudden phone calls summoning him to rejoin the team.

He fell into the role of back-up to the back-up of injured starters. He was always happy to be with the ball club, but too many days were marked with uncertainty, doubt, and waning self-confidence as he rode the bench. He was called up again when the roster expanded in September but spent too much unsatisfying time in the dugout.

His fourth year was more frustrating than fun. He spent every week one more hit or two fewer outs away from a permanent position in the major league. Phil Pate spent the day of his college graduation going two for five. He stood on second, watching a new pitcher come lumbering in, and he seriously considered his options. He knew he had a decision to make in the coming months — did he want to keep bouncing between the major and minor leagues, or did he want to look for a job with his new degree and teaching certificate?

"You wanted to see me, sir?" Jason asked.

Coach Pate looked up from the papers he was grading. He imagined Jason modestly dressing in his closet, the air smelling of cleaning supplies. The cramped, dimly lit space crowded with the mop, buckets, brooms, and bleach.

"Yeah, Jason, come on in," he said, leaning back in his chair. "That was some fancy base running out there today."

"Did I read the signals wrong?" Jason asked, worry creasing his young face. "Was I not supposed to steal home?"

Coach Pate smiled. "Yes, boy, you were supposed to steal home," he assured him. "I gave you the signal. I'm talking about you getting to third. That was heads-up base running."

"Thank you, sir."

The older man stared intently at Jason's face, a practiced expression that somehow reflected both serenity and suspicion. "I guess you have a long walk home?" the coach finally asked.

"Yes, sir."

"You sure I can't give you a ride this afternoon?"

"Thank you, sir, but I would rather walk."

"Sure, I understand." Coach Pate stood and stepped from behind his desk. He started to walk Jason out but paused and put his arm on the boy's shoulder.

"One more thing—"

"Yes, sir?"

"I wish you'd think again about college—"

Jason had heard this before. "Yes, sir. I—"

"Don't just 'yes, sir' me, Jason," Coach Pate interrupted, frustration in his voice. "Listen here. I can help you get a baseball scholarship, maybe even a track scholarship. Let me get another Iowa State scout out here. Let them talk to you this time. You could get an education. Get a degree. Maybe in agriculture, come back here and help your family, your people. And you could keep playing ball."

"Thank you for your offer," Jason said softly, "but I am not expected to go to college."

"I know," Coach Pate continued, "but keep one thing in mind. I got that waiver from the state to let you play on this team because I recognized your talents. It'd be a shame that after I went to all that trouble, and after months of coaching, you'd just walk away at the end of the season."

"Yes, sir," Jason responded. And then he walked away.

A SMALL, excited group waited for the players outside the building—friends, family, and girlfriends, radiating the energy of the game, their eager voices quick and high.

Jason worked his way through the crowd, excited words and back slaps pouring down on him like a strong summer shower. Nodding as he approached Adam and Faith, the three shared wordless looks for a moment before ambling away.

They continued in silence along the sidewalk of the small city street, past small businesses and shops. A passing pickup honked, the back jammed with kids who called out to Jason and waved. Smiling sheepishly, he returned the wave and watched the truck disappear around the corner. Adam and Faith looked on in disbelief. Although his friendship with the English was allowed, Jason knew they didn't understand why the other kids were so excited. He simply shrugged, and they continued on in silence. Faith glanced up at Jason, but he shifted his gaze from her, his thoughts a dozen miles away.

As the three continued along a gravel road carved between two fields of browning Iowa corn, an Amish buggy appeared on the distant horizon.

"It's Aaron Ropp," Jason said in their native tongue, a regional variation of the Amish Dutch more like their Ohio cousins than their Pennsylvania ancestors.

"Where is he going, I wonder?" Faith said.

"I know where," Adam said, a sly smile curling around his eyes.

"Where?" Faith asked.

"He's rushing to watch a baseball game, maybe," Adam teased with a giggle.

They exchanged waves with the buggy driver as he passed.

"You played well today," Adam said.

"Thank you. I was very lucky."

Faith smiled. "You were also very good."

Jason was embarrassed. "Thank you, but my teammates played well, and they made it easier for me." He paused to return her smile. "Having you and Adam there also made it easier for me."

"Isn't it time to stop playing baseball?" Faith asked.

"We have just a few more games before we play West High. If we win, then we play the district games," Jason explained. "If we win again, we will play the state finals. I will be done in a few weeks."

"No," Faith said intently, as she stopped walking. Jason stopped to listen. "When will you stop playing games? When will you end your rumshpringa and join the Order? When will we..."

Each of them was poised to say more when they both turned to Adam. He, too, had stopped walking. He returned their stare, eagerly awaiting their next words, eyes wide and curious. He took several long, awkward moments to realize why they were waiting. With a dignified nod, he continued down the gravel road, his fists shoved into his trouser pockets. Faith and Jason followed.

"My birthday is in June," Jason finally replied, "and you know I don't have to join until after that."

"Yes, but can you not at least act as you should?"

"It is only baseball. Just a game. Some boys my age drive cars. They drink. They go to the movies, and watch television, and read magazines and English newspapers."

"And do you want these things of the English? Television and magazines?" she challenged.

"I just want to play baseball." Jason looked away, embarrassed by the conversation.

"But what of us?"

"We will be married," he responded quickly. He assumed she knew the answer. Or was she questioning the idea? With a surge of panic, he realized he couldn't tell the difference.

They'd known each other their entire lives and had been in love for as long as either could remember. She meant everything to him.

Faith studied his eyes. "I hope so," she said, her voice just above a whisper. "I hope so."

"Hey!" They looked up to see Adam gesturing from several respectful yards away. He pointed toward an approaching open wagon.

"It is Eino Ward," Adam said over his shoulder as he jogged toward the wagon. "Let's catch a ride."

Jason and Faith turned to join Adam, who was already on the wagon, his little legs dangling over the end.

Jason was lost in his own thoughts and dreams as they rode silently in the wagon.

"I hope so," Faith repeated. She, too, seemed lost in her thoughts and dreams. "God willing."

As the sun slowly set on the Yoder farm, soft flames of lamplight flickered to life. Jason waved goodbye to Adam and Faith and made his way toward the house. Jason thought of the tremendous effort his mother put into growing as he passed through the massive garden that covered much of the side yard and all of the back yard.

For many women in the community, the family garden helped bring in extra money, but for Grace Yoder, her garden income accounted for a significant portion of the household budget. This late in the season, almost all of the tomatoes and peppers had been harvested and either canned or sold. Jason had cleared and replanted the cole crop section more than a month before.

Seasonally, other sections included celery, okra, squash, and, of course, corn. Jason had determined that pollination was more likely to occur if types of plants were cultivated closer together.

"The bees are all but gone," he had said to his mother when he introduced the idea of manually pollinating other plants, "so we've got to do something to help the process along."

So instead of the long lines of a half dozen rows stretching the length of the garden, Jason planted corn in a more compact square, where the plants could better pollinate each other and protect each other from the wind. For the stalks on the outside rows, he took the time to manually pollinate.

He built raised beds for carrots, turnips, and different types of potatoes. Dead and drying vines that had been picked clean of green beans, butter beans, and wax beans snaked through the lattice frame Jason had built.

"More goomeedas, less lawn," Grace said that spring, as she watched Jason spade thirty more feet of lawn into garden. "When you're married, and your children need a yard to play in, you can turn this back into lawn. Until then, I would rather watch you pick beans than watch you cut grass."

"Yes, Maam," he responded as the shovel pierced the grass. He dropped to his knees and started to shake the dark dirt from the clumps of thick grass roots.

The garden had huge sections dedicated to cucumbers, red and green peppers, and onions. Jason and his mother harvested and canned all summer long. The previous year, Grace had canned more than 2,500 jars of relish, enough to sell year-round. The first farmers' markets of the year were particularly popular places to sell to the English, Mennonite, and even other Amish.

"People want a taste of summertime, even when summertime is months away," she had told Jason, as he loaded the buggy with cases of relish, "and that's what my cucumber relish is: the taste of summertime in a jar."

They had sold more than one hundred jars at the March farmers' market in Riverside. The recipe included cucumbers, red and green peppers, and onions, all grown in the Yoder garden. Her unique combination of spices included a few drops of green food coloring to "help it look more natural," Grace had whispered to Jason when she first showed him the process.

The English, both locals and tourists, loved her cucumber relish. It was also especially enjoyed at weddings, funerals, barn raisings,

Sunday lunches, and other gatherings of Plain People. Each year she canned more than the year before and managed to sell them all. But she was always hesitant to can too many, for fear of not being able to sell them.

"It's good," she explained to Jason, "but not so good that I want to eat it two or three meals a day for weeks if we have jars we don't sell."

"How about you, my little man?" she asked as she patted his cheek. "Do you want to eat cucumber relish with every meal?"

"No, Maam," he smiled. "I eat that much cucumber relish, maybe I turn into a cucumber. Make it hard to do my work, what with being green and no arms."

She laughed and pulled at the back of his suspenders. "How would you keep your pants up without those big, strong shoulders?"

"No work for me," he laughed. "I would just sit around while you feed me more relish."

The accident had limited Grace's mobility, so Jason often did tasks that were usually considered "women's work." Grace was blessed that her only child worked at cooking and canning with the same enthusiasm that he plowed, dug, hammered, and lifted.

As he softly stepped inside, the fading light of the gloaming hour found Grace at the kitchen table, surrounded by bills and ledgers. She silently stared at a ledger and then turned her attention to a bill. She studied it for a few moments before moving it to a growing stack of debits.

Concern and helplessness creased the corners of Jason's young eyes as he made his way upstairs.

Jason knelt by his bed. "Lord, you have given me physical strength, and I honor your gift with my hard work and effort," he prayed aloud. "You have given me the gift of Jesus, and I honor your gift with my faith and my dedication. Lord, it is through Christ I ask that I please be able to help my Maam. Let my strength lift her up from her trials and difficulties. I ask this in Christ's name. Amen."

Settled under the covers, he pulled the quilt up to his chin and remembered the afternoon his Maam put in the final stiches. She and other women of the community worked on the quilt for what seemed like weeks, before it finally met with her approval and was laid upon his bed. He passed his hand across the complex quilting as he reflected on his prayer and wondered how God would answer. He had every confidence the Lord would respond, he simply wondered how.

His most vivid dream that night wasn't unusual. Words and emotions swirled in both English and Pennsylvania Dutch. He was running down a dark road he didn't recognize. Suddenly, he was twenty feet tall, walking across a pasture with long strides, a bull under each arm. Somewhere in the distance, a woman called out, lost and afraid. In mid-step, the bulls transformed into metal barrels and then into huge baseballs as the pasture became a ball field. Jason found himself in the outfield. The field got bigger, and he grew smaller.

"Shmase doe rriva!" He looked to throw, but he didn't know where. He continued to shrink, and he was forced to pull his hands out from under the crushing weight of the massive orbs. Without warning, the sky opened up, and baseballs fell like white rain, becoming a snowstorm of round spheres.

"Eekk leeba deekk," Faith's voice said, from far in their past.

"Love?" he asked. He looked, but he couldn't see her. Beyond the shower of baseballs, he felt the sound of hymn singing, black carriages parked outside the window.

"Gelt," his uncle whispered softly. "May gelt."

"More money?" Jason didn't understand. "How do we get more money?"

Baseballs plopped onto the grass around him, and he looked up to see base runners circling the field like the tilt-a-whirl at the county fair. He picked up a baseball, and it blurred into a twenty-dollar bill.

All around him, baseballs transformed into paper currency and swirled across the field in small tornadoes of wind. The ball field was covered knee-deep with money. As he scooped at it with his glove, the bills became leaves that blew up into the sky and reattached themselves to a lonely copse of trees standing where the seats should have been. The trees—ash, oak, and elms—had baseball bat branches and leaves of currency. He thought it curious that there were so many trees near the playing area, but he was too sleepy to walk over to them. Instead, he lay down in the field of money. As he closed his eyes, the money became grass and dried to hay as he fell into a deep sleep where dreams no longer troubled him.

Chapter 2

The morning sun washed the Yoder farm in a warm orange glow. Pulling on his well-worn gloves, Jason walked toward the barn, ready to get to work. He reveled in the physical exertion the farm demanded.

All his life, he'd heard that hard work glorifies God, and in the deepest fibers of his muscles, he believed it. He lived it every day. God gave his family the countless tasks that a farm provides, and God also gave him the strength to perform those tasks.

He and his family glorified the Lord when they brought in the bountiful harvest the Lord supplied. The land beneath his feet had belonged to Yoders for more than one hundred years. He was as much a part of the land as the land was a part of him. And that would never change.

SKIP SCOWLED at the hundreds of acres of stubby, harvested cornfields.

"What a barren wasteland."

"Hush."

"Where are we? We haven't seen a town for, what's it been, ninety miles?"

"Less than five minutes." Annie smiled. "You're being ridiculous."

"I don't see why Dorothy was so eager to get back here. If I had my choice, I would've stayed in Oz."

"That was Kansas."

"Mmmm. Lake Wobegone?"

"That's Minnesota. We're in Iowa."

"Mmmm. So farmland and Amish? Got it."

Skip and Annie had left the city hours before. Driving slowly down a narrow Iowa road, surrounded by harvested cornfields, they were nearly two hundred miles from Carl Sandburg's City of the Big Shoulders and twenty-five miles west of Dubuque on the outskirts of Dyersville. They had already passed the long-abandoned construction site of what was supposed to be a celebrity couple's new home. The TV star and her ex-husband movie star had begun the mansion decades before. The empty hulk of a building was gradually collapsing onto itself, the perfect metaphor for the failed marriage.

"Seriously, where are we?"

"I told you, we're in Iowa. Go left up there," she gestured.

"I knew I should have paid attention to where we were going."

"You haven't paid attention to anything but the team in months," she replied. "You've been out of contention since the All-Star break, and you've been in a bad mood every day."

"Don't remind me," he said, shaking the memories from his head. "I'm sorry."

"You get so caught up in the what of the game that you forget the why of the game."

"What why?"

"Why? Because you love it, that's why. It's not about a trophy or a ring, or anything else. It's about loving the game for the sake of the game."

"It's kinda about winning, too, you know—"

"I know."

"Especially if we don't want to get fired. If we start next season the way we ended this season, we'll have plenty of time to drive around the country next summer, because I'll be out of a job."

"I know," she said. "What do you always say? 'Don't worry about the pitch count, worry about quality pitches.' Don't worry about wins and losses, worry about quality games. You have quality games; the wins will take care of themselves. And you have quality games by loving the game. Take the next right."

"I'm sorry, did you not watch any of our games this season?" he asked, slowing the car to look at her. "Quality is not a word I'd associate with the team occupying the bench behind me."

She snorted.

"You laugh, but other than a few standouts with big salaries, we literally have the definition of journeyman players. The team lacks cohesion, and I don't know how to provide that with so little talent on the field. I have infielders who are allergic to leather. The bullpen has no depth. I've seen better rotations on a Ferris wheel."

She snorted again.

"Yeah, keep laughing. I'm serious. Come July, if I don't have this team turned around and making serious progress, we're in Mesa full-time, and you and I will both be watching the games on TV. I have no idea what I'm going to do to stop that from happening." After a moment of silent driving, he mumbled, nearly to himself, "I feel like the captain of the Titanic. I can see the iceberg coming, but there's nothing I can do about it except go down with the ship."

He glanced to his left and did a double-take.

"What is that?" he said, stopping the car in the road.

"'If you build it, he will come,'" she giggled, struggling to contain her excitement.

"Is that the— "

"Yes!" she said, clapping her hands. "'Baseball, Ray, baseball,'" Annie quoted, attempting a deep-voiced impression of James Earl Jones.

"The Field of Dreams from the movie?" he asked, still dumbfounded.

"Yes! Turn left, right there, and turn right into the parking lot."

The ball field was nestled into the cornfield. Off to the right, down the first base line, behind the small wooden bleacher, the farmhouse stood.

"It's exactly like the movie."

"Yes!" she exclaimed. "It's been thirty years, and look at it! It's still the same! 'People will come, Ray, people will come,'" she said, attempting the impression again.

He was still in shock, but they parked and made their way to the field, moving slowly as though just waking from a dream.

"This is the love of the game, Stephen," she said, using his given name, her arms wide as she gestured at the field. "For the sake of the game."

The infield was populated with businessmen in dress shoes and ties who were standing near other men who clearly hadn't exercised in decades. Grandparents with grandchildren played in the outfield while children of all ages ran the base path and played in the infield.

Like a B12 shot coursing through his system, the simple and pure love of the game strengthened Skip's whole body as he felt it return.

Not far from the businessmen, three boys in their early teens caught Skip's eye as he made his way to the infield. One of the boys was on the pitcher's mound, another catching behind the plate while the third stood in the batter's box.

"Hey, partner, that's no way to throw the ball," Skip said, approaching the mound. He took the ball from the boy and knelt down. "Let me show you a grip Dennis Eckersley taught me. Here, like this," he said, handing the ball back and moving the boy's fingers on the ball. "And step like this when you shift your weight."

Rising, he looked on with approval as the boy went into his windup.

The boy pitched the way Skip demonstrated. The batter swung and missed as the ball darted away from him.

Skip rushed toward the plate, calling out to the batter. "Now wait a minute, you can't swing wildly at every pitch."

Skip remained at the Field of Dreams for hours — coaching every person who picked up a ball or carried a glove. He graciously signed autographs and posed for photos as more than one kind soul offered encouragement or consolation concerning his team's prospects and the coming season.

His disposition was temporary. His typical concerns for the team would soon darken his attitude, like storm clouds washing out a Sunday afternoon game. But he was back in his element and happy, for as long as it lasted. Perhaps this really was a magical place.

SKIP THOUGHT hard about the self-serve fruit stand long after they had driven away.

The hand-lettered "organic fruit" sign had caught Annie's eye when they passed the Amish farm. As Skip approached the stand, he saw that it was little more than a simple card table with a tray of purple fruit. A small, hand-written sign was taped to the top of a plastic bucket: "Raspberries: $4.50. Grapes: $4.50. Please leave the money in the bucket."

The large tray held just a few quart containers, so he expected to see bills in the bucket, but there were none. The bottom of the bucket was covered in change, pennies mostly, with a few silver coins but few quarters. Confused, Skip checked the price again and considered the possibilities.

Perhaps the farmer was watching, and he collected the money

after cars drove away. Perhaps the tray wasn't full at the start of the day, and instead the few containers were all there were.

Skip hated to think that people driving by would take the fruit without paying, or worse yet, steal the cash. He hated to think that people would take advantage of such obviously trusting and honest people.

He dropped a twenty in and carried a quart of raspberries and a quart of grapes to Annie waiting in the car.

"You have to try these," she said as he drove. "It's so, so clean and natural. Here—" She fed Skip a few berries. "Aren't they amazing?"

"Mmm-hmm," he nodded as the fruit dissolved in his mouth. "They're great." He wondered about the bucket. Perhaps the pennies were simply there to keep the container weighted down. Maybe the coins were all the change they'd collected over the summer. What sort of people would rip off an Amish family over a few bucks? Exploit their naiveté and trust?

"I haven't been easy to get along with," Skip said, interrupting the silence. They'd ridden the past twenty minutes without speaking.

"I know you're frustrated," Annie said. "I know this season took a lot out of you." He could feel her silent, steady gaze as he drove. "Get back to basics, right? When you've gone through these slumps in the past, you've always said it's about getting back to basics."

"I suppose," he agreed.

"Even beyond the basics, it's about loving the game," she said slowly. "What's it going to take for you to love the game again? Pure love of baseball like all those kids back at the Field of Dreams?" She watched him drive. "Manage because you love baseball, Stephen. Anything less, and you disrespect the game." He glanced at her. "We don't need the money. God knows I don't want you hanging around the house all day. But if you're not doing it because you love it, then you're just wasting your time. What about getting off the field? Have you thought about a front-office job?"

"Like Joe? Trade in the uniform for a tie? It's like throwing away the banana and eating the peel." He shook his head. "I'm not cut out for an office. No, when I leave managing, I'll be done with baseball."

She smiled. "You'll never be done."

"If I don't turn things around, the organization will be done with me."

That afternoon, before arriving in the small town of Kalona, they impulsively stopped at a small Amish grocery store.

They pulled into the six-car gravel parking lot wedged between the store and the owner's front yard. Skip wasn't impressed with the nondescript, cinderblock building, but they had stopped at Annie's insistence. Dead, dried flowers populated some of the simple beds around the stubby store, while half the beds were neatly cleaned out. Signs on the side of the building warned other drivers: "DO NOT BLOCK HITCHING POST."

Skip appraised the store as they entered and was struck by the stillness of the air and the dull, natural lighting of the skylights. Rows upon rows offered everything an Amish family would need, and a tourist could want: cloth by the bolt and needles and thread to sew it; hatbands and bonnets, ribbons, small children's toys, pencils and notebooks, twenty-pound bags of flour, ten-pound bags of sugar, and one-pound bags of candy.

Annie wandered the small store for some time before finally making her way to the counter, her arms full of handmade soap, snacks, and a quilted pillow.

The two women behind the counter looked like clones in their identical wardrobe and hairstyle. One of the women was speaking to Annie as Skip approached.

"She had gall bladder surgery yesterday, and not three hours later, he slipped off a ladder and broke a leg and sprained a wrist," she explained.

"Oh, my," Annie responded with a sympathetic shake of her head.

"So we are collecting a few things for them—" the woman nodded her head toward a large box on the floor near the counter with the words "Grocery Shower" spelled out neatly on the side, half-filled with food items—"to see them through until they are both back on their feet again."

"Forgive my ignorance," Skip began, "but is charity like this common with the Amish?"

The woman smiled kindly. "If someone needs help, then we help them; that is what the Bible tells us to do. We do not consider it 'charity;' this is just neighbors helping neighbors. And why would someone not accept the help if they need it?"

"That makes sense," Annie said.

"We help our neighbors like this, but many Amish also help strangers through groups that help with disasters and such. We help the poor and needy around the world that way," she explained in a gentle tone, as she bagged Annie's items. "But as I said, this is just neighbors helping neighbors. Where would any of us be without the help of our neighbors and the community?"

"Do Amish people ever turn down offers of help?" Annie asked, fumbling with her purse.

"It happens. Not too often, but sometimes," the woman replied. She glanced at the other woman, who was ringing up another tourist, and who, on closer inspection, looked like a younger version of her, and gestured at an item on the counter. "Mee-sin oss foon sell," she whispered. "Da lecht. Hop ken may."

She smiled as she turned her attention back to Annie. "Some people are too proud to ask for help. Or too embarrassed, depending on the situation. Sometimes, people have problems, and they do not even know there is a problem." She handed Annie the bag.

Annie pulled a fifty-dollar bill from her wallet. "I'd like to help," she said.

"That is not necessary, and it is not expected of you."

"I'd still like to help," Annie repeated as she handed over the bill.

"Thank you," the woman replied. "God bless you," she said as Annie made her way toward the door.

Skip lingered at the counter. With thoughts of the fruit stand still on his mind, he slipped a hundred to the woman and wordlessly walked away.

As ANNIE and Skip stepped from their car, several Amish teenagers rolled by, standing up on odd-looking scooters. The push-powered, two-wheel contraptions were like bicycles without pedals or seats, a small metal platform between the wheels.

Moments later, an Amish horse and buggy rumbled down the small main street lined with one-hundred-year-old two-story buildings.

An assortment of old and new businesses occupied the storefronts, some catering to the locals, but many were designed to appeal to the tourist trade. Judging by the pedestrian traffic along the sidewalk, tourism was a booming industry. Cafes and antique stores were alongside an insurance office and a dentist. A hardware store filled half of the next block, and a banner on the front proclaimed, "Gingerich's Hardware: Celebrating 100 Years of Service."

"Where do you want to start?" Annie asked, quickly scanning the shops. "Did you see—"

CRACK!

The sound of a bat hitting a ball carried on the air like the smell of smoke from a fire. As a hunting dog responds instinctively to a gunshot, Skip's head snapped around to face the echo. The wind carried the sound of a cheering crowd, and his wife's voice faded into a distant, blurry sound. He slipped into his comfortable "baseball zone" and struggled to see what he was missing as the voices rose as one.

"Stephen!"

Skip roused out of his distraction. "What?" He continued to look for the source of the sounds.

"Go," Annie said with a wave of her hand, acknowledging she'd lost him. "Go to the ball game."

"Thanks, hon," Skip said quickly. He brushed her cheek with a hasty kiss as he turned away.

SEARCHING for a seat in the crowded bleachers, Skip glanced toward the pitcher's mound. The old phrase "a man among boys," entered his mind as he gauged the pitcher's size compared to the teammates on the field.

A look at the scoreboard told him there were two outs, the score tied 1-1 in the top of the fourth inning. He watched as the pitcher fired a strike that crashed into the catcher's glove with a violent pop of leather.

Skip's eyes widened, and he froze halfway between standing and sitting. Spellbound, he remained that way as the pitcher went into his windup. Skip looked on in amazement as the ball broke in a nearly magical way, freezing the batter in place. Effortlessly, the pitcher unleashed a breaking ball that seemed to drop straight down in the strike zone, unlike anything Skip had ever seen.

Questioning what he'd just witnessed, Skip sat as the teams quickly change sides.

The pitcher selected a bat, put on a helmet, and moved toward the plate. As he approached, the catcher stood with his arm out, signaling for an intentional walk.

"What are they doing?" Skip asked out loud to no one in

particular. The pitcher began throwing balls to the catcher's outstretched glove.

"That's an intentional walk," said an old man near Skip.

"I know that," Skip snapped. "Why put the go-ahead run on base in a tie game? Why take the chance? Why not pitch to him? He's only the pitcher."

The old man's eyes wrinkled into a smile. "You ain't from around here, are you?"

The batter took ball four and flipped the bat in the direction of his dugout as he bounced down the line toward first base.

"No, why?"

The old man gestured toward the ball field, his smile growing wider. "That's Jason Yoder. He gets walked all the time. They know if they pitch to him, there's a good chance he'll hit it out of here."

Skip shook his head as the boy took a step or two away from first base. The next batter hit a pop-up to shallow right field. Jason stood with a foot on first base, leaning toward second.

"What's that kid doing?" Skip asked. "He's not trying to take second? He's gonna get cut down."

"Watch," the old man said with glee, unable to hide the expectation in his voice.

Jason tagged up and was halfway to second before the outfielder threw the ball. With blinding speed, Jason slid into the bag, underneath the second baseman's late tag. The crowd roared its approval.

"I...I don't believe it," Skip muttered.

The old man cackled with delight. "Ain't he amazin'?"

The pitcher looked warily at Jason before the next batter hit a pop-up on the first pitch.

Out of habit, Skip glanced over to see the coach give Jason signals with quick movements of his hands as the young man watched intently. When the pitcher went into his windup, Jason floated down the baseline like smoke on the wind. He was safely at third before the catcher could respond.

With the next pitch, Jason bounced away from third as though stealing home, but the batter hit a pop-up to end the inning.

As play continued, Skip had trouble accepting what he was watching. Pitchers like this weren't supposed to be good base runners, Skip thought. And base runners weren't such good pitchers. Jason maintained his prowess through the subsequent innings, overpowering batters with both speed and expert ball control.

At the top of the seventh and final inning, Jason struck out the first player with pitches that were nearly impossible to hit. The next batter somehow managed to make contact and put the ball in play. But when the third baseman didn't field it cleanly, the batter reached on the error.

The next batter smashed a line drive back at the mound. Despite his follow-through leaving him in an awkward position, Jason managed to pull the ball from the air, turn his body, plant his foot, and fire the ball to first to double up the runner. It was like the delicate motion of kitchen curtains dancing near an open window.

Skip was startled to see such graceful, big-league moves on a high school field.

To lead off the bottom of the inning, Jason's teammates first struck out and then hit a fly ball to center. The home team coach and the crowd shouted encouragement as Jason walked casually from the on-deck circle toward the batter's box.

Jason stepped to the plate, swinging his bat loosely as he sharply appraised the pitcher.

"They're gonna pitch to him this time," Skip said to his new companion.

The old man nodded knowingly. "They'll regret it."

Jason took the first pitch, a called strike. The second pitch he drove deep to center field. The crowd leaped to its feet, screaming as Jason took off running with the fluid motion of music. He rounded second before the ball bounced high off the center-field fence.

The center fielder gathered the ball, turned, and threw it to the cutoff man near second base. The second baseman relayed the ball to the catcher, but Jason rounded the bases so quickly, there wasn't a play as he crossed the plate.

The old man giggled as Jason's teammates rushed toward him. "What'd I tell you?" the old man said, clapping his hands. "I told you."

Skip said nothing. He stared in silent fascination.

As PLAYERS MADE their way toward the nearby school, Skip saw the coach finish a conversation with a local reporter.

"Hey, Coach," Skip called out as he rushed across the field, "can I talk with you a minute?"

"Skip Anderson!" Coach Pate responded in surprise. "I'll be, Skip Anderson. What are you doing in Iowa? Are you lost?"

Coach Pate's engaging smile helped Skip feel at ease. Most people were star-struck meeting a major league coach.

"I'm on vacation," Skip said as they shook hands.

"Did you see this game? How's this for a vacation?"

"I saw it. Your pitcher—" Skip pointed to the young man as his voice trailed off.

"Jason Yoder. He's something else, isn't he? The best ballplayer I've ever seen."

"He's one of the best players I've ever seen," Skip said. "He's astonishing. The complete package. His ball control, his presence on the field. His bat."

Coach Pate beamed. "Welcome to Iowa. I get to watch him play every day. You ready for this? His ERA is .079."

"His Earned Run Average?" Skip was sure the local coach had misstated a ridiculously low number—it was better than most of the pitchers on Skip's team.

"That's it. Point zero seven nine. Today's run was unearned. Our shortstop has hard hands sometimes. Jason has only given up a handful of hits all year. He has four no-nos this season alone."

"Four no-hitters?" Skip said incredulously.

Coach Pate nodded. "Of course, high school games are seven innings. But every game he had more than enough in the tank to go another two innings."

"Amazing," Skip said, shaking his head in wonder.

"You want amazing? He turned seventeen last June. He has no errors at all. I've never seen him mishandle a ball. His batting average is around .520." He nodded at Skip's reaction. "Yes. Five. Two. Zero. He has nearly thirty stolen bases. The best baseball instincts I've ever encountered. Amazing isn't the word to describe Jason. There isn't a word. Trying to describe Jason is like trying to describe wind."

"He's a baseball machine," Skip whispered. "And this kid is in high school? Where's he going to college?"

"He isn't going to college. Technically, he's not even in high school."

"I don't understand."

"I got a religious waiver from the Iowa High School Athletic Association so he could play on my team. He only has an eighth-grade education, and he's not going any further. He's Amish."

"Come again?"

"He's Amish. They don't go past the eighth grade in school, and they don't go to college. The ones that do go don't go there to play baseball," Coach Pate said as he started to follow his players who were walking toward the school.

Skip stepped quickly to keep up.

"If he's Amish, what's he doing playing ball? Why isn't he—" Skip gestured, groping for the words, "off being Amish?"

"Because he doesn't have to," Coach Pate explained with a laugh. "Teenagers aren't full members of the Order."

"What's that mean?"

Coach Pate stopped walking and turned to face him. "On Amish farms around here, there are cars parked next to buggies," he began.

"Yeah, I've seen that."

"The cars belong to the teenagers. They give them up when they join the Order. They give up cars," he gestured toward the school, "and he'll give up baseball."

"You mean to tell me that boy is going to walk away from baseball because he's Amish?"

"He'll put down his glove and pick up a pitchfork. He'll turn eighteen, and then he'll get baptized and join the church. Some days I look at him, and I wonder if he'll even miss it," Coach Pate said, shaking his head slowly.

"So why does he play?"

"He must like it. He came to me last year and asked if he could play. He started at the beginning of the season, about three months ago. Before that, he'd never played organized ball of any kind."

Skip opened his mouth to respond, but no words came out. He closed his mouth again.

"This'll be the first time in this school's history that we may win the state title," Coach Pate continued. "Baseball's a team sport, but not with this kid. Jason is a team."

"Or a franchise," Skip added. "What do his parents say about him playing?"

"Not much," replied Coach Pate, "they don't know."

"They don't know?"

"That was part of the deal Jason and I worked out," he explained. "His father is dead, and his mother knows he plays baseball, but not that he's playing for the high school team." He smiled. "I'm under the impression the entire town is conspiring to keep the truth from Grace Yoder and her brother-in-law."

"Why?"

"Amish are afraid the other kids would be a bad influence. All things being equal, they're probably right."

"What do you mean?"

"Kids today? Even here in Iowa, the public schools aren't great,"

Coach Pate said. "I'll tell you, Jason's special. All the Amish are in one way or another."

"He seems to get along with your other players and the fans in the stands," Skip said, glancing around them. "I mean, no one makes fun of him."

"Of course not. He's probably related to half the town, in one way or another. Heck, my uncle was Mennonite. My granduncle was Amish. Half the kids in this town are only a generation or two away from the Order, so they're not going to make fun of him. And one other reason."

"What's that?"

"He's one of the best baseball players to ever tie on cleats, and they know it."

"I'd like to meet him," Skip said as they arrived at the school.

"He may not want to meet you."

"Why not?" Skip asked, somewhat surprised.

"He's not joined the church yet," Coach Pate patiently replied, "but he's still Amish. Don't get me wrong: Jason's the most polite person I've ever met. Just don't expect him to be too talkative. I've never met an extrovert Amish. They are a quiet and reserved people, and Jason is one of the most taciturn in this whole county."

Skip nodded. "I understand," he said, but he didn't understand.

"Honestly, during a game, he can go four, five, six innings without saying a word," Coach Pate explained. "Not a single word. Then he walks to the plate and drives a triple like you'd scratch an itch."

"I'd still like to meet him."

"I'll tell him," Coach Pate said. "Just don't be surprised if he doesn't have a lot to say." The high school coach disappeared into his school.

Chapter 3

Skip quickly dialed his cell phone and cast a furtive glance over his shoulder, waiting for the call to go through.

"Hope? Skip Anderson." The words poured out of him. "I've found the answer to our problems. You won't believe him. I can't believe him, and I've just seen him... Yes, a player for next year... No, I've not been drinking, and I resent that. Wait until you see him. I—"

Jason came out of the door, looking around. Skip saw him and did a double-take, surprised to see a ballplayer transformed by Amish clothes.

"I gotta go," Skip said quickly. "Tell Henry I called. I'll explain later." He hung up the phone.

Jason began to walk away.

"Jason," Skip called out as he rushed over to the boy, hand extended. "How you doing? Skip Anderson."

"Yes, sir," Jason said, taking the offered hand. "I'm Jason Yoder." Skip was struck by the width and grip of Jason's young hand. "Coach

Pate said you wanted to speak with me. I am sorry the Cubs did so poorly this season."

"Yeah, well, it was a tough season," Skip replied, instinctively slipping into his "coach" mode. "But we had a lot of injuries to overcome. This was a rebuilding year."

"Well, I hope next year is better," Jason said, turning away. "Good-bye." He began walking away before Skip even realized it.

Skip ran to catch him. "Hold on. Can I talk with you for a minute?"

"I need to get home," Jason said over his shoulder, walking quickly.

"Let me give you a ride?" Skip said.

"No, thank you."

"Can I walk with you?"

"That would be up to you."

"I'll be right back," Skip said, looking around and realizing he'd left his wife behind.

Jason paused to stare at him, intelligent light shining silently in his eyes.

"No," Skip said. He didn't want to upset the boy, but he was so excited by the raw talent standing before him that he didn't want him to get away, even for a moment. Skip didn't know what to do. "You keep walking. I'll catch up."

Wordlessly, Jason continued on his way, as Skip hurried off to find Annie.

"Stephen," she said sternly, anger darkening her features as she leaned against the car. "What happened? You've been gone forever."

"I'm sorry, honey," Skip interrupted. "I'll explain later. We have to hurry. Get in."

THE COLORS of the small coppice at the edge of the cornfield interrupted the otherwise barren landscape. The reds of the hard maple were more intense than the brilliant reds of the red oak. The leaves of the bur oak and hickory were still yellow, while the yellows of the ash had begun to turn purple. The elm and soft maple had more yellow leaves on the ground around them than on their empty branches. The white oak were sprinkled with brown leaves that would remain until spring. The bright red Virginia creeper and sumac leaves stood in stark contrast along the edge of the tree line. A flock of goldfinches, pine siskins, and common redpolls passed above them unnoticed, on the way to somewhere warmer.

Walking along the gravel country road, Jason and Skip paid no notice to the display. Adam shuffled along a few respectful yards behind them, his hands casually in his pockets. A few yards behind Adam, Annie drove the car very slowly.

Jason stared straight ahead as Skip turned sideways to gesture while he talked. "You know who I am, so believe me when I say you're one of the most talented ballplayers I've ever seen."

"Thank you, but the team deserves most of the credit." Jason offered a small, disarming smile.

"Horse sh—" Skip said, before catching himself. "I— I disagree," he said quickly. "You have incredible bat speed, ball control— You're a coach's dream. A pitcher who can hit, or a hitter who can pitch."

"I thank you again," Jason said, guarded. "Why are you telling me this?"

"Because I want you to understand that I'm completely serious when I say that I want you to play baseball for me," Skip said.

Jason stopped walking and turned to face Skip. A few paces behind them, Adam stopped as well. Annie stopped the car.

Jason opened his mouth, said nothing, and closed it again. He shook his head slowly as he turned and continued walking.

"Thank you, no," Jason said. "That would be impossible."

"Did you just say no to the Chicago Cubs?"

"Yes, sir," Jason replied softly. "As much as I would like to, it would be impossible."

"Stop saying that," Skip snapped. "If you want to, why can't you?"

"I— I have plans, responsibilities."

"You're seventeen years old. How many responsibilities can you have?"

"I am expected to join the church," Jason explained. "And I plan to marry. I must help my mother with the farm."

"How many farms can you buy with a million dollars? Or five million? Or ten?"

Jason stopped walking again to stare at Skip.

"But don't think about the money," continued Skip. "Wouldn't you like to play against the best players in the world? Have you ever asked yourself, 'am I good enough?' Do you want to spend the rest of your life not knowing? Here's your chance to find out."

Jason considered Skip's words. "Am I good enough?"

"I think so."

Skip looked at him expectantly as Jason said nothing. Finally, with a dismissive shake of his head, he said, "My mother would never allow it."

"I'll handle your mother," Skip said, sensing Jason warming to the idea. At least that's what he hoped he was sensing. He really had no idea what the boy was thinking, so he plunged ahead. "I'm sure she's a reasonable woman. What do you say?"

"You would talk with her? And with my uncle?" His accent was pronounced when he said the last word.

"Right now if you want," Skip said eagerly, afraid to let the golden moment slip away.

"No," Jason quickly replied, his expression caught between fear, excitement, and dread. "Tomorrow."

"Fine," Skip said. "I'll talk with them tomorrow. Will you come play baseball for me?"

Jason's thoughts were hidden behind an expressionless, dispassionate stare, perfected by generations of grandfathers.

Jason and Skip stood amid empty fields, bathed in the headlights as the last shadows of the day disappeared into darkness.

"You talk to my mother and to my uncle, then I will decide," he finally said.

THAT EVENING in their hotel room, Skip was yelling into his phone at the Cubs general manager. "How much, Henry? Just give me a damn answer. How much can I give the kid? No agents, no negotiations. You tell me, and I'll offer it to his mother. How much?"

Skip fell silent, growing angrier as he listened.

"He's Amish, Henry, not an idiot. We can't give him the minimum. If his family thinks we're taking advantage of him, he won't play. Besides, when people see him, we'll look like thieves exploiting the kid. Let's keep it simple. How about a million-dollar signing bonus and one million for the season?"

"You're not hearing me. He's the best I've ever seen. Ever. We have to give him the money, or he won't play. It's that simple." He nodded silently. "If you don't trust my judgment, you might as well hire a new manager. I'm not an idiot, either. No. I don't need any help, I can handle it. I'll call you tomorrow. Good night, Henry. No, I don't need your help. No, I don't need her help, either. Good night."

He ended the call with a stab of his finger.

"I need help."

Annie's mouth dropped open. "But, you just said—"

"I know," Skip interrupted, reaching for his car keys. "I don't need Henry's help. I need a different kind of help."

COACH PATE OPENED the door to Skip, who stood in the silver glow of the front porch light.

"Thanks for seeing me, Coach."

"My pleasure, Coach, come on in," Coach Pate said, holding his door open.

After exchanging pleasantries and sitting in the handsome living room, Coach Pate got down to business.

"You talked with Jason?" Coach Pate asked.

"Yeah," Skip said, "and now I have to talk with his mother and uncle."

"Ah, yes," Coach Pate said, leaning back in his chair. "Grace and Isaac Yoder. He's her brother-in-law."

"You know them?"

"Sure," Coach Pate replied, locking his fingers behind his head. "Nearly everyone in the county knows everyone else. Amish and non-Amish. Evidently, none of them are telling the Yoder family about Jason playing for me."

"I want Jason to come play for me."

"I figured as much," Coach Pate nodded. "What did he say?"

"He might, but I have to talk with them first."

"Now, that is surprising," Coach Pate leaned forward at the news.

"Why?"

"It's like I told you before," Coach Pate said. "He's not a full member of the Order; this is his rumshpringa. He intends to join the church. I didn't expect him to leave and play major league ball."

"Rum-what?" Skip asked, the strange words swimming in his mouth.

"Rumshpringa," Coach Pate repeated slowly. "It's the running-around time. Amish teenagers aren't born in the church; they aren't automatically Amish."

"They aren't?" Skip interrupted. "But I thought he was Amish."

"Don't get me wrong," Coach Pate quickly responded. "Jason is Amish. He's as Amish as his great-great-grandfather— "

"And dressed just like him," Skip interjected.

"And dressed just like him, probably," Coach Pate continued with a smile. "Like his great-great-grandfather, his trousers still have buttons, not a zipper. He has hundreds of years of traditions he's carrying around on those young shoulders. He's Amish, but he's not a member of the church."

Skip nodded, trying to absorb the history lesson.

"Young people, teenagers, are born into a family and a community, but not the church. To join the church, they make an adult, conscious decision to become Christian." Coach Pate cocked his head. "I don't suppose you've heard the hymn, 'I Have Decided to Follow Jesus'?"

Skip smiled ruefully. "Is that the one they play on Sundays instead of 'Take Me Out to the Ballgame'?"

Coach Pate chuckled. "People aren't born Christians because their parents are Christian. Someone may be raised Hindu or raised Muslim because his parents are Hindu or Muslim or because he lives in a Hindu or Muslim country, but Christianity isn't like that."

"But— the USA is a Christian country—"

"Is it? When did you last go to church?"

Skip cast his eyes downward.

"Try not going to mosque in some Muslim countries. In those places, you're Muslim because everyone else is Muslim. Here in the US, you may be surrounded by Christians, but that doesn't make you a Christian, no more than standing on a ball field makes you a pitcher. You may think you're a ballplayer, but you're not until you actually play ball."

"OK, I get your point," Skip conceded as the lesson returned to the ball field he understood.

"The Amish are Christians. They are Anabaptist," Coach Pate

continued, pronouncing the word slowly. "They came out of the Reformation in sixteenth-century Europe."

"And brought their clothes with them."

"And brought their clothes with them," Coach Pate repeated, "and their farm equipment, and their recipes, their slow pace of life, their faith, and their rules and traditions and everything else. They believe that the sprinkling a child receives at its christening in most denominations isn't sufficient."

"I was christened as an infant in a Methodist church," Skip offered, finally glad to connect to what he was learning.

"And does that make you Methodist?" Coach Pate asked, his forehead furrowed.

"No, not really," Skip conceded.

"No, not really," Coach Pate nodded. "And the Amish don't think so, either. So as Anabaptists, they believe you have to be baptized again—ana—again—baptized. Jason's not been baptized. He's running around. This is his rumshpringa, the time before he becomes an adult and joins the church. He's sowing his wild oats."

"And everyone is OK with this?" Skip asked.

"It's not exactly encouraged, but it's not discouraged," Coach Pate answered. "Remember when we met, I told you about the cars parked in front of Amish homes?"

Skip nodded silently.

"The kids drive the cars during the rumshpringa. Just like Jason plays ball. Other kids do other things they probably won't be proud of later. This is the Amish way of getting things out of their system before they get baptized, join the community, get married, have kids, move on, and never look back at our world."

"That's something else I don't understand. What's wrong with our world?"

"Do I really need to answer that?"

"You know what I mean."

"I know what you mean," Coach Pate conceded. "The Amish believe there are two types of people, them and us," he explained.

"They call themselves unser satt leit, our sort of people. Everybody else—you, me, everybody—is aanner satt leit, the other sort of people." Coach Pate walked across the room and picked up the family Bible from a coffee table. He thumbed through the pages as he returned to his guest. He read aloud: "'Therefore come out from them, and be separate from them, says the Lord, and touch nothing unclean, then I will welcome you.' This is what they believe. Our world is unclean. You're asking him to leave their separate world and enter ours. This isn't about a boy and his way of life or family traditions. This is about a boy and his relationship with God. You're talking about him walking away from everything he believes God wants him to do." He slapped the Bible closed and returned it to the table. "Good luck."

"I'm not out yet. I still have a few more strikes. What will his mother say?"

"What do you think? Jason didn't want his mother to know he was playing with high school kids. How do you think she'll feel about major leaguers?"

"Not good," Skip said. This was getting more complicated than he expected. "What do I say to Grace Yoder? Will you help me?"

"I'll try," Coach Pate replied, "for Jason's sake. But it's not just Grace Yoder; you'll need to earn his uncle's trust, too."

The two talked late into the night. One eager to learn, the other willing to teach.

As Skip pulled into the driveway of the Yoder farmhouse, colorful shirts and dresses on a clothesline snapping sharply in the autumn wind, he recalled Coach Pate's parting words the night before: "Christianity is about following Jesus, deciding to follow Jesus, like the hymn says. The Amish understand that, probably better than many other Christians. They decide to follow Jesus. And they do it the way the Bible says, peacefully, passively, humbly, gently. With grace and forbearance. Being a good Christian is difficult; doing it the way the Bible actually says is nearly impossible. In our world, the Amish are among the best, most authentic followers of Jesus around."

Skip had shaken his head with disbelief. "Why haven't I heard any of this before?"

"Where are you supposed to hear it?" Coach Pate asked. "Over-politicized Christian radio? In church? If you happen to wander into a church." He smiled. "Few Christians understand the Amish. Even fewer non-Christians. They look funny and they talk strange, and that's all most people know. They're odd characters in movies, and they make furniture and jelly. But understand—they don't lie, and they nearly always go out of their way not to be rude. If they start to get rude, you've pushed them about as far as they're willing to go."

Skip kept Coach Pate's words in mind as he and Annie made their way to the Yoder door.

"How's this for an Amish vacation?" Skip asked, gesturing grandly at their surroundings.

"It's not exactly what I imagined, that's for sure," she replied with a small frown. "And I don't understand why I have to wear a dress. What's wrong with jeans?"

"The Amish don't like women in pants," he said. "You don't want to offend them in their own home, do you?"

⚾⚾⚾⚾ ⚾⚾⚾

JASON ANSWERED moments after the knock. "Good day, Coach," he said, shaking Skip's hand. "Thank you for coming."

"I'm a man of my word. This is my wife, Annie," Skip said, gesturing.

"Welcome."

Isaac and Grace stood in the hallway as the three entered.

The home was surprisingly modern but noticeably austere. Glancing past the simple dining area, Skip glimpsed a living room with a pair of easy chairs and a mismatched couch. Two Bibles sat on the nearby coffee table. Skip was struck by how orderly the rooms looked. There was nothing superfluous, but there were comfortable pillows on every wooden chair. An old oak desk in the corner was covered with mounds of paperwork, folders, and envelopes. Several windowsills held small, colorful glass figurines that refracted colored light into the rooms.

Each room had at least two skylights cut into the ceiling, providing adequate illumination for the late morning. The ceiling fixtures weren't traditional lights; they appeared to be wick gaslights enclosed by silver metal screens, the sort found on campground lanterns.

There was a faint odor of gas, but more than that, the Yoder home smelled clean. Not the smell of chemical cleaners, but a natural and fresh aroma. The floor, the furniture, their clothes—everything was immaculately spotless. Skip thought the room suitable for an operation. Or a museum.

"These are the English you invite into your mudder's home?" Isaac asked in accented English.

"Yes, Onkel," Jason replied. "Stephen Anderson and his wife, Annie."

"Thank you for agreeing to see me, sir," Skip said. He had no way of judging Isaac's age; beards seemed to make most Amish men look older.

Isaac nodded, his emotions hidden behind gray hair and an expression as somber as his surroundings.

"This is Jason's mudder, Grace."

"Welcome," Grace said as she invited them in with a gesture of her hand. "Please excuse me, I will get some lemonade."

"May I help you?" Annie asked.

"That would be fine," Grace said, nodding. She led Annie into the kitchen as Isaac and Skip sat at the dining room table. Jason remained standing.

Isaac turned his stern countenance upon Skip. "And what can I do for you, Mr. Anderson?"

"I'll get right to the point, Mr. Yoder. I want Jason to play professional baseball for the Chicago Cubs."

Isaac shot a withering glance at Jason, who squirmed under the gaze. "That would be impossible," the older man responded.

"Respectfully, sir, it's not impossible. It's very simple. He signs a contract for a million dollars, and he plays."

Standing at the door with a tray of glasses, Grace inhaled sharply at his words. Recovering quickly, she made her way to the table as Annie followed her in with a pitcher of lemonade.

Isaac glared as though Skip was tracking muddy manure through an operating room.

"I am a simple man, Mr. Anderson," he said gruffly. "We are simple people. You do not understand our ways."

"I recognize and respect your rule book," Skip said sincerely. He paused, licking his lips before continuing, struggling to get his mouth around the word, "Your...Ordnung."

Annie snapped her head around to look at Skip.

"I know rules are meant to be followed," Skip said. "But the Ordnung allows Jason to choose jobs other than farming, right?"

Skip shifted his gaze to see Annie's eyes widened in shock.

"Ya."

"Does it prohibit a career in baseball?" Skip asked.

"In some communities back East, the Ordnung does prohibit adults from playing baseball."

Skip's stomach dropped. Coach Pate had failed to mention that. His no-hitter had just been busted by a grand slam.

"The Ordnung for our community says nothing about baseball," Isaac continued. Skip exhaled, not realizing he'd been holding his breath. "But baseball is a child's game for little boys and girls." He waved his hand dismissively. "Jason is a man. He must put away childish things and behave as a man should."

"Do children play with toy tractors and have their own little gardens where they play at farming?" Skip asked.

"Ya."

"They play at farming and grow up to be farmers. They play at baseball and grow up to be professional baseball players. What's the difference?"

"One is living the word of God, one is not. Working the land is the calling of the Lord," Isaac said. "If Jason works among them, then he is not separate from them. He could face the meidung."

"The shunning. I understand. Excommunication. But to receive the meidung," Skip pronounced the word slowly, "he must be a member of the church, and he isn't."

Out of the corner of his eye, Skip saw Annie raise her glass to her mouth, then stop. She lowered it without drinking.

"His mother is a member," Isaac said. "He would jeopardize her place in the community as well as his."

"This is his rumshpringa?" Skip asked, ignoring Annie's shocked expression.

"Ya."

"Then the elders may be a little more forgiving, at least until his birthday. You could look at it like he's gone off to work someplace else."

Isaac sat stoically, saying nothing. Skip took his silence as a go-ahead sign and swung away.

"I want you to understand. I truly believe that Jason has a gift from God. A gift of speed, and agility, and ability. It'd be a sin to not let him use God's gift."

Isaac stared intently at Skip for a long time before responding.

"Who is to determine what is a sin, Mr. Anderson? You? Me? People in Chicago? Do you trust da people in Chicago? Do you trust people, Mr. Anderson? Strangers? Trust them with your life?"

"I, ah..."

"What about your world can his mother and I trust, Mr. Anderson? My brother's only son. I should encourage him to live in your world? Do you understand why we want to have nothing to do with your world?"

"I, ah..." Skip repeated.

"Your world is nothing but sin and temptation, Mr. Anderson. Temptations that distract us from da Lord. We take our eyes from da Lord, we bring shame to ourselves, or worse," Isaac said. "I am talking about sin, Mr. Anderson. Sin in the world that can swallow the soul and condemn us forever. Is that what you want for Jason, Mr. Anderson? That is not what his mother and I want for him or for any of us. But that is what happens when we stop thinking about da Lord. We stop thinking about da Lord, we start thinking about the world, and we bring shame to da Lord. What does your world have for us? Shame? Sin? Temptation? We need not even be in the world, it is all there, waiting for you on your television." Isaac finished with a wave of his hand and an expression of disgust usually reserved for the contents of an outhouse.

His eyes locked on Isaac's, Skip said nothing.

"What good is it? Let that into my house? Naaah," he said with a shake of his head and another wave. "And the internet? For one good thing that comes into my home, it also lets in fifty more dirty things. And for what? So I can know what the temperature is outside? That is why I have a thermometer. Naaah," he said again. "You can keep your internet and your computer and your television. My conscience is clear. Life is difficult enough without bringing all dose worthless things into it. You can keep it all, and keep your baseball."

Skip swallowed, considering Isaac's words. He licked his lips before speaking.

"I know I'm not unser satt lleit," Skip said slowly and carefully. "I'm anner satt leit."

Annie stared at her husband. Grace and Isaac exchanged glances.

"Jason has been given a gift, a tremendous ability to do things few people in the world can do," Skip continued. "I want to help him use the gift God gave him." He paused to let the silence of the room prevail. "I give you my word that no harm will come to him," he pledged. "I will protect him with my life."

"Yes, Mr. Anderson, I believe you will, but who will protect his soul?"

Skip had no answer. Isaac turned his attention to his nephew, who was concentrating on the floor, studying the immaculate linoleum for answers.

"And do you want to go play the games of children?"

Looking at his uncle, Jason considered the question for so long that Skip thought he must not have heard it. Finally, he nodded slowly. "Maybe, Onkel, I think so. But it is more than that."

"You would leave us to go be among them?" Grace asked, her words soaked in sadness.

"Not forever, Maam. I would come back. I would earn enough money to take care of you. Then I would come back."

"You say that now, my son, but I wonder if you will be able to. We will not change," Grace said, "but you will."

They looked at each other for a few moments before Isaac wordlessly stood up and walked into the living room.

Annie looked to Skip, who shrugged in ignorance.

Skip and Annie glanced at Jason, who shrugged his massive shoulders.

Momentarily, Isaac returned, a Bible in his hands. He placed the heavy tome on the table and remained standing as he opened it. The others looked on as Isaac moved the pages until he found what he was looking for.

"Proverbs," Isaac pronounced and then locked eyes with each of them around the table. He began to read:

"'Every word of God is pure: he is a shield unto them that put their trust in him. Add thou not unto his words, lest he reprove thee, and thou be found a liar. Two things have I required of thee; deny me them not before I die.'" Isaac stopped to let the words sink in. Again, he looked from face to face before he continued.

"'Remove far from me vanity and lies: give me neither poverty nor riches; feed me with food convenient for me: Lest I be full, and deny thee, and say, Who is the Lord? or lest I be poor, and steal, and take the name of my God in vain.'"

Annie appeared struck by the solemnity of the words delivered in Isaac's deep baritone. Skip wasn't sure what was going on, but he didn't think it was good.

"'Remove far from me vanity and lies'," Isaac repeated reverently. "'Give me neither poverty nor riches,'" he glowered at Skip, "'feed me with food convenient for me: Lest I be full, and deny thee, and say, Who is the Lord?'" He closed the Bible and looked at Jason. "'Lest I be full, and deny thee, and say, Who is the Lord?'"

The room was silent.

"Is that what you want, Jason, to be rich and full, and to deny the Lord?"

"No, sir."

"Riches can drive you away from the Lord. The eye of a needle, ya?"

Jason nodded in understanding. "Yes, sir."

Isaac turned to Skip and Annie. "Excuse us, please," he said.

Isaac, Grace, and Jason filed into the kitchen, leaving their guests alone. Although they closed the door behind them, Skip and Annie could hear them talking in their throaty native language.

"How do you know so much about the Amish?" Annie whispered.

"Coach Pate told me a few things last night."

"A few things," Annie said, shaking her head.

"What do you think?"

"You didn't learn this much about my family before we got married," Annie said. "I hope he's worth it."

"He is," Skip said. "He is."

Isaac, Grace, and Jason returned from the kitchen. Skip glanced at Jason for a clue, but the boy only shook his head and shrugged his wide shoulders.

Isaac remained silent for a long, tense moment.

"I will not give you my blessing, Jason," Isaac said. "Nor will your mother. You are old enough to make your own decisions," the patriarch said. "You will do what you wish."

"Thank you, Onkel," Jason said.

"We will leave you now to do your business in private, like a man," Isaac said. He turned to Skip and Annie. "Mr. and Mrs. Anderson, God be with you."

Grace struggled to contain her emotions as she and Isaac moved from the room.

"So that's it," Skip said to Jason. "You'll play for us?"

"I do not know, Coach Anderson," Jason replied. He stroked his chin thoughtfully. "I have not made up my mind."

"What? I don't understand. Your uncle said—"

"He said it is my decision. I still must decide."

"When?"

"I don't know," Jason said. He shrugged. "Soon."

ALREADY IN THE CAR, Annie appeared to be deep in thought when Skip got in and closed the door.

"He'll come around," he said, trying to assure himself. "What's wrong?"

"I wonder if you're doing the right thing."

"What do you mean?"

"He's so...innocent," Annie began slowly. "They all are. Taking him out of his protected community... Exposing him to the outside world—to ballplayers, of all people. I wonder if it's not more dangerous than you might think."

"He's not so innocent," Skip argued. "He listens to the radio. He knew who I was, for crying out loud."

"Stephen, has he even seen a three-story building? Or an elevator? Or a four-lane highway? And you want to take him to Chicago? Chicago?"

She stared intently at him. He had no response.

"Is winning the World Series worth putting that innocent young boy into such a dangerous situation?" she said at last. "I know you'd trade your soul to the devil to win, but would you trade his?"

"Annie, I will take care of him," he responded, trying to convince them both.

"I hope so, Stephen. I hope so."

Like a water glass staining a wooden table, Skip's confidence evaporated, leaving nothing but worry.

Chapter 4

The rising sun found Jason and Faith walking along the edge of a drying brown cornfield. A respectful distance behind them, Adam walked even slower, his hands in his pockets.

"What does this mean?" Faith asked, her delicate features creased with worried confusion.

"We may have to wait a little longer before we marry," Jason said, struggling to find the right words.

"Why?"

"In just a few years playing baseball, I could make more money than I would in my entire life."

"Baseball?"

"Professional baseball players are paid very well."

"I don't believe it," Faith said, shaking her head dismissively. "It's a child's game."

"The pay is very good, but that's not all. I enjoy baseball. The challenge of hitting the ball. And throwing it fast and hard and straight. Catching and running."

"Years?" she repeated with a tone he'd never heard before. "But our plans? Our dreams?"

"With that money, I could help my mother," Jason explained, his tone betraying his excitement. "I could buy more land. Help my uncle. I could help your parents. Your brother."

"To do that, you must go be among them," she said. "What will God think?"

"God gave me this skill and this opportunity. Perhaps he wants me to go."

"What if this is a test?" she asked, her voice rising with worry. "Have you thought of that?"

"No," he said, taken aback, "I haven't."

"What if this is a test of your faith, like so many stories in scripture?" Faith grew more agitated. "What if God does not want you to go, and this is the devil tempting you? Will you still go?"

"I do not know."

"What about your mother?" she asked. "How will you take care of her if you're far away in Chicago?"

"I...I do not know." He studied her eyes, searching for answers he could not find. "You would help her, as you always have. I...I can hire someone—with the money—" His mind raced like a yearling colt across a pasture.

Faith stopped walking and looked at him as though seeing him for the first time and not liking what she was seeing.

"Is this what our people do? Hire others to care for our parents?" she demanded. "You will go away and then come back? Can you remember anyone who has done that? While your mother and I just wait for your return? My life waits, while yours goes on?"

Her face flushed red with emotion.

"You have your decision to make, yes? Well, so do I."

"AM I COACHING A FUTURE MAJOR LEAGUER?" Coach Pate asked Skip as the high school team warmed up. Skip had helped Annie to a seat before joining Coach Pate near the dugout.

"You'll have to ask him," Skip replied. "He hasn't told me what he wants to do."

"It may take a while." Coach Pate said. "Days. Even a few weeks."

"Wonderful. What am I supposed to do until then?"

"Interested in a busman's holiday? My assistant coach is on a field trip. I have another uniform in my office."

"Honestly?"

"Sure. Come out and teach us a thing or two," Coach Pate said. "The kids would get a kick out of it."

"Well..."

Minutes later, Skip walked out of the dugout, wearing the team's uniform. He caught Annie's eye as she looked up from her book and shook her head, smiling. Skip grinned self-consciously as he made his way onto the field. He joined Coach Pate near the first base line where players were warming up.

"I was thinking about Jason while you were changing," Coach Pate said, watching the boys sprinting around the outfield. "I don't know how he does what he does half the time, but I'll tell you this, he's the most coachable player I've ever seen." He met Skip's gaze. "If you and I in our playing days were as coachable as he is, I'd have had a real career, and you'd already be in Cooperstown.

"I never have to tell him twice. He does exactly what I say. Sometimes, it's like I don't even have to tell him once. I can just show him a change in his stance or grip, and it makes a difference. But really, it's like adjusting the lighting on a van Gogh or turning up the volume on a symphony. Easily ninety-eight percent of the time, I just stand here and watch him play.

"But understand, if he plays for you, he'll do exactly what you tell him to do. Exactly. Without question. That's how the Amish are. If I had more players with his dedication, I'd win the state championship every year.

"What am I saying, 'win the championship?' We still have to win a few more games before we get there. You want to head out and give the boys some tips?"

Skip started toward the field. "Be glad to, Coach."

Like a shepherd tending his flock, Skip moved from player to player, offering advice, cajoling, encouraging, and teaching the players new ways of approaching their positions. He continued his tutelage right up to game time.

"Play ball!" the umpire called out.

Jason jogged out of the dugout, nodding to Skip as he passed.

"Where's he going?" Skip asked, confused.

"Right field."

Skip's face registered alarm. "You don't rest him between starts?"

"He doesn't need to rest between innings," Coach Pate asserted, shaking his head. "I keep telling you Skip, he's not like the rest of us."

"Yeah, I know," Skip said to himself, imagining the possibilities as the boy jogged across the field.

Throughout the game, Jason put on his usual baseball exhibition, going three for four. A double, driving in two runs and his normal excellent fielding all helped the team go into the seventh inning leading 9-3.

"Ok, boys, let's hold 'em," Coach Pate called to his players as they trotted onto the field for the final inning. He turned to Skip. "What do you think of high school baseball, Coach?"

"Not bad," Skip replied. "Jason's playing a fantastic game."

"Just another day at the ballpark for him," Coach Pate said. "Have you noticed how much looser his uniform is than the other players'?"

"Yeah, I did."

"The Amish think it's wrong to show off their bodies," Coach Pate explained. "I had to get a uniform two sizes too big. And look at him. You can imagine how hard that was. And the Amish don't use zippers. I had to have snaps sewn onto his pants. There are a lot of little rules like that. Keep that in mind." Clapping his hands, Coach Pate turned to the field. "Let's hold 'em, boys, let's hold 'em."

Later, with the game decided and the teams preparing to shake hands on the infield, the conversation continued.

"You've done a great job coaching him," Skip said.

"I can't take too much credit." Coach Pate considered his words for a moment. "You remember, he's only been playing for about four months, right?"

"Yeah," Skip said with a slow shake of his head. "It's hard to believe."

"I don't know when he would have even seen a real baseball game before he showed up here," Coach Pate said. "His baseball instincts are unreal, but I still had to teach him a lot of really basic rules. All of his baseball education is from the radio or the newspaper. It would be like learning to drive by looking at pictures of cars. I did my best, but I'm sure there are things he still doesn't know."

"We'll work out those details when we have to. You've made him a great player," Skip said. "I could make him a hall of famer." Coach Pate nodded in agreement. "Can you talk to him for me?"

"I've done all I can to encourage him," Coach Pate replied. "I don't think he'll listen to me anymore. But I'm willing to try."

"I seemed to get through to Isaac," Skip said. "I don't know what else to say to Jason."

"I told you he may take a while to come around. I'll do the best I can to convince him."

"He's the best ever," Skip said. "He could make a fortune."

"Pride and greed," Coach Pate said quietly.

"What?"

"Pride. Greed. Gluttony, envy, anger, sloth, and lust," Coach Pate continued. "The seven deadly sins. You won't win him over by appealing to those. He'll come around in his own time for his own reasons. If he comes around at all."

ANNIE AND SKIP relaxed side by side above the covers of their hotel bed. She read a guidebook while he held his phone, waiting to place his call.

"You're sure you don't mind me working?"

"Did you know Buddy Holly and Ritchie Valens died in Iowa?" Annie replied, not looking up.

"No, I didn't. You don't mind?"

"And the Big Bopper, too."

"The day the music died?" he asked, his curiosity suddenly piqued.

"Mmmhmm," she replied as she continued to read. "And one of the Everly brothers was born here."

"So Iowa still owes rock and roll two musicians?" he asked.

She smiled. "That's one way to look at, I suppose," she said, not looking up.

"You're sure you don't mind?" He had to keep asking.

"Sometimes, they look like little undertakers in their dark clothes," she said, refusing to meet his eyes. "Like little undertakers slowly walking to a funeral."

"Listen, if—"

"I don't mind. It says here that sometimes the Amish wear regular clothes as a disguise, so they can blend in with the tourists."

"Seriously? I don't believe it."

"It's true."

"No, it isn't."

"No, it isn't," she admitted, smiling with her eyes.

"You do mind?"

"We're on vacation, why would it matter to me if you keep working? We're entering a world of permanent work and permanent vacation."

"You do mind, don't you?"

"It doesn't matter if I mind or not," she chirped, turning the page. "You're going to do what you have to do. So there's no point in me minding. Star Trek's Captain Kirk was born in Iowa, too. Or will be, eventually. Not far from here."

He completed the call. "Henry? Skip Anderson," he said. "Listen, buddy, we've got a problem with the kid."

"What problem?" Henry asked. Skip could hear him sit up in his chair. He had his full attention now.

"He wants to think about it," Skip said.

"A million-dollar signing bonus, and he wants to think about it?" Henry asked incredulously.

"He has a few more games to play with his high school team, so I'll stay here and keep an eye on him. Work with him a little. We're not leaving until I sign him."

Skip watched Jason warming up on the pitcher's mound when a well-dressed man called out.

"So, how does somebody try out for this bush-league team?"

"Dave!" Skip said with a smile, rushing to greet him. Jason stopped to watch their interaction. "What are you doing here?"

"No, Skip," Dave responded, shaking Skip's hand, "the question is, what are you doing here? Henry told me where you were. You've finally run away from the Cubs forever to coach high school kids in Iowa."

"Did Henry tell you about the boy?"

"He might have mentioned him," Dave replied.

"That's like him." Skip shook his head. "The lying snake can't keep a secret. He sent you."

"Now wait a minute, Skip—" Dave said, holding his hands up defensively.

"He sent you here to check up on me, didn't he?" Skip demanded.

"No, not in so many words," Dave said slowly. "I volunteered to take a look at him."

Skip's next words exploded with enthusiasm. "You won't believe it, Dave, you just won't believe it."

"Let me see him. I'm looking forward to a demonstration."

"Boys, come here for a minute," Skip called to Jason and the stocky boy in the catcher's gear.

"Dave Watson, this is Jason Yoder and Mark Branderstatt," Skip said with a gesture. With his blond hair and muscular frame straining his uniform, Branderstatt looked like a smaller version of Jason. Skip continued as they exchanged handshakes. "Dave's my bench coach. Jason, show him what you can do."

Jason and Mark returned to the field as Dave and Skip looked on.

"What do they feed 'em out here? Oats and the blood of human sacrifices?" Dave asked. "Look at the size of them. It looks like you're coaching a team of superheroes. Is that what you've been doing here in Iowa, Skip? Coaching superhero kids?"

Skip wasn't amused. "Real funny. Why don't you give him something to throw at, Dave? Grab a bat and head out there."

"Are you kidding, Skip?" Dave said, shaking his head. "I have three batting titles. I might seriously hurt that kid if I make solid contact with an aluminum bat."

"I'm not too worried," Skip replied, throwing the bat to Dave. "Batter up."

Dave caught it and took a few practice swings as he walked to the plate. Like Skip, Dave was a well-liked player's coach. He understood the player's lives and careers because he'd already traveled the path they were on. Like Skip, he retained the physique of his playing days. His massive shoulders filled his tailored suit so precisely that it looked like the hanger was still in the jacket. He waited for the pitch with condescending patience.

"Give him your fastball, Jason," Skip called out.

Jason nodded in acknowledgment. He leaned back and fired the ball.

Dave was frozen as the white orb blurred by and smashed into Mark's glove with a pop. Dave stumbled backward with a look of shock. "Wh— Wh— What was that!?" he sputtered.

"His fastball," Skip replied with a wry smile.

"I have extra padding in my mitt," Mark said matter-of-factly, throwing the ball back to Jason. "And my hand's still swollen after a game."

"Get back in there," Skip called out. "Here comes his breaking ball. You hear me, Dave? He's throwing a breaking ball." He looked out at Jason and gestured. "The deuce!"

Jason responded with a nod. He dug at the ground with the toe of his shoe. He stepped to the rubber, went into his wind-up, and delivered the pitch.

The white blur hurled directly to the center of the strike zone. Dave swung assuredly at the space where the ball should have been, but instead, the ball smacked into Mark's glove against the ground.

Skip laughed at Dave's reaction. "Looks like it's rolling across a table, doesn't it?"

Ignoring him, Dave muttered through gritted teeth, "Playtime's over, kid. Time to get busy." He took off his suit coat and threw it onto the grass. The crumpled jacket cost more than the annual maintenance budget for the ball field under it.

Dave missed everything. With great exertion, he swung and missed pitches low, high, and right down the middle. Fastballs, change-ups, curveballs—Jason threw them all past him. Dave finally swung so wildly that he corkscrewed around until he fell down.

"That's enough fun for now, boys," Skip said, walking onto the field near home plate. "What do you think?"

"OK, Skip," Dave said with resignation. "I'll admit it, he's pretty good, but I haven't swung a bat in years."

"Wait until you see him hit," Skip said.

Minutes later, Jason stood at the plate, taking practice swings. His teammate, Hank Utz, was on the mound, pitching from behind a protective screen. Skip and Dave watched from near the dugout, Dave holding his dusty jacket over his shoulder.

A year older than Jason, Hank Utz was as large as Mark Branderstatt. He and Mark settled into their positions as Jason prepared for the pitch.

With each pitch, Jason swung effortlessly, and the ball either smashed into the outfield fence or cleared it all together. As he found his rhythm, the ball sailed further with each swing.

Skip and Dave exchanged looks but said nothing.

Skip's sympathies went out to the kid pitching, who was clearly rattled. Pitching to Jason had to be tough for even the best high school pitchers. Skip hoped the kid wouldn't melt down before they were done. As Skip looked on, he watched the effects of good coaching. The boy paused and collected himself before putting every ounce of his fiber into the next pitch.

Skip and Dave scrutinized Jason's fluid swing as the ball cleared the center field fence by twenty feet and landed deep in the cornfield surrounding the ball field.

Again, Utz pitched as hard as he could.

Jason crushed the ball again with a brittle crack. It impacted like a meteorite ten yards beyond the previous ball. Utz continued to pitch—

CRACK! CRACK! CRACK!

Each ball landed further in the field than the other.

"Coach," Utz pleaded exasperated. "Don't make me keep going."

"OK, that's enough," Skip replied. He turned to Dave. "Amazing, isn't he?"

"Maybe."

"Maybe?" Skip was shocked.

"I don't want to kill your party, Skip, but that's a high school pitcher he's slapping around out there," Dave said, gesturing with his bat at the field. "And it's a metal bat."

The realization slowly spread across Skip's face. "Oh, no. No, no, no. No. How could I be so stupid?"

"What are you gonna do?" Dave asked.

"Obviously, I have to see how he'll hit against big-league pitchers."

"You'll have a chance to find out," Dave said. "Henry and Hope will be here tomorrow to see the kid. They're bringing a couple of the guys to give him a real tryout."

"Jason's ready for them," Skip said as he watched Jason talking with his teammates. He wasn't even sweating. "I hope."

GRACE JOINED Jason at the table and placed the family Bible between them as he ate breakfast. She had been praying deeply for her only son.

Like every other day, they had been up for hours. Like all Amish, they prayed while doing their chores. She studied scripture while he shoveled manure.

Life is supposed to be simple for plain people, she thought, preparing his eggs. She was sorry his young life had become much too complicated. She couldn't imagine him leaving his home, leaving the community. Nor could she imagine living without him, not after living without his father all these years. Losing him after losing his father might be too much for her to bear.

"'Do not weary yourself to gain wealth,'" Grace read aloud from the Bible. "'Cease from your consideration of it.' Proverbs 23:4." She closed the book and looked at him as though the matter was decided.

Jason looked at his eggs.

"Maam," he said at last, before shifting his gaze to meet hers. "I know what's going on with the money and the bills."

"Do you now?" The sadness in her eyes betrayed her false smile.

"I have heard you and Onkel Isaac talking about it," he admitted. "I've seen you looking at the bills. I understand what you've been doing. The relish. The farmers' markets. The vegetables. I understand."

A silent tear slipped from her eye.

"Property taxes," she whispered, just loud enough for him to hear. "Property taxes are so high, and I am behind. I did not want to worry you, my little man.

"That horrible man. That Mr. Baker." She slowly shook her head at the memory. "I know the Lord tells us to forgive, but that Mr. Baker took my money, our money, your money. I invested the money with him, because others in our community invested, and he had so many Amish investors from Indiana. And he took our money. He robbed us as surely as if he had a mask and a gun. I try to forgive, but I'm glad he ended up in jail."

Like her words, her tears came freely.

"Isaac has helped. Renting out more of the land helped. I didn't sell it, because you would need it someday. But we are thousands of dollars behind. Thousands. Oh, my son, my boy. I call out to the Lord, asking for his help."

Jason dropped to his knee beside her and took her hand in his. "I am your son. I will always be Jason Yoder, son of James and Grace Yoder." He held her hand against his face. "This will always be our home," he said, looking deep into her eyes. "Your home. Until the day the Lord calls you to be with Jesus in his home. To be with Daa."

"My little man." She smiled through her tears. "Since your father went home to be with the Lord, it has just been you and me in this house. We would not have made it without your uncles, cousins. We are all family, but I am your mother, and you are my little man. But not so little anymore." She wiped her face with her apron. "Now you are my big man." She cradled his cheek in her hand. "I'm so satisfied with the man you have become."

He is so much like his Daa, she thought, in every way. She recalled the countless times she had watched James shuffle out to the barn, Jason following in his footsteps. Now her breath caught each time she saw her son lumber the same path, wearing his father's clothes.

Gone so long, and his spirit still such a presence in their lives. Every room held memories of him, the house still carried his smells. It was as though her husband had gone out to the barn just a few moments ago and would be right back.

His side of the bed was still as warm as her feelings for him. Remarriage was out of the question.

And now their son was the age they were when they fell in love. Each day, she saw her son and remembered his father moving the same way, smiling, laughing.

James at seventeen could lift anything. He once outran a horse for hundreds of feet, laughing the whole way, before it caught up to him. Had she told Jason that story? She couldn't remember.

Each day Jason looked more like a twin than a son, as he grew in spirit and in size. It broke her heart anew to realize he'd spent more of his life without his father than with him.

"So much like your Daa," she said, smiling sadly.

"I think about him every day," Jason said. "I miss him so much."

"I do, too. He's with God."

"I wish he was with us."

"Yes, I do, too." She nodded slowly. "Listen."

She held him by the shoulders and looked deep into his eyes. Simultaneously he was seven and seventeen years old. He was the man before her, and the newborn son handed to her by the midwife.

"Please don't let the taxes influence your decision to play the baseball. The Lord will take care of me and of you."

Your Daa would be pleased to see the man you have become, she thought.

"Maam," Jason murmured, with his disarming smile. "Like you said, one day, the farm will be mine."

She nodded slowly. So much like his Daa.

"These taxes will be mine. The garden. This house." He looked around. "These will be my responsibilities. Maybe it's time I be responsible and do what I need to do. Maybe it's time I be your big man."

She kissed his cheek. "Maybe it's time you go do your chores, my big man." She hugged him with every muscle in her body, pressing her head against his warm, firm chest. Just the two of them, as it had been for all these many years.

THAT AFTERNOON, Jason and Skip walked near the right-field fence. In uniform, Jason carried his glove and a ball, while Skip, dressed in his street clothes, carried a small metal bucket.

"I still don't understand," Jason said with the bewildered tone usually used to describe the shenanigans of the English. "If they want me to play, why do I have to try out?"

"Because they don't trust me," Skip replied.

"But you're the manager."

"I'm also desperate to win the World Series, and you're seventeen years old," he explained. "So you'll give them a baseball demonstration, OK?"

"OK."

"That's the attitude." Skip tossed a ball to Jason. "You're on. Do it just like I said."

Jason remained near the warning track, stretching and twisting with nervous energy.

Skip crossed the field toward home plate where a small group gathered. Uniformed players warmed up on the field, but nearby stood several office men, their dark suits incongruent on the green grass of the field. Among them, Dave wore a casual polo shirt and slacks. Beside him stood a smartly dressed woman in a business suit. She captured Jason's attention as he studied the group. He had never seen a woman dressed that way.

Her skirt stopped just before her knees, like a photo of a blue wave breaking on a white, pristine beach. Her dark shoes seemed wrong for the ball field, but she was clearly comfortable standing in the grass and dirt in shiny heels that stood above the grass like black icepicks.

Amish women always dressed plain and modestly, Jason thought, as he watched her speak to the men next to her. Vacationing Englishwomen almost always dressed in immodest shorts or dungarees. Those few who wore skirts or dresses looked nothing like this woman. He'd never seen anyone who looked like her. He never imagined any woman could look like her.

Her auburn hair tumbled about her head like leaves from the trees. Her strong shoulders gave her an athletic appearance, but Jason noticed she clearly had the legs of a woman. Bare legs, without hose or stockings or anything. She commanded respect from the others around her, and she was obviously used to it.

He couldn't stop looking at her.

Several uniformed players warmed up on the field as Skip made his way toward the suits. The letters on their backs spelled out the names he heard on the radio and read in the paper. Cubs pitcher Stan Kinnick was on the pitcher's mound, throwing hard to catcher Rico Austin. A third player, Dale Cody, swung a bat, warming up. Dale Cody had arms like kitchen table legs.

The stands were already filled with half the town, Jason's teammates, and their families. Coach Pate stood nearby. The air buzzed with anticipation and excitement.

Jason put away distracting thoughts and focused on the task at hand. He needed to do just what Coach Anderson asked of him, and things would all work out, is what Coach Anderson had told him.

Jason felt he had no other choice but to believe him and to trust that God's will would be done.

○○○○ ○○○○

Skip approached the office staff with an icy glare. "Hello, Henry, what brings you to Iowa?"

Henry Hinkley was a petty man, constantly convinced he was being slighted by others. His combover wrapped around his head like a massive fusilli noodle. A small man in size and spirit, it seemed he had gone into professional sports, not for a love of the game, but because he hated athletes. His entire career appeared to be dedicated to wielding power over men who reminded him of the jocks he believed had mistreated him in high school, but who, in reality, had no idea who he was. Skip hated Henry, and they both knew it.

Henry glared at Skip. "Is that your million dollar boy out there?" He gestured to Jason, who was stretching in the outfield.

"That's him," Skip replied, nodding.

"No one this young has ever played major league ball," Henry said.

"Actually," Dave interjected, "the youngest major league player was Joe Nuxhall. He was fifteen when he pitched for the Reds in 1944."

Henry turned his wrathful eyes toward Dave as though seeing him for the first time. "Who?"

"Joe Nuxhall. During World War II," Dave said, dismissively. "I looked it up."

"Amed Rosario was seventeen when the Mets signed him," Skip added.

"Yeah, but they didn't start him at that age," Henry argued.

"Andruw Jones was nineteen when he started with Atlanta,"

Skip replied. "Julio Urías was nineteen when he started for the Dodgers. Harper was twenty when he started for the Nationals."

"But you're talking no minor league work at all? Nobody is that good."

"Eighty to plus-plus across the chart," Skip replied. "He's an ace, a number one starter, and I expect him to start opening day."

"Ha," Henry said contemptuously. "The highest rating in every category? You're out of your mind."

"Isn't that stretching it a little, Skip?" Hope Chambers, the Director of Player Development, asked with her practiced, disarming smile. "Eighty across the chart? He looks more like a thrower than a pitcher."

Hope was everything Henry wasn't. She was kind, caring, and considerate to the players and the other members of the organization. Born into a baseball family, her uncle was on his way to Cooperstown before she was born. She attended college on a full athletic scholarship, double majoring in sports management and business. She intended to be the first female general manager in major league baseball; she was simply waiting for Henry to be fired. Henry was convinced Hope hated him. He was right. Everyone in the organization hated Henry Hinkley.

She beamed at Skip, expecting him to back away from his seemingly outrageous claim.

"He can do things with a baseball most of us have only imagined," Skip replied as Henry shook his head dismissively. "He's a five-tool player. A five-tool pitcher. Players like Jason aren't rare—they are unheard of." He turned his attention to the field. "See for yourself."

He walked onto the infield and called to the other players, "OK, men, take a break."

The others moved away as he laid the bucket on home plate. He whistled sharply to get Jason's attention. Jason, who was standing in the dirt of the warning track in front of the 385 feet sign on the fence, nodded in response.

With a short step, he whipped his arm and fired the ball toward the infield. The blur of the ball arched above the grass and, with one hop, smashed into the bucket at their feet. The people in the stands rose as one and exploded into cheers.

"Geez," one of the suits exclaimed, jumping backward as the spinning bucket bounced across the dirt, brought to life by the ball crashing around inside.

"What kind of throw was that?" said another suit.

"I'd say pretty damned accurate," Skip replied. "The best arms in baseball can't do that." Skip adjusted the bucket and waved at Jason, who delivered another rocket from the warning track. Again the ball crashed into the back of the metal bucket, the force causing it to stand up. Skip radiated satisfaction, studying the astonished expressions of the others. He turned to the outfield, whistled, and gestured for Jason to come in. "Wait until you see him on the mound," he said.

Moments later, Jason prowled the mound, catcher Rico Austin behind the plate. Dale Cody flexed his table leg arms while taking practice swings.

The others gathered around the baseline, where Dave held a radar gun.

"It's just batting practice, Cody, batting practice," Dave called out. "Take the kid downtown."

His eyes locked on Jason, Cody took a final few practice swings and spit.

Jason looked to Skip for reassurance. Skip offered an encouraging nod and a small shake of his fist.

Cody grunted as he swung and missed. The crowd exploded into cheers.

Dave released his breath in one long, slow sigh. He held up the radar gun for the others to see. 108 MPH.

"Tha—Tha— that's impossible," Henry sputtered in disbelief. "Your radar's broken."

Dave pointed the radar at Henry and held it up again. 0 MPH.

"No," Dave said, "it's working all right." He winked at Hope, who smiled in return. He aimed the gun at Jason.

Jason pitched, and Cody swung and missed again. Dave held up the radar gun. 107 MPH.

Jason went into his windup and fired the ball past Cody's wild swing. The crowd exploded with excitement after every pitch. 108 MPH.

Henry sputtered like a 1964 Johnson Evinrude outboard motor. "Bu— Bu— Bu— But how is this even possible?"

Repeatedly, Jason pitched, and Cody swung and missed.

"Swing hard, Cody," Dave yelled, "in case you get lucky and make contact!"

Once Jason found his rhythm, the pitches got faster.

107 MPH. 108 MPH. 109 MPH. 110 MPH.

"This is the most incredible thing I've ever seen," Henry whispered.

"At that speed, it's like trying to hit a BB with a pool cue," Dave said. "I bet he can take that fastball into the seventh or eighth inning."

"Does he have other pitches?" Hope asked calmly.

"You want my scouting report? He's obviously got an eighty fastball," Skip responded. "I'd say his changeup and slider are both eighties, too. Like I said, eighty across the chart."

"Three eighty pitches?" Henry replied. "That's preposterous. Unheard of."

"Fine," Skip deferred. "Call it a plus-plus changeup and a plus-plus curve. Whatever you want to call it. All of his pitches, his command, his makeup, are all just like his fastball. He has laser-like focus and ice water in his veins." He turned to the field. "Jason, hold it a second."

"Cody, he's going to throw his changeup," Skip said to Cody after making eye contact with him. "Do you hear me? He's throwing a changeup."

"What are you doing, Coach?" Henry asked as Cody nodded in acknowledgment, confusion on his face.

"Watch," Skip said, gesturing at Jason. "He doesn't just paint the corners, he moves into the corners, hangs drapes, and arranges the furniture."

Jason nodded and fired. Cody swung early and awkwardly, completely befuddled. Several suits chuckled.

"What are you doing?" Henry yelled.

"You think I did it on purpose?" Cody yelled back, defensively.

Skip looked at Jason and nodded. "Throw it again." He looked at Cody. "Here it comes again. The changeup. Let him know when you're ready."

Cody spit, took a few practice swings, got into his stance, and nodded. Jason nodded in return and pitched. Again, Cody's timing was off. He stumbled a few steps forward and sprawled into the dirt.

"Keep throwing, Jason," Skip said. He turned to Henry and Hope. "Knowing the pitch doesn't make a difference," he explained. "He'll have them chasing breaking balls and out in front of off-speed pitches. Fastball, changeup, slider— it's impossible to tell them apart. All of his pitches appear exactly the same, more so than any other pitcher I've ever seen. He also has more movement and better control than most veteran pitchers."

"How does he do it?" Henry challenged.

"Look at the size of his hands," Hope said with a gesture. "The ball disappears into his hand." She turned to Skip. "What is he, six-six, six-seven?"

"About that," he responded, shrugging.

"Look at him, Henry," she said, taking Jason's measure. "Do you see his muscles? He's a giant."

"More mass, more gas," Dave agreed with a shrug. "He can grip it and rip it."

"With his kick, he's halfway to home when he finally releases the ball," Hope said.

Skip nodded. "His release point is significant. Also, watch his mechanics. Look at his shoulders and hips."

"Yes," Hope said, "look at his shoulders and hips. He's rotating his hips while his shoulders are still closed."

"Precisely," Skip said.

"I don't get it," Henry said.

"He's a high-level pitcher," Hope said. "His arm is moving into acceleration while his hips are opening— what, close to forty-five, fifty degrees?" Skip nodded. "But his shoulders are still closed. He stretches the muscles of his core and puts his whole body into the force of the pitch. All of this weight and muscles act like a slingshot."

"More like a trebuchet," Dave interjected. "A counterweight trebuchet."

"What are you talking about?" Henry said.

"I looked it up. It was a type of medieval catapult that used a counterweight to sling stuff hundreds of yards. Jason uses the torque of his body, his shoulders and hips, better than any player I've ever seen."

"Look at his shoulder tilt," Skip said, pointing to Jason. "He's keeping the pressure off his elbow and not doing damage to his body with every pitch. It means his physical recovery time between starts isn't typical.

"He could throw like this all day, and there's nobody here who can hit him. There aren't a dozen guys in the league who can get the bat on one of his pitches. He's like Koufax or Tom Seaver."

"You're thinking starter?" Hope asked Skip, without taking her eyes from Jason.

"Like I said, I'm looking to start him opening day," he responded. Hope nodded in silent agreement. Skip noticed she still hadn't stopped staring at him.

"How is he out of the stretch?" she asked.

"See for yourself," Skip replied. "Jason, pitch from the stretch."

Jason acknowledged the request with a nod and changed his stance before pitching.

"Same velocity, same movement on the ball. He's as consistent as a heartbeat," Skip said. "It will seldom matter because he won't have that many get on base."

"What a freak," Henry said with a shake of his head. "And he can hit, too?"

"He's the best hitting pitcher since Babe Ruth," Skip replied.

"Let's see him at the plate," Hope said.

Skip and Dave shared concerned, conspiratorial looks, both of them wondering if Jason could actually hit major league pitching.

"Yes," Skip repeated quietly to Dave, "let's see."

Chapter 5

J ason stood near home plate, wearing a batting helmet and absentmindedly swinging the bat as he studied Kinnick on the mound. With his dark hair, features, and eyes, Jason thought Kinnick looked like a medieval Spanish knight preparing for battle. He was throwing hard.

Unbidden, the words of his father came to Jason: Watch close, they'll show you what they're thinking.

Can it be that simple? Jason thought. Joe Kinnick was one of the best pitchers in the game, and the way his body shifted for off-speed pitches was so obvious Jason could see it from across the field. He looked around to see if it was some sort of test, but no one else appeared to notice.

It had been years since he'd hit a baseball with a wooden bat. He'd used the aluminum bat to hit softballs with the other kids and when he played with the high school team. Working his fingers on the grip, his hand pressing against the knob, memories flooded over him like a warm summer rain. He loved the feel of the wooden bat, the brand Mjollnir burned into the barrel. It felt real, natural. And he loved what the wooden bat represented.

He'll show you what he's thinking.

Why was Kinnick so obvious in his delivery? Jason looked to the suits for answers, but they were talking to each other.

Scanning the crowd, Jason finally found Faith and Adam in their usual places near the stands, a small smile slowly splitting his face like the dawn chasing away the darkness.

Faith offered a wave and smile as Adam nodded stoically.

Nodding, Jason continued to smile as he gave the bat a strong, confident swing. The crowd roared. He took a few more swings before resting the bat on his shoulder to watch Kinnick's now-familiar motions.

Kinnick stopped throwing, put his meaty hands on his hips, spit, and offered a glare that would wither most men like fresh-cut alfalfa in the noon sun.

The crowd buzzed with excitement.

"OK, Jason," Skip called to him. "Let's go."

Jason nodded confidently to Skip and stepped into the batter's box. Like a warm breeze on a cool afternoon, silence settled over the field in anticipation of the pitch.

Kinnick wound-up and fired the ball across the plate. Jason watched the ball smack into the catcher's mitt.

He couldn't believe it was so easy. It was a hard pitch, but not as fast as he expected. It wasn't an off-speed pitch; that was obviously different. *So what is going on?* Jason wondered.

As the crowd shouted encouragement, he took a few practice swings and stepped back into the batter's box.

Kinnick pitched again, grunting with the effort, and Jason watched the strike shoot by.

Kinnick's body mechanics were so obvious for his off-speed pitch that Jason thought it was intentional.

Quietly murmuring concern, the stunned crowd was too shocked to offer even perfunctory support.

"I thought he could hit," Jason clearly heard a suit say across the silent field. "He's not even swinging."

Coach Pate quickly stepped forward to speak to Skip, before jogging on to the infield.

"Are you OK?" Coach Pate asked Jason.

"Yes, sir," Jason said.

"What's the problem? Are you afraid of this guy?"

"No, sir, not too much. Just a little surprised."

"You can hit him, can't you?"

"Yes, sir."

"I know you can. You can hit him. You can hit anyone they put in front of you. You have nothing to worry about, so just settle down." Coach Pate spoke calmly and gently as he placed a firm hand on Jason's shoulder. "Keep your eyes on the ball, lead with your hands, keep your weight back, and swing through the ball. Fundamentals. Got it?"

"Yes, sir."

"Good. And have fun. That's why you're here."

Coach Pate slapped Jason's back pockets and walked off the field. Kinnick spit, leaned towards the catcher, and pitched.

Jason whipped the bat so quickly that it struck the ball with the cracking sound of a snapping broom handle. As one, the crowd exploded with excitement.

Kinnick pitched again, and Jason smashed the ball again. It cleared the center field fence by five feet. Kinnick looked like he was trying to swallow the next baseball. He spit, leaned, stood, and fired the ball to the catcher.

CRACK! Jason placidly watched the ball disappear into the corn beyond the fence. Suddenly his teammates raced each other to the field, eager to retrieve mementos of the hitting display.

CRACK! CRACK! CRACK! Kinnick pitched with all his strength, and effortlessly, Jason drove each ball over the fence and into the field.

"He sits back on the pitch, quick hands," Dave said.

"He uses his hips and weight for power," added Hope.

"See how long he keeps his bat in the strike zone?" Skip asked.

"Has he ever played football?" Henry asked.

Skip glanced at Coach Pate for an answer.

"I don't think he's even touched a football," Coach Pate replied.

"Keep him away from football scouts," Hope said.

"No one else knows about him," Skip said. "No scouts. No recruiters. No one. Just us."

The rhythmic sound of the ball exploding off the bat was hypnotic. They returned their attention to the action on the field. Having found his rhythm, Jason was driving the ball dozens of feet over the fence, seemingly with no more effort than it took to swing the bat.

Jason's teammates cheered with each crack of the bat and laughed moments later as the ball impacted in the mud with a loud thump. They joked and frolicked as they jockeyed for the home run balls with the distinctive MLB logo and the commissioner's autograph.

"Just us," Skip repeated.

"He's seventeen?" Cody wondered aloud. "The change in my pocket is older than this kid."

"He may be seventeen, but he's definitely no kid," Hope said.

Kinnick reached into the bag at his feet for another ball but stood up empty-handed. "Hey, Skip," he called out, "we're out of balls."

The stands exploded in delirious excitement.

Skip whistled and waved to Jason and Kinnick, and the two trotted from the field.

"Whatever it takes, we have to sign this kid," Henry said breathlessly.

"Let's not get ahead of ourselves," Hope added in her normal calming tone. She silently studied Jason as the young man walked toward them. "But I'm fairly certain an acceptable agreement can be reached. He certainly appears to be as advertised. I understand your excitement." She smiled disarmingly at Skip.

Looking past Hope and Henry, Skip watched as Coach Pate approached Jason, and the two began to talk. Skip couldn't hear them, but he could see an unusual expression cross Jason's face as he pointed to the distance, and Coach Pate turned to look.

"He's worth every penny," Henry said, caught up in the excitement. "We have to sign him."

Craning his neck, Skip tried to see where Coach Pate and Jason were looking. He observed only a brown cornfield past the outfield fence, the kids eagerly searching for balls among the remains of harvested cornstalks.

"Sounds simple enough," Skip said, watching the coach and player in their animated discussion. But he was learning that nothing about Jason Yoder was as simple as it sounded.

"Is this true, what they say?" Grace asked Jason after dinner. Earlier that afternoon, an elder had stopped by to tell Grace about Jason playing with the high school team, and with baseball men from out of town. Was he really playing in English baseball games?

"Yes, Maam," Jason replied.

"You lied to your mother?" Isaac asked, his countenance clouding like a spring storm sky. "To me?"

"No, Onkel," Jason denied quickly. "I did not lie. I just did not tell you all of the details."

"You did not lie," Isaac said, shaking his head sadly. "But you did disappoint us. Is this what comes of the baseball? You stop telling the 'details'?"

His words wounded Jason like a wasp sting on the face.

"I am sorry, Onkel."

"My boy, I am sorry," Isaac replied softly, his emotions buried beneath his graying beard.

Jason remained silent in his shame of disappointing his family.

"How long has this gone on? Playing baseball with the English?" Grace asked.

"Four months."

Isaac and Grace looked at each other in shock. Isaac rose slowly and walked around the room, his weathered hand stroking his whiskers.

"And who were these other baseball men?"

"Mr. Anderson works for them," Jason responded. "They came to watch me play."

"Public demonstrations," Isaac said with a sad, slow shake of his head. "You crowd the fence, and now someone tells your mother what you do." He raised his hands in exasperation. "Next the Bishop comes here, is that what you want? To bring shame on your mother's house?"

"No, Onkel. I—"

"I?" Isaac interrupted. "What is in the middle of 'pride?'"

"I," Jason replied with a guilty tone and downcast eyes.

"I. And where is God? Do you forget joy?"

"No, Onkel." Jason studied his uncle's eyes.

Isaac sat as he held up his thumb. "Jesus is first." He raised his index finger. "Others are in between, and you are last," he added as he raised his middle finger. "Do not forget God, my boy, do not forget God. Keep God in your heart and in all things."

Jason nodded, considering the words he'd grown up hearing. The importance of others—of community— was woven like a thread into every aspect of Amish life. Jason knew he was crowding the fence, he knew he was at the limit of what their community would accept. But he was only playing a game, safe within the confines of the foul lines.

After more than five silent minutes, Grace stirred.

"If you will play the baseball," Isaac finally said, sadness in his tone, "you must go."

"What?" Jason said, shocked by his uncle's unexpected response. "Go? I do not understand."

"You bring disruption to our community," Isaac said slowly, suddenly very weary. "To your mother's home. This must not be."

"I want to help Maam. Help with the farm."

"Help how?"

"The...the money they will pay me..." Jason struggled to explain. "The money— will help—" He fell silent. He didn't wish to shame his mother. Didn't his uncle understand?

"I cannot tell you what to do," Isaac said. "Pray and ask the Lord for guidance. You must choose a life and live it."

JASON STRUGGLED with his choice for days.

His final minutes before sleep each night were dedicated to prayer and seeking the Lord's will for his life. But when he opened his eyes, he felt as lost as he did when he closed them.

The usual comfort found in physical labor remained elusive as he went about his chores. Normally, he easily lost himself in his work, as the Lord intended, but he lost himself in the efforts of baseball just as easily. Strangely, it felt natural and unnatural to work or play baseball. The comfort of each seemed lost.

He assumed the more he played baseball, the more likely he would decide to remain at home. He thought the more seriously he considered Coach Anderson's offer, the easier it would be to reject it.

But as he played the last few games of the regular season, he realized he wanted to keep playing. Like the early morning mist burning off with the rising sun, he felt his options coming into focus.

He went twelve for fourteen with four home runs and three

stolen bases. He was ashamed to admit that he enjoyed his teammates carrying him from the field on their shoulders after the final regular-season win. Coach Anderson told him as a Chicago Cub, he shouldn't expect to be carried off the field, but he could expect to be buried under a pile of teammates when they won the pennant.

Even more than baseball, or his mother, or the Order, his thoughts returned to Faith.

Faith.

With hair as golden as corn silk and eyes the color of caramel, she had grown to be as beautiful in appearance as she was kind in spirit.

Like the blessing of his natural strength, she was blessed with a compassionate heart. Still, he knew she had absolutely no interest in leaving the Order, and even less interest in anything associated with the English. Her love of God, the community, and her family was one of the traits he found so attractive.

How could he leave and not see her for months on end? He tried to imagine the loneliness of being away from her, away from everything he knew, but the thought simply sat in his mind like a black emptiness. He couldn't conceive it.

There was also the money. He had great difficulty getting his mind around the money he could earn playing baseball. Baseball. Onkel, Faith, everyone was right; baseball was a children's game. But he played so well that they were willing to pay money for him to do it. They would give him money and freedom and possibilities. He was as amazed as everyone else by the possibility.

He loved throwing the ball with such speed and precision that it was impossible to hit. He always knew he was good, but thanks to Coach Anderson, he now had an idea just how good. He made the major league players look foolish when they tried to hit him. His father's dipsy-doo pitch was impossible for anyone to hit. He wished his Daa were there to see it.

He imagined all of the players he'd heard announced on the radio or read in the newspaper, trying to hit his pitching—trying and failing. He was thrilled by the thought of him—Jason Yoder—

throwing the ball past some of the greatest players ever. He knew he could do it. He knew, as surely as the sun would rise in the morning, that with a touch as soft as well-worn leather, he could put the ball right where he wanted it to go, with nearly every pitch.

He felt the life of a cow in his fingertips while milking. His whole body experienced the muscles and twitching nerves of a horse when it leaned against him as he cleaned a hoof. In the same way, his fingernails in the stitching could make the ball do precisely what he wanted.

He would throw the ball past all of them.

Hitting was even easier. Life on the farm had given him the strength and skills he needed on the diamond. Swinging a bat was like swinging an ax. Easier, because the weight wasn't all in one end. So no matter the speed of a ball, he knew he could get the bat around as fast as he needed to.

Kinnick was one of the best? His delivery was as clear as spring water.

Driving the ball was as easy as driving a team of horses. And they would give him more money than he could imagine for him to do it.

He loved the feel of the bat making contact with the ball. He wanted the feeling again.

THE AFTERNOON SUN warmed the crisp autumn air as well as the capacity crowd for the final game of the Iowa High School League State Championship.

The Kalona Eagles won the first game of the best of three series—4-0—when Jason pitched a three-hit shutout and drove in two runs. With Jason playing third, the Eagles surrendered the second game 3-2. Their entire season came down to one final game.

Coach Pate and Skip stood in the dugout, watching the teams

warm up on the field. The unseasonably warm air was filled with the sound of baseballs popping into leather gloves and players yammering easily to each other.

"This is it," Coach Pate said to Skip. "Win or lose, I want to thank you for your help." He offered his hand.

"No, Coach, thank you," Skip said, exchanging the handshake.

"I've told you just about all I know about the Amish," Coach Pate said. "I still don't know what Jason will do, but if he agrees to play, you should be ready."

"I hope so."

"By the way, you know he hasn't had any vaccinations or inoculations?"

"What?"

"Yeah, some Amish don't believe in it."

"So what's that mean?"

"He needs to be inoculated. He could come back at the end of the season with God knows what— chickenpox, whooping cough, probably mumps, measles— if he introduces the viruses into the community, he might kill some older people."

Skip was appalled. "What are you talking about?"

"A fair number of Amish don't believe in vaccinations— they'll avail themselves of modern medicine when they need to— but most don't get the basic shots. I don't even know if they get tetanus shots on a regular basis. I hope so, but I honestly don't know."

"Now I've heard everything," Skip said, rolling his eyes.

"Yeah, I know. That's why I'm telling you," Coach Pate said. "You'll need to make sure it's taken care of during his contract physical. Make sure the doctor gives him his shots because if the doctor doesn't ask, Jason probably won't volunteer the information."

Skip nodded. "Right, I'll take care of it."

"He's obviously healthy as a horse," Coach Pate said, gesturing to Jason. "I wouldn't be surprised if he's not seen a doctor since he was born. My exemption for him to play also exempted him from the required physical on religious grounds." He winked. "I don't expect the Chicago Cubs to be so accommodating."

They returned their attention to the team, though after a moment, Coach Pate asked, "Have you noticed how he affects the way the whole team plays? He changes the tone of the locker room, the field, the bench. Their mental attitude is different when he's on the field. His ability gives the team a confidence beyond their skills. He's taught them how to focus on the game. He's also taught them how to be winners. I've never seen anything like it."

"Neither have I," Skip agreed, as he considered the thousands of players he'd seen over the years. "Neither have I. He's one of the best ever on the mound and at the plate. He's a pitcher who hits in the number four position for power. He is easily the best hitting pitcher since Babe Ruth."

Coach Pate smiled.

"What is it?" Skip asked.

Coach Pate took off his hat and ran his hand through his hair. He shook his head but continued to smile. "It's just funny hearing Jason talked about in the same sentence as Babe Ruth," he said, a touch of awe in his tone. "Jason Yoder, from Kalona, Iowa. I knew he was something special. I just knew it."

"How is he such a good hitter? What's his secret at the plate?"

Coach Pate returned his hat to his head. "You don't think I haven't asked him? Repeatedly?"

"What's he say?"

"He just shrugs and says he can see what's coming before the pitch."

"What's that mean?"

"I have no idea. If you figure it out, let me know." Coach Pate thought for a moment. "Actually, it usually does look like he knows what the pitcher will throw before the pitch. I don't think I've ever seen him strike out. Fly out, yes, usually deep down the foul line, but never strike out. He's never swung at a bad pitch. Ever."

"Is he a 'guess hitter'?" Skip asked. "He looks more 'see the ball— hit the ball.'"

"You'd think he's guessing, but how can he?" replied Coach Pate. "Pitchers he's never faced before, he just walks up to the plate and gets base hits. He has astonishing bat speed; I've never seen anyone get the barrel around as fast as he does, but there's more to his hitting — I just can't figure out what it is.

"Almost as impressive as his bat? He's never made an error. Not one, in the entire time he's played for me. His baseball instincts are spot-on. I've never seen anything like it." He smiled. "I'll try to stop saying that, but you get the point."

Skip nodded.

"He's purely present, every moment he's on the field, he's present, you know what I mean?"

Skip nodded again.

"He's completely connected to the movement of the ball. Hitting, pitching, fielding. He doesn't make mental errors, ever. He's in a Zen-like state with a focus I've never seen at any level of the game. I've never seen his type of focus anywhere else in the world, actually.

"You know that vicious, evil curveball of his?"

Skip laughed. He knew Jason's curveball would be as difficult to hit for major-leaguers level as it was for high school boys.

"He walked in with that," Coach Pate continued. "I hardly helped him with it at all. I gave him a couple of pointers, a few suggestions about his delivery and release— how to hide the pitch from the batter. But that was all him. He was born with that curveball." He smiled and nodded at Skip. "I think about that a lot. That curveball. That wicked curveball. And he just does it. Hitting coaches, pitching coaches, they can help make improvements, build on natural talent. But that curveball..."

"I know what you mean," Skip said. "A lot of guys have trouble with curveballs."

"You don't have to tell me," Coach Pate said. He slowly shook his head in wonder. "Watching him play, watching those curveballs, it's like watching a lightning storm. Completely controlled and completely out of control, unimaginable power. A breath-taking wonder of nature."

As if awakening from a dream, he looked Skip in the eyes. "And then he walked onto my field and asked if he could play baseball for me. I tell you Skip, I wasn't much of a believer before, but I am now. Jason is a tremendous work of nature, a creation of God. There's no other explanation. You don't just climb down off a horse and buggy, walk onto a baseball field, and be as naturally good as he is. It's impossible. God reached down and touched this farm boy and gave him skills that many men would sell their souls for. Skills that he just takes for granted. Skills that are going to walk off that field and back onto that horse and buggy and disappear into the Iowa countryside, if you don't do something."

Skip realized he had never heard so much talk about God in his life. It was as though the religion of the Amish brushed off on their neighbors, and in turn, on everyone who came in contact with them.

"I said everything I could to convince him to go to college," Coach Pate was saying. "I didn't even think of professional baseball. I talked with him, after that exhibition he put on for your bosses, but I don't know if it did any good." He looked at the field for a few long moments before returning his gaze to Skip.

"Let me tell you something else," he continued. "I don't know how he even knew the rules of the game. The Amish go to libraries, of course, just like everyone else. But I know for a fact he had never played in an organized game until he walked onto our field, four months ago.

"Try to wrap your head around that, Coach," he said with a smile. "What we're watching on the field is pure, raw ability, with whatever coaching I've been able to offer. With you and your staff, and the best of everything, he could become the greatest that's ever played the game. He'll shatter all the records. He'll become legendary. He'll have his own room at Cooperstown." His voice trailed off, and they returned their attention to the kids on the field.

Jason held a bat horizontally, chest high, a hand on either end. A laughing teammate dangled from the center of the bat, doing chin-ups, a foot off the ground. Others gathered around, cheering.

"He'll make his decision based on what you say to him, not what I say," Coach Pate said "I begged him to go to college, and he wouldn't even consider it.

"But can you imagine," he said slowly, "now that you've watched him play, all that God-created ability and skill, just disappearing?" He locked eyes with Skip, and said earnestly, "Don't let that happen, Coach. Do whatever you need to do to give him a chance to be the greatest baseball player of all time."

IN THE DUGOUT, Skip and Coach Pate clapped and called out encouragement to Jason on the pitcher's mound.

Clearly agitated, he was throwing more balls than normal.

Wiping his brow, he glanced at the runner on second and then at the runner several steps away from first. Both boys reached on fielding errors, the result of the team feeling their nerves. Jason stole another look at the scoreboard to confirm his team's 1-0 lead in the seventh and final inning.

Toeing the rubber, Jason went into his wind-up. In a sudden blur he whirled and whipped the ball toward the second baseman, the runner diving back to the bag too late to avoid being tagged out.

"Out!" cried the outfield umpire as he gestured. Coach Pate and Skip clapped in response and shouted encouragement. The massive crowd rose to their feet in anticipation of the final out.

Jason stalked the mound nervously as the batter took a practice swing and stepped to the plate.

"Two outs Jason, two away." Coach Pate said, clapping his hands.

Jason wound up and fired the ball to the catcher.

"Ball," shouted the umpire.

Jason's expression remained unchanged as the catcher threw him the ball. He stared intently at the catcher, looking for the sign.

"Settle down, Jason, settle down," Coach Pate called out.

"Take it easy, boy," Skip yelled, joining in and clapping his hands. He turned to Coach Pate. "What are you going to do?"

"He has to finish it win or lose," Coach Pate replied, flashing the catcher several signs. "I don't have anybody else to send in."

Jason leaned forward, watching the catcher give the signals. He nodded, stood, went into his windup, and delivered the pitch.

"Ball two!"

Jason instantly turned his back on home plate and walked around the pitcher's mound, head down, as though looking in the grass for answers.

"Come on, Ump," Skip yelled at the umpire. "What ballgame are you watching?"

"Easy, Skip, that's not a major league umpire out there," Coach Pate whispered uneasily. "that's an Iowa high school umpire."

"It's alright," Skip replied calmly. He turned back to the field. "Come on Blue, let's see a little consistency," he yelled louder than before. The umpire glanced toward the dugout, but said nothing.

Jason caught the ball, looked at Skip, and then at the people around the field. Near the bleachers, Faith waved with her finger tips and smiled, while Adam nodded calmly in his usual way.

Jason offered a weak smile and turned back to the game. Wiping his face, he leaned in for the signals, paused, went into his wind-up and fired the ball.

"Strike one!" called the umpire.

Jason's sweaty face was covered with relief.

The crowd cheered and applauded.

"That's more like it, Jason," Skip called. "That's the way."

Jason caught the ball, went quickly through his wind-up, and pitched.

"Ball three!"

Skip rushed from the dugout, Coach Pate fruitlessly grabbing at his arm.

Skip charged the field releasing obscenities like colorful balloons over a parade.

"That's the worst damned call I've seen in my entire baseball career," Skip screamed, closing in on the umpire.

Dumfounded, the umpire slowly removed his mask. "You're arguing balls and strikes with me?"

"You can't even see the baseball, how can you call balls and strikes?" Skip yelled. "You're the dumbest corn-pone, hayseed cracker, trailer-trash I've ever seen. What are you doing on this field? Why don't you get back up on your tractor and drive back to your cornfield!"

"Coach, I don't know where you think you are," the umpire calmly responded, "but I think you need to sit back down."

"You stupid S.O.B., you're so stupid you don't even know when you're being insulted," Skip said quietly, staring the man in the eye. "Knock the corn cobs out of your ears and listen to me. You don't know baseball, at all, corn-pone. Go back to your filthy pigpen and say hello to your mother for me."

"This ain't Wrigley Field, Coach, this is my field, and you can get the hell off it," the umpire said, matching Skip's tone. He stepped back and gestured as he yelled, "You're out of here!"

"You're throwing me out?" Skip howled. A vein on the left side of his head began to grow. "You small-town hick. You're a disgrace to baseball. My grandmother could call a better game."

Coach Pate was by Skip's side. "Let's go, Coach," he said, pulling Skip by the arm.

The crowd cheered as Skip shook him off and stomped away.

Coach Pate pulled Skip close to him and whispered sharply, "What was that all about?"

"It'll take the pressure off Jason," Skip replied. "He'll keep his confidence up; he'll think it's the umpire and not him."

"It's a strange way to boost his confidence," Coach Pate muttered.

"It'll work."

JASON WATCHED Skip storm from the dugout and toward the school before the umpire resumed the game. He held up three fingers on one hand and one finger on the other as he yelled, "Three and one!"

Jason took a deep breath to settle his nerves. "Don't matter who's batting," his father said, "you're just throwing the ball to the catcher." Calmly, Jason went into his wind-up. Paused. "You just throw it hard and fast like I showed you."

Jason fired the ball down the center of the strike zone.

"Strike two!"

The crowd roared approval.

"That's the way, Jason, one more strike," Coach Pate said, clapping. "Just one more pitch, buddy."

The air had the energy of a summer electrical storm.

Jason looked in for the sign. As he straightened and moved into his wind-up, the deafening crowd quieted in anticipation.

Time and again, Coach Pate had drilled into his team the simple science of baseball. As the ball approached the plate, physics took over: the force of the pitch and the force of the swing combined to generate the distance the struck ball traveled.

The moment the ball left the bat, Jason realized that for all the home runs he'd hit, he'd never before given up a home run as a pitcher. Turning to watch the ball fly out of the infield, in the back of his mind, he wondered if Coach Anderson would still want him after he gave up a home run and lost the championship.

Seconds later, it was pure chance that Jacob Miller got anywhere near the fly ball as he raced it to the fence. A six-foot senior already accepted to the University of Iowa, he was playing his last high school game, and Jason knew he desperately wanted to win the state championship. Jason also knew by the trajectory the ball would go over the fence, and Jacob only had one chance.

When he reached the warning track dirt, Jacob took a long stride, planted his left foot on the fence, and stretched his gloved hand to the limit as his extended body crashed into the fence. He fell backward with a somersault, sprung to his feet and stabbed his snow cone catch triumphantly above his head. He held the glove aloft as he screamed and galloped toward the infield.

The bleachers erupted into pandemonium.

The pain in Jason's chest told him he'd been holding his breath, and he finally exhaled. He allowed a small smile that grew out of control as his teammates converged on him. Coach Pate and the few players on the bench rushed onto the field and jumped onto the growing pile of players on Jason.

Jason squirmed his way to the top of the pile. Before he could take two steps, his teammates hoisted him into the air and lifted him onto their shoulders. This was the greatest moment of his life. Jason smiled widely and looked for Faith in her normal spot. For a moment, he thought he saw her, but her golden hair quickly disappeared into the sea of people.

Chapter 6

That evening in his hotel room, Skip opened the door to find Jason outside, dressed in his Amish garb.

"Jason. Come in," Skip said, gesturing to a chair.

Jason removed his hat as he entered.

"Thank you, Coach," Jason replied. He addressed Annie sitting at the table. "Mrs. Anderson."

"Hello, Jason," Annie said.

"What's on your mind?"

"This tournament," Jason said. "Winning the championship. I want to keep playing. I want to play for the Chicago Cubs."

Skip clapped his hands sharply one time in celebration. "Outstanding." He extended his hand to Jason. "Welcome to the organization."

"Congratulations," Annie said.

"I will play baseball for you," Jason said, shaking hands, "but I will continue to follow the Ordnung."

"The Amish rulebook?"

"Yes, sir, the Ordnung is more than just rules," Jason explained. "It is a guide on how to live a plain and holy life. We live by the Ordnung, and I will continue to as I play baseball, just like I did when I played for Coach Pate."

"What does this mean?"

"I will live my life as unser satt leit," Jason continued. "In the way of my people."

"In the way of your people," Skip repeated, nodding.

"I will keep God in my heart at all times," Jason explained.

"Of course," Skip replied quickly.

"I will wear plain clothes when I'm not on the field."

"Okaaaay..."

"I do not know what I will do for church every other week," Jason said, glancing around the hotel room, searching for elusive answers.

"I'm sure you'll do the best you can," Annie offered helpfully.

"I will be among you," Jason said, "but I will still try to remain separate from you English."

"OK," Skip said, "but can you try not to call us 'you English'?"

"I will try," Jason replied stoically.

"I GOT HIM, HENRY," Skip yelled into the phone. "We sealed the deal with a handshake."

"Good news," replied Henry. "Give me his number; I'll give him a call."

"He's standing right here," Skip said. "Hold on."

He passed the phone to Jason. "Here, talk to Henry."

"Yes?" Jason asked tentatively, the phone cradled in his hands, inches from his head. "Yes, sir. I— I would like to play baseball for the Chicago Cubs." He listened and began nodding. "Yes, sir, I am

Amish. I do not know, sir, I do not know Coach Anderson well enough to say. I don't know. What? Yes, sir."

Jason quickly gave the phone back to Skip, seemingly eager to be done with it.

"Yes, Henry?"

"We have some problems with the contract," Henry said. "I'll explain it to you when I see you. When are you coming back?"

"Annie and I will be in Chicago in a few days. Don't spoil this, Henry. Jason Yoder is exactly what this team needs. I'll talk to you later."

Jason appeared distracted as Skip ended the call.

"What's wrong?" Annie asked.

"I've never talked on a telephone before," Jason said, looking with sadness at the instrument of his undoing.

"What?" Skip was incredulous.

"Why not?" Annie asked gently.

"I have never had anyone to talk to."

Annie stared hard at Skip. He knew she was angry about the way Jason was being affected. But what could he do? He had a World Series to win.

Jason and Faith sat near a creek where the warm afternoon air gently stirred the surface of the water, the dappled sunlight playing across the small waves. Just out of earshot, Adam was fishing.

"I am going to play."

"I know."

"I still love you."

"I know."

"I will come back."

"I know you think so." She smiled sorrowfully.

Jason looked at her. "What do you mean?"

"Many leave, few ever come back," Faith said wistfully. "You will be among them, you will change."

"My love for you will never change."

"That may be so, but if it isn't enough to keep you here," she said with a small, sad smile, "will it be enough to bring you back?"

Emotions swirled freely in his head like dandelion seeds on the wind. His simple life was growing complex and conflicted, and he felt helpless to do anything about it.

They rose and began to walk.

"Would you stay if I asked you to stay?"

"I cannot stay. I have to try. And the money."

"When will you leave?"

"Not until February. I have to get the farm ready."

"So, we will have five months."

"We could get married before I leave. We could marry in a few weeks." They stopped walking.

"And live with your mother until you leave?"

He nodded.

"And I stay with her after you are gone?"

"Yes."

"And if you never come back?"

"I will."

"Then that is when we will marry, after you come back. Have you thought about if the lot of deacon or minister were to fall on you?"

"The Lord knows what is best," Jason replied.

"Yes, the Lord does, but do you? Are you ready to accept all of the responsibilities that come with marriage? You can not play children's games and live like an adult. Not in our community."

Frustrated, Jason simply looked at her, but she began to walk again. He had imagined them together so many times that to him, it was already real. He couldn't understand why she didn't agree.

He glanced at Adam, who gently moved his fishing pole, the line splitting the surface of the water, and shrugged.

Jason watched Faith walk away.

⚾⚾⚾⚾⚾

"WHAT ARE YOU SAYING?" Skip asked sternly.

He sat at his cluttered desk in his equally cluttered office, Henry standing over him.

"We're not paying the Yoder kid the million signing bonus."

"What?" Skip yelled, leaping from his leather chair and knocking over a stack of scouting reports.

"The organization can't risk that much on a complete unknown," Henry said. "An absolutely untried unknown."

"Unknown?" Skip repeated, his eyes closed, shaking his head as though he'd never heard the word before. "Unknown? Henry, you saw him."

"I know I did," Henry said, "but we just can't afford it."

"First you can't risk it on an unknown, now you can't afford it? Which is it?" Skip demanded, crossing his arms in defiance. "I told him he'd get a million."

"We're signing him to a minor league contract and scaling back his salary to the league minimum, too."

Skip exploded, slamming the desk with both hands. A stack of papers fluttered to the floor like leaves. "The hell you will. Listen to me, you worthless sack of horseshoes. I told Jason he'll get the bonus, and you're going to give it to him."

"What are you, this kid's agent?" Henry sneered.

"I'm not letting you take advantage of him." Skip sat back down.

Henry smirked, perspiration on his upper lip. "Honestly, Coach, what's your interest in the kid? Why do you care about his signing bonus?"

Skip pushed aside a clipboard on his desk, put his elbows down, a hand up, and spread his fingers wide. "You see this?"

"What? Your hand? So what?"

Skip stood, holding his hand out in front of him. "I don't have a World Series ring. This team hasn't won a World Series in more than a century," he said. "This kid will win us one, but only if we treat him fairly. You screw around with Jason, if he thinks we've lied to him, he'll stay in Iowa, and we have another losing season. If he and his family think they can't trust us, can't trust me, he'll never play. Is that what you want?" Henry was silent. "I didn't think so. We're going to pay him every penny we promised him, and he's going to win this organization the Series. Got it?"

Skip looked hard into Henry's eyes. Henry held his gaze for a few moments and then looked around the small, cramped office.

"Yeah, I got it," Henry said at last. "I'll find the money somewhere."

"Good," Skip said, relieved. "It'll be worth it. You'll see."

"THEY'RE TRYING TO SCREW HIM," Skip said to Annie later that night.

"Why?"

Annie sat on the couch, sewing. Skip carried a tray loaded with drinks and a bowl of popcorn.

"Because they can," Skip said, putting the tray on the spotless coffee table. "They're trying to save a few bucks by taking advantage of a new player, and they're rubbing my face in it."

"You?" Annie looked up from her sewing. "Why are you taking it personally?"

"I gave him my word. I promised him the signing bonus."

"Is that all?"

"What do you mean?" He looked at her blankly.

"You gave Isaac and Grace your word, too," Annie reminded him. She returned to her sewing.

"So?"

"You told Grace you would protect her son. Sounds to me like you're doing a good job of it already."

"He's going to turn this team around."

"I hope so. Ta-da!" She held up her sewing: the pants of a Cubs uniform. "I took off the zipper and added buttons."

"Great job," he said.

She folded the pants and began putting away the sewing kit.

"I wonder if it's really worth it," he said, half to himself.

"What? The buttons?" Annie asked. "He'd look awfully funny out there in his suspenders and hat."

"No. Signing him at all." He waved his arms. "With everything that's going on, Henry, the Ordnung, next season. All of it."

"Are you starting to regret this?"

"I'm just thinking out loud," he mumbled defensively.

"Let me do the thinking for you," she said. "Do you have a Series ring?"

"No."

"Have you celebrated your sixtieth birthday yet?"

"No."

"Then it's not time to retire yet, is it?" she asked, an expectant tone in her voice.

"No."

Skip knew that Annie could recite the conversation like she knew the rule for the infield fly. "Honestly." She moved toward him. "What am I going to do with you?" She hung her arms around his neck and hugged him. "You want a championship, or you want to open a restaurant in Mesa. You want to break the curse...you want to break Henry's neck."

"I want to do that stuff all the time," he muttered. "That never changes."

"A little consistency," she said, with a sly smile, "that's all I ask for."

"I consistently love you," he said, kissing her forehead.

"That's good enough," she replied, kissing his chin.

"Worry about Jason in the spring," she said between kisses. "Worry about Henry tomorrow. Worry about me right now."

"It's a deal." He smiled.

"Where's my bonus?"

"Right here..."

⚾⚾⚾⚾ ⚾⚾⚾

DAYS GAVE WAY TO WEEKS, and weeks slipped to months.

Knowing that his time in Kalona was limited, Jason relished each moment. More than ever before, he understood that his life and community, his skills and ability, were all gifts from God. He intentionally enjoyed his efforts on the farm, focusing on the labor and the Lord. Each evening before his prayers, he contemplated the completed day as his life slowly inched away from all he loved and toward the dark unknown of the future.

When not working, Jason spent his precious time socializing with Faith, Adam, and other Amish young people. They gathered for group sings, volleyball, and a trip to Cedar Rapids to watch a rodeo. But the largest get-together was for Lillian Graber and Samuel Bontrager.

The first buggies arrived with the rising sun Tuesday morning. They paraded into the Miller farm from every direction like massive black ants.

When Jason entered the barn, Grace on his arm, whispered comments followed him like wheat gavels behind a reaper. Everyone knew about Jason and the baseball men, of course, but they couldn't guess what he would do. They knew that when individuals left the Amish, they seldom returned.

Jason knew the story of the man who left not only the Amish but his bride of several years. The man was among the English for decades, his wife living like a widow. One day he suddenly reappeared, broken and sick, returning home to die. Of course, she took him in, the community accepting his repentance, and she nursed him until he passed away.

Jason couldn't imagine leaving for so long. The idea of missing traditions like weddings was almost too sad for him to consider. He knew that Samuel spent the previous two weeks riding around the countryside, extending invitations in person, as men in the community had done for hundreds of years.

Nearly a dozen families traveled from Davis County. Several families made the trek all the way from settlements in Illinois and Indiana.

Held in the home of Lillian's neighbor, the ceremony lasted nearly four hours. Singing began when the main preacher took the couple to a room for the questions and continued until they returned nearly twenty minutes later. The service was a little longer than normal—the bride's brother was the fourth to speak, and he had a lot he needed to say.

Ordinarily, newlyweds moved in with the bride's family, but Samuel had a grandparent's house, so that night would be her last under her parents' roof. Most of her belongings had already been moved to her new home with her husband. Her father himself delivered her hope chest. The newlyweds would get up the next morning, help with the cleanup, and then move to their new home, just a few miles away. The coming months would find them visiting relatives on the weekends as they settled into married life. But that was to come—Tuesday night was for reveling.

"Jesus performed his first miracle at a wedding party," Grace had told Jason, as he loaded the case of relish into their buggy, "obviously the Lord wants us to celebrate weddings." So they celebrated all day and into the night.

With the celebration so late in the season, the family had run out of homegrown celery and had to rely on store-bought for the traditional wedding celery salad.

Like a Sunday lunch, people ate in shifts. Plates were hardly washed and dried before they were passed out again. Seats were vacant for less than a moment before someone else slid in.

The marriage feast for nearly two hundred people included a dozen chickens, four ducks, mashed potatoes, massive bowls of thick, buttery noodles, a dozen loaves of bread, countless rolls, and vegetables from gardens, some fresh, most canned. Jason and Grace provided a case of her relish. Jason would retrieve the jars, emptied and cleaned, after the celebration.

Dessert involved seventy-five pies, fruit, doughnuts, and several wedding cakes, including a special one from the bakery in Iowa City.

Several volleyball nets adorned the yard. Games were grouped by age, with the smallest children playing on lower nets. A higher net had several married couples on each side.

Eck ball was falling out of favor since the boys got to be too competitive and rambunctious when they played. Instead, corn hole was growing in popularity because both girls and boys could participate.

When young James Gingerich brought out a softball and bat, Jason heard the murmur pass through the group, but he didn't recognize the tone. Surely they weren't judging? What did they expect of him? He didn't play ball to compete. He played to be the best he could be, as the Lord intended.

Glancing at the young faces around him, he realized he just wanted to make the maed and buwe happy. He enjoyed children almost as much as he enjoyed baseball.

He took the proffered ball, and with the speed of a match bursting into flame, dashed from the group and ran to the open yard, the pack of laughing and yelling children chasing behind. In a clear section of grass, Jason patiently tossed the ball underhand to each child while others fielded. As a little girl chased the ball, he smiled to himself and remembered that baseball would always remain a child's game.

When five o'clock slowly approached, Jason took Faith by the hand, and they joined other unmarried couples returning to the barn. According to tradition, Lillian Bontrager played matchmaker and invited Jason and Faith, as well as two other couples, to sit together on her side of the table.

The supper of warmed leftovers, as well as roast beef and baked oysters, was accompanied by singing and harmonicas. Served by the older married couples, supper lasted until nearly seven o'clock, and singing continued for hours after.

Throughout the celebration, Jason savored each moment as though it was a small, tasty morsel. More than once, as he looked at the faces that had surrounded him his entire life, he considered the meaning of community.

He was reminded of the day many of them had gathered at the Brenneman farm. When a stroke confined Amos Brenneman to a wheelchair, the community gathered—but rather than raise a barn, they created a concrete walking path around a pasture. His family used it nearly every day to push Amos and his wheelchair in the afternoon sun, while his grandchildren of all ages rode behind on tricycles, scooters, or in wagons. A few hours of work made a permanent improvement in the lives of generations of family members.

Jason wasn't even gone yet, and he missed the feeling of community. The emotions pulled so sharply that he felt a literal pain in his chest.

Throughout the long wedding celebration, Jason spoke with dozens of well-wishers while happening to overhear only one uncharitable comment: "What does scripture say? 'When I was a child, I spake as a child, I understood as a child, I thought as a child: but when I became a man, I put away childish things.'"

Jason couldn't see who spoke, nor could he place the male voice.

"Baptized or not, it does not matter; he is still at risk of falling from grace, dragged down by sin and temptation," the voice continued, matter-of-factly. "If he leaves the community, he will not come back. The draw of the world is too much. Too strong. It is like wading into a stream that looks slow-moving, but once you are in it, the current is too powerful to escape, and you get swept away. Swept away to your destruction."

SKIP CONSIDERED the nature of God as he walked from the kitchen to the garage. He clearly didn't think about God in the way Jason seemed to; it just never entered his mind. He thought about God in the context of damning bad hops, bad calls, bad luck, and bad days. There wasn't talk of God when he was growing up. Even less talk about Jesus. Was God dependent on how one is raised? He was baptized as an infant in the Methodist church, but he didn't know what made Methodists different from Baptists, Presbyterians, or Catholics. He was in churches for his wedding and a niece's christening, but had he been any other time since? He didn't think so. Would his next visit to a church be his own funeral?

He couldn't imagine why he would go to a church. He never needed God, not in his playing days during a slump or while battling injuries, and not coaching. He didn't really believe Jason was a "gift from God" to help him win a pennant. If he lost his job without Jason, so be it. He'd get another one. Maybe he needed to be a bench coach again, anyway.

If there was a God, surely that God had more important things to do than worry about Stephen Anderson or the winner of a baseball game. Did he and God have a tacit understanding? He wouldn't bother God, and God wouldn't bother him? He honestly hadn't even given it that much thought. So if it was a question of faith, then he had faith in himself.

He knew some players crossed themselves—players who weren't even Catholic—others who gestured or offered silent prayer. He didn't think God cared if a backup shortstop was hitting .210 or .212. Did Jason's God care about Jason's ERA or on-base percentage? Was God actively involved? Was Jason blessed? Really blessed? Many people thought so, but who knew?

Skip couldn't remember how long he'd been sitting in his car. He only remembered getting in after he entered the garage. He started the engine and began to drive.

There were a lot of Christians. And among Christians, there were so many different ideas of God—they couldn't all be right. So if some were wrong, which ones?

What if the Amish were the only Christians to get it right? There were a lot of Catholics, but not a lot of Catholic priests. What if the priests were the only ones who were right?

Why did Christians knock on doors in the evening and on weekends, bothering people?

It seemed like there were a lot of Christians on TV talking about things they were against and not the things they were for. There seemed to be a lot of people calling themselves Christians who didn't act anything like Jesus. There were some Christians who weren't very nice, but really nice people who weren't Christian.

Some Christians were obsessed with talking about prayers and public displays and saying Merry Christmas. Is that what Christianity was about? Skip didn't care if they called it a Christmas party or a holiday party as long as they served shrimp.

He'd heard about Christians doing a lot of really crappy things. The holy rollers on TV and Christian protestors. They seemed to spend too much time judging people.

Some Christians didn't like gay people. He didn't understand that. What was the big deal? As long as they kept coming to the games during losing seasons, he didn't care who they were. They could have gay pride parades in the stands if it meant they bought tickets to be there.

Did the KKK burn crosses because they were Christians? Or because they didn't like Christians? Why crosses?

Didn't Christians torture people throughout history? The Middle Ages, maybe? What about the stories of anti-abortion Christians attacking women's clinics? Shooting doctors. And why did those Christians publish those graphic pictures? Skip shook his head in disbelief. That was messed up, he thought. Christians didn't like abortion, but who likes abortion?

He tried to think of Christians he knew and people he knew who might be Christian. What if they were all wrong? What if everyone just died, and that was it? There would be nothing else. What if some people lived good lives because they were trying to get into heaven, but there was no heaven? Was that such a bad thing?

I could ask the team chaplain, Skip thought. What was that guy's name? Father somebody?

He found himself sitting in his car again. He got out and started walking.

I'm a good person. Isn't that enough? I'm a person of high morals. I recognize right from wrong, don't even push gray areas. I try to do the right thing.

Hab seemed to be a good guy, and as a Muslim, was his God a different God? Hindus had a lot of gods. What did Buddhists have?

Skip didn't know.

Jesus Christ. What about Jesus?

People could believe in God without Jesus, but he didn't think people could believe in Jesus without God. Could you believe in Jesus and not be a Christian? Could you be a Christian and not believe in Jesus? How do you decide who a Christian is?

There was so much suffering in the world, life was so difficult for so many people, and where was God? Where was God during the Holocaust? During famine in Africa? During genocides, or tornados, or floods? Where was God when children suffered needlessly?

Where was God when children had cancer, brain tumors, abusive parents; where was he during gun accidents or when all sorts of horrible things happened to children?

He knew he wasn't the first, nor would he be the last, to ask questions. Maybe God would get more converts if the answers were a little more clear.

Why did some people need God while others didn't? Every game, every career, had to end eventually, and not even God could change that. All the prayers in the world couldn't fix a torn UCL without surgery.

He stared out the window at the landscape below, and politely declined the flight attendant's offer.

The 9/11 terrorists thought they were doing God's will. They had to be out of their damn minds. Fly an airplane full of people into a building? That wasn't God; that was just crazy.

Maybe God was like a ball club. Different religions at different positions. So a Muslim plays one position and has very little in common with a Christian or Jewish guy in other positions. But they are all on God's team.

Made as much sense as anything. More sense than blowing yourself up.

Was God just calling balls and strikes, like an umpire? Or was God a manager, guiding the action on the field? Players could do what they want, within parameters, but if necessary, the manager had the final say?

What about hell? Were terrorists in hell? If they weren't, what was the point of hell?

God sent people to hell because they didn't believe in God? That didn't make a lick of sense to Skip. He and Annie donated a lot of money to children's issues and did a lot of work with children's groups each year. Surely that counted for something?

God would send him to hell for not caring about Jesus, and God would reward Christians because they were Christians, but who didn't do anything to help suffering children?

If that's really who God was, Skip didn't want anything to do with it, he thought, as he made his way to the taxis.

Did God really punish people? Bring down wrath upon an entire country, a whole civilization? Individuals? Did God really punish people for reading, thinking, believing, doing the wrong thing? What if they intended to do the right thing, but did the wrong thing, did they get halfway punished? And what about heaven? If he lived in a desert like the Muslims and Jews and Jesus, then he'd probably imagine heaven to be someplace cooler, too.

Maybe he should ask Jason about this. But he felt a little silly being a grown man talking to a seventeen-year-old boy about the nature of God.

"1060 West Addison," Skip said, sliding into the taxi.

"Wrigley?"

"That's right. The employee entrance."

The cab driver glanced in the rearview mirror.

"I'm a Sox fan."

"Nothing wrong with that."

He glanced again. "You doin' the best you can wit what you got, but I can't see the Cubbies goin' too far next year."

"Like you said, we'll do the best we can," Skip said, his eyes searching for a different topic. "Is that a Jesus picture on your dashboard?"

"That's right. I don't care how biga tip you give me; I ain't praying for the Cubbies. That ain't gonna happen," he said, smiling to show missing teeth. "Don't you know God hates the National League? God loves the Sox."

"Sure, that's why they traded Sosa years ago. Seriously, though, tell me more about God."

"Ha. Wha'chew wanna know?"

"Whadya wanna tell me? I'm listening."

"God saved my life. Saved me from being a drunk, drug dealer, drug user. Runnin' in the streets wit all sorts of people I shouldn't a been runnin' wit."

"Did God change your life? Or did you change your life?"

"That's all God, man, I couldn'ta done it alone. And I was alone. Lost my family, lost all my friends drinkin' an smokin' my life away. I had to hit bottom, stop diggin', before I could finally see up. I couldn'ta done it alone. God the only one listens when you strung out, hungover. So badly broken ain't nobody could put you back together again 'cept God. So I got busted. Had to dry out and get clean in jail. Then I call out to the Lord, and he helpt me."

"So you think God hears you when you pray?"

"Of course God hears. I ain't prayin' to myself. It's easy fo' God to be around on good days. When you singin' in church an' listen' to preachin' an' all. But the bad times, the dark of night, when evil is knockin' at yo door. When you alone and all you hear is screamin' and cryin' and dyin' all around you. That's when you cry out to God, and he hear you. God right there wit you. When there is nothin' but evil around you, God is there."

Skip wondered if Jason believed the same thing about the nature of God. He tried to remember if Jason had ever mentioned God, or did he only talk about the Ordnung?

"Scripture say do not despair," the driver said, his eyes looking at the rearview mirror more than the road. "Cry out to the Lord, and he will rescue you. And he does. Lord may not be able to help you outta bad times right then—he the Lord, he ain't no magician who can pick you up someplace an' whisk you away.

"But he be right there wit you, walkin' beside you through the valley of the darkness. When you think you alone, and ain't nothin' but evil all around, the Lord is there. When there's rapin', killin', and evil all around you. You ain't alone; the Lord is there. 'Do not be afraid,' Jesus says. Do. Not. Be. Afraid. Yeah, I called out to the Lord, and he answered. Sure as shit, he answered.

"Next thing you know, you arrived. Just like now. You here."

"What do you mean?"

"We here, Coach. Wrigley Field. That'll be $28.50." He put the car in park. "I know you searchin', I can see it on yo face." He turned sideways on the seat and gazed intently into Skip's eyes. "You don't look like you hurtin', but you look like you thinkin' hard about somethin'. You chasin' answers that may never come. That a hard way to live. A hard way to live. I'll pray for you, Coach. If the Sox can't win, I'll pray you bring the trophy back to Chicago."

"Thanks." Skip handed over a crisp bill with the picture of U.S. Grant. "Write down your name. There'll be two tickets for you at will-call on opening day."

"Seriously?"

"Seriously."

"Thanks, Coach," he said as he handed over a battered business card. "I appreciate it. Why you wanna do that for me?"

Skip smiled. "God knows."

Chapter 7

B efore returning to the barn, Jason found a large box on the front porch. His smile grew with every discovery as he unpacked dozens of T-shirts, hats, cups, stuffed bears, and other souvenirs emblazoned with the Chicago Cubs logo.

A snowstorm that covered the infield and seats of Wrigley Field also blanketed the Yoder farm, driving the work inside. Sky the color of dirty lamb's wool told Jason it would be snowing when he left the barn later.

He hung his overcoat on a nearby nail and squatted in the center of the barn to scratch the barn cat behind the ears.

"Goot kots," he whispered as he offered a final scratch and straightened up. Purring, the cat wrapped itself around Jason's legs. Jason calmed his breathing and stared at the far wall.

It's just you, God, and the ball, nothing else, his father's voice echoed in his mind.

James Yoder had once stood in front of the tarp that was spread across a stack of hay bales. He waved a bat, giving his son a target.

"Don't matter who's batting, you're just throwing the ball to the catcher. Don't think about the batter, think about God and what you want the ball to do."

After a moment, Jason went into his wind-up and pitched. With a loud SMACK, the ball crashed into the tarp and the startled cat disappeared into the shadows.

He retrieved another ball from the bushel basket, paused, and began his wind-up.

SMACK!

He wished he could talk with his Daa.

SMACK!

If his Daa were here, would he still make the same decision?

SMACK!

He would secure his future, protect the farm, perhaps for generations to come. Maam would never have to worry again, about anything.

SMACK!

He could pay property taxes for the entire district for a decade.

SMACK!

But at what cost?

SMACK!

What cost?

SMACK!

"Gott segen eigh."

SMACK!

"So now you will take my only son to Chicago?" Grace asked, shaking her head, her unresolved bitterness smoldering through the room like an ember.

Skip stood with Isaac and Grace in the Yoder's cozy kitchen, the outdoors covered in a thick coat of snow, the sky as cold and gray as week-old ashes.

"Actually," Skip responded sheepishly, "I'm taking him to Mesa, Arizona, first."

"What?" Grace demanded, anger flashing in the corners of her eyes.

"Spring training. Mesa, Arizona. It's the first address I sent you. That's where we'll be. He's staying with Annie and me. He'll be back here the last week in March, and then we go to Chicago."

With a vacant expression, she nodded her head slowly. Isaac stoically placed his arm around her.

"Take care of my boy, Mr. Anderson," she said.

"I will," Skip replied sincerely. "You have my word."

"He is not a boy anymore, Grace," Isaac said. "He is a man. He will make his own choices."

The gas lights hissed at Skip like a slowly leaking balloon.

Jason entered, wearing his blue shirt and simple black suit. His hands held his formal hat and a small suitcase.

"Goodbye, Maam. Onkel. I will write every day."

Skip could see Grace's sadness, but any other emotions were deeply hidden.

"Goodbye, son," she whispered and kissed him goodbye.

"Be careful among them, boy," Isaac advised.

"I will, Onkel," Jason responded somberly.

⚾⚾⚾

"I KNOW it's hard leaving home, Jason." Skip spoke into the uncomfortable silence. "I know how you feel."

The highway hummed as Skip drove past the snow-covered countryside. Jason looked beyond the hood of the car, staring at the horizon. Long minutes passed before he glanced at Skip.

"My family has worked our farm since 1847," he said simply, before returning his gaze to the distance. "My father and his father before him. My urgrossvadder's grandfather had to leave Switzerland because the government opposed us. Said we could not worship the Lord in the way we are called to do. We are simple people who only wished to be left alone, but we had to leave our homes, sail across the ocean, and find new homes in America.

"My urgrossvadder was beaten and jailed because he would not leave the farm and fight in the war with the other states. My grandfather also was beaten because he would not leave and fight a war. Today I am leaving to play baseball."

Skip opened his mouth to speak, and then closed it, unable to find a response to Jason's turmoil. Yet again, another aspect of Jason's life was much more complex than it appeared.

"That is how I feel," Jason said, staring at nothing.

Skip pulled the rental car into the Cedar Rapids Airport parking lot as Jason looked around anxiously, panic on his face. "What is this?"

"The airport," Skip said as he turned off the engine and opened the door. "Next stop, Mesa, Arizona."

"I can't travel on airplanes."

"Excuse me?"

"I cannot fly. The Ordnung prohibits airplane travel."

"You're kidding?"

Jason stared at him, saying nothing.

"Wait a minute," Skip argued. "You mean to tell me you're not getting on the plane?"

Silently, Jason blinked his blue eyes.

"At all?"

"I cannot fly," he repeated.

"This is going to make road trips to the coasts difficult," Skip said to himself as they got back into the car.

"I will ride on the train or in automobiles."

"I don't see us driving to Mesa. We better find a train station." Skip closed the car door. "I can't wait until we play L.A.," Skip mumbled, starting the car. "San Francisco...the Marlins...the Mets..."

AFTER A SCAN OF THE INTERNET, a series of phone calls, and assistance from the staff of the traveling secretary, Skip was able to secure train travel from Kansas City to Flagstaff. Skip felt he was finally getting out of his bad news slump when he booked the most expensive and roomiest Superliner Bedroom Suite available on the Southwest Chief.

The twenty-four-hour journey into the American West would be more comfortable than he anticipated, but it still began and ended with dull drives across uninteresting interstates.

Hours later, when Skip and Jason entered the crowded train station toting their luggage, curious passersby glancing in their direction, Jason slowed to gawk at the surroundings. "I have never ridden on a train before," he said, looking around in wonder.

"The world's full of little miracles," Skip said, distracted. "You don't know what you're missing by passing on the plane."

"The Or—"

"—The Ordnung. I know. Come on."

They found the suite and saw that it was designed for four passengers and provided a pair of private toilets, sinks, and showers.

"Between the two of us, we're almost thirteen feet long and easily four hundred twenty pounds, so we'll need as much room as we can get," Skip said, appraising the accommodations.

The suite offered each of them a sofa, armchair, fold-down table, and the choice of sleeping in an upper or lower berth. Neither Jason nor Skip opted for the upper berth— Skip didn't want to risk his knee climbing the ladder, and Jason didn't trust the design.

"I'm a big guy," he said, smiling. "I'm not so sure it can hold me all night."

They began their ride on opposite sides of the suite, Jason staring out the window at the passing landscape, Skip on his computer, the fan blowing on him.

"That is cold air and hot air?" Jason asked, still astonished.

"At your fingertips."

"I'm not used to air conditioning," Jason said. "It makes it feel like November."

Skip processed Jason's words for several long seconds. "What do you mean, you're not used to air conditioning?"

"I know what it is, of course. But we don't have electricity, remember? I have only been in a couple of places that have air conditioning. It is not easy to get used to."

"Well, after a few weeks in Arizona, you'll probably get used to it."

Jason nodded silently and shuffled the unopened and unread newspaper on his lap.

"I have a friend, Samuel, he is a bookworm," Jason said. "He reads everything. Me, not so much. I read the sports page during the season, box scores. Stories about the Cubs."

"When you say things like that, that's when I know you're a real ballplayer."

"What do you mean?"

"You'll find out," Skip said.

Sometime later, he closed his laptop and asked, "You getting hungry?"

"I can eat any time."

"You and your mom have regular mealtimes?"

"Yes, sir, most days," Jason said. "But I can always eat."

Once seated in the dining car, Skip told Jason to order whatever he liked, "courtesy of the Chicago National League Ball Club and the Ricketts family."

"Ha," Jason laughed at the menu. "Look at that, 'Seafood Catch of the Day.' Shrimp and crab cakes." He looked out the window at the barren landscape rolling past. "Where do you think they caught those shrimp today?"

Skip chuckled at the boyish humor before scanning the menu. He and Jason both had steaks, but Jason ate twice as fast as Skip, so he also ordered the catch of the day. "They caught it when the man loaded the box onto the train," he said with a smile as he wiped up the last crumb with his sixth dinner roll.

After dinner, reflecting on his day as the train rolled west, Skip was put in the mind of baseball's golden age, long since passed. The Polo Grounds and the Brooklyn Dodgers. Cigars, telegrams, and porters. Wool uniforms, leather belts, sanitaries, and stirrups. When did league officials stop caring about stirrups? And when did men start wearing so much jewelry? The 1970s? He didn't like being that kind of manager, so he never mentioned that he hated when players wore necklaces during games.

When the train jostled, Skip glanced over to see Jason sleeping through it. Jason fits perfectly with the era of railroads, Skip thought.

"The Amish don't look at time the same way you or I do," Coach Pate had said a few hours earlier when Skip called seeking guidance. "He's used to a different pace of life. They measure time by seasons and whole days, not hours and minutes. To most of the world, life is like a football game, with time rigidly divided into segments. For the Amish, life is more like baseball—tasks take as long as they need to take, and people don't rush to finish. Even if they might be in a hurry, they nearly never appear to be. An Amish person who's ready to go will drop a half dozen different hints before he admits he's ready to go. That's just how they are."

"OK."

"You know why Amish don't drive cars? It's so they are forced to move slower. Honestly."

"Slower?" Skip said, exasperated. "I'm on a train, Phil. I feel like Connie Mack or Leo Durocher."

Coach Pate laughed.

"There's a conductor, Phil, a conductor. Because I'm on a train in the nineteenth century. Jason wants slow, he's got it."

"Their rules force them to move at a different pace. For example, most Old Order Amish allow the use of push scooters but not bicycles. A scooter lets you carry things from the store, but a bicycle allows you to move too quickly, so it's forbidden."

"Maybe I should take a look at this rule book," Skip said.

"I sincerely respect your effort," Coach Pate replied. "It's reassuring that you care enough to ask."

"You think you can get me a copy?"

"Not a chance. There are more rules like that than you can possibly imagine. The ones you've heard about aren't even close to scratching the surface. The thing is, most of these rules aren't written down. If they were written, they'd be in German.

"Remember, a direct translation of Ordnung is 'order or discipline or organization.' They've lived a certain way for so long, there's no need for them to write it down. It's not written that we grow up, get a job, get a car, get married, get a mortgage; this is just how we live life. Their Ordnung is the same thing—it's how they live life. And as you're learning, their way is dramatically different than our way of living life.

"You don't bunt to get a base runner when you have a ten-run lead. You just don't do it. It's an unwritten rule, right?"

"Right."

"Their whole lives are governed by unwritten rules." He paused to let the example sink in. "But, all the rules make sense to them. They'd probably make sense to you, too, if you stop and think about them. See? You need to slow down, stop and think about the rules."

Skip was still thinking about the Amish rules while a sports talk show droned on from his computer when Jason spoke for the first time in three hours, startling Skip.

"You seem different in person than you did when I heard you on the radio," Jason said slowly. "But in other ways, you're exactly the same."

Skip closed his computer. "How do you mean?"

"When men talked about you on the radio, they said many of the Cubs' problems were your fault," he said.

"Yeah, I've heard that, too," Skip said with a wry smirk.

"And I listened to you on the radio, talking about the team, and about baseball."

After several seconds of empty silence, Skip finally said, "OK."

"I listened to games on the radio, and it didn't sound to me like many of the losses, or even the team's record was your fault. It seemed many of the players just didn't play good," Jason said.

"Well, things happen."

"I don't know all the rules or the things you do as the coach, but I noticed, when you talked about games, you didn't blame the players who made mistakes. You are not even blaming them right now. You always talk about the bigger picture—how to play the game. 'The fundamentals are what is important,' you always say." He looked out the window at the landscape rushing past. "Before Coach Pate, it had been a long time since anyone taught me how to play baseball."

"So I've heard," Skip said.

"I played with older boys." Jason smiled. "I am pretty sure there's a lot about the game I do not know. There's a lot I do not know about a lot of stuff. I think, if I make mistakes, you won't blame me, either."

"I don't intend to."

"One of the reasons I am willing to play for the Cubs, besides the money, is to learn more about the game. I want to see if I am good enough to play against major league players. But I just want to play. I want to learn about the game and to play."

Skip looked at Jason. "You'll do just fine, sport, don't you worry."

When their train journey was over, and they were loading their bags into the town car in Flagstaff, Skip struggled to get his bag into the trunk.

Jason teased him. "Maybe you need Carlos to come help you."

"Who's Carlos?"

"The man on the train who made up our beds and brought us coffee and doughnuts," Jason said, surprised. "You gave him money. You didn't ask his name?"

"No, I didn't."

"We say paying respect is more important than paying money," Jason said before climbing into the car, leaving Skip speechless on the sidewalk.

"Hello," Jason said to the driver, "I am Jason, what's your name?"

⚾⚾⚾⚾ ⚾⚾⚾

ANNIE MET Jason and Skip near the door of their Mesa apartment. "I bet you boys had an interesting trip," she said.

"I've never seen a cactus before," Jason replied.

"Or a train," Skip interrupted as he kissed Annie hello. "Or a train station. Or a limo. It's like leading an innocent lamb through a city of wolves."

Annie cut a glance at Skip. "Chicago will be exciting then, won't it?" She turned to Jason. "I bet you're hungry?"

"Yes, ma'am."

"Anything you can't eat?"

"No, ma'am."

"Then I'll see what I can find," Annie replied.

Jason remained standing near the door as he looked around his new surroundings. "Do you have a television?" he asked.

"You're joking, right?" Skip responded, incredulous. He exchanged a look of confusion with Annie.

"No, sir."

"Jason, honey," Annie said softly with a gentle gesture. "That's the television."

"I have heard about television."

"But you've never seen one?"

"I have never been in an English house before."

"You haven't missed much," Skip quipped. "You can watch TV later. Right now, let me show you your room."

Annie continued toward the kitchen. "I'll get supper on the table."

The meal was punctuated with sounds of cutlery scraping on dishes from the head of the table—Jason, with knife and fork flying, inhaled food as fast as he ran the bases.

Annie shot a raised eyebrow at Skip. Jason looked up from his plate and paused as Skip and Annie turned their eyes to him.

Jason released a huge belch. He offered an empty stare for a moment before lowering his head and continuing his systematic destruction of the casserole. Skip had already witnessed Jason's culinary habits, so he looked at Annie across the table to gage her reaction. She glanced at Jason again and silently shook her head, before continuing her meal.

Later, as Skip and Annie lay in bed, Annie whispered, "He's like the child I've never wanted."

"Only he's seventeen."

"Like a giant baby. Or a baby giant. He's darling—"

"But?"

"He's just so—" She struggled to find the word. "He's strange."

"He takes some getting used to," Skip admitted.

"He's going to take a lot of getting used to."

"I appreciate it."

"What?"

"Your willingness to get used to him, your patience, everything," Skip said and kissed her forehead.

"All in a day's work," she smiled, then giggled. "That belch—"

"Yeah, I should have warned you."

"Did he eat like that on the way here?"

"He ate nonstop. Like a war refugee."

She laughed.

"Yeah, you laugh, but I may have maxed out a credit card. They had to stop the train to reload it with food. Twice."

"He'll fit right in on the team," she said, still giggling.

"I'm more worried about that television thing."

"It's spooky in a way," Annie said, her brow wrinkled thoughtfully. "What else doesn't he know?"

"What else don't I know?" Skip asked. "Phil Pate told me about Jason's world, but I didn't realize we'd be teaching him so much about ours."

"I'm beginning to better understand Grace and Isaac's fears."

"I just have to be careful with him, that's all."

"And patient," she added.

"I get him out on the field tomorrow, it'll all be worth it."

"I hope you're right," Annie said before she kissed him goodnight.

He lay beside her for hours, remembering the journey from Iowa. She was right. She was always right. Like all sports wives, she carried more than her share of household responsibilities. She kept a level head and even keel, which allowed her to keep everything in perspective. So yet again, she was right. Jason was like a giant baby. He had a charming sense of humor and superhuman patience to match his superhuman athletic ability, but he was utterly clueless when it came to simple aspects of living.

No matter what happens, this will be an exciting ride, Skip thought and slipped into a dreamless sleep.

Jason's small suitcase remained unopened on the chair where Coach

Anderson had put it. Jason struggled with where to hang his hat before deciding to rest it on the case. He stared at the quilt on the bed, like trying to place a familiar face. The design clearly wasn't Iowa Amish.

The pattern wasn't something he recognized. It wasn't Barn Swallow, Center Diamond, Double T, Feathered Star, Sundance, Steppingstones, or his favorite, Pinwheel. He remembered the Wedding Ring design and thought of Faith. Faith. He recalled Lillian and Samuel's wedding and thought of Faith as he considered the quilt.

Perhaps it was a pattern from Ohio or Pennsylvania. He studied it intently, but the quilt surrendered no clues. He leaned down and passed his hand across the surface, as though stroking the side of a horse. The stitching was as rough and course as a gravel parking lot. The quilt was fake, the kind sold to English tourists in front of an abandoned gas station.

Fake.

Nothing was as it seemed in the English world. It was all lies and falsehoods. Deceptions. Like photos of food in a magazine, appearing real, but little more than pretending. Like the games of children. Coach Anderson and Mrs. Anderson were kind people, but the English all seemed to live in a fantasy world. The other passengers on the train and in the stations, all the people he saw, they seemed to have a false sense of urgency and held misplaced values. He had watched man after man rush to get on the train first, only to flop down in a seat and do nothing. He saw rudeness and selfishness in the actions of nearly every person around them, and yet the English seemed to have no idea they were acting badly. Rudeness was routine for them.

He remembered seeing a seabird years ago, standing alone in their field. He wondered how the bird came to be so far from its coastal home. Was it injured? Stunned? Or just horribly bewildered? He watched it take slow, tentative steps. Was it looking for kernels after the corn harvest? Or just trying to find a way back to a familiar setting? He watched it as the evening sun set until his chores called him away. The next day the bird was gone.

He slipped his boots off and carefully laid down on the bed. He clasped his hands on his chest and stared at the ceiling.

He was that bird. Bewildered. Lost. Alone. Far from home and far from the flock of others like him.

What had he gotten himself into? When he had agreed to play baseball, he hadn't thought about the time when he wouldn't be playing. Off the field, in the dressing room, traveling from game to game. Waiting. Now, it was all he could think about. The dry, sad times between games. All of the worldliness and spiritual emptiness he would encounter while he waited for the next game, the next opportunity to use his gifts.

He'll practice tomorrow, he said to himself. No matter how bad things might get among the English, at least tomorrow, he'd be back on the familiar ground of the ball field.

Chapter 8

Jason's enormous fingers nervously worked the brim of his hat. Skip had walked him from the car, through the administrative offices, and down a hallway that opened directly onto the field.

The thick grass felt like expensive plush carpet beneath his feet.

"It is big. Real big."

"Yeah, it seats 15,000. Get used to it. Wrigley seats 41,000. It's nearly four times bigger."

Jason turned in a small circle, taking it all in.

"The field is not much different than you're used to," Skip said.

"Mmmm, it is bigger, too," Jason replied matter-of-factly.

"This is why they call it the big leagues." Skip smiled until he noticed Jason's expression. "Listen to me." Jason continued to look around. Skip snapped his fingers. "Listen."

Jason turned his attention to Skip.

"The pitcher's mound, same height. Same distance to the plate. Same distance between bags." Skip gestured at the infield. "This is exactly the same you're used to, so don't let it get into your head.

Don't be intimidated." He turned and waved at the outfield. "That is bigger by a few dozen square feet. Your wheels are so fast it won't matter." He waved both hands above like a magician casting a spell. "This is bigger than Wrigley. You hear me? This field is bigger than our park. Left field, right field—both are 360 feet. At home, left field is 355, and right field is 353 feet. So you pull it, you're still gonna clear the fence and put it in the tenth row. Look—" He gestured to center field. "The wall is 410 feet. At Wrigley, dead center field is 400 feet, and the wall is eleven and a half feet tall. It's more than you're used to but not as far as that cornfield back home."

Home. Jason nodded. He wondered what his Daa would say about the field. Had his Daa ever been to Chicago?

"The only distance that matters is the six inches right here." Skip pointed to his temple.

Jason cocked his head sideways, confused. "Your head?"

Skip closed his eyes and shook his head slowly. "No, son, your head." Skip tapped Jason's temple. "The six inches between your ears. Don't play in your head, just play the game you know how to play."

Jason flashed a smile. "That makes more sense."

Skip gestured at the stands. "Don't pay any attention to what goes on up there. Don't get distracted. I know it's easier to say than to do but try to ignore them. You're used to ignoring people, right?"

"I do not like being rude," Jason said, nodding. "But I understand what you're saying. English tourists always want to take pictures of the Amish, and we have to pretend that they don't."

"That's the attitude. Look around. Get used to it. And then pretend it's not there." He started walking. "Come on, let's go look at the clubhouse. It's not as nice as Chicago, but it's better than some visitor locker rooms you'll see in the season."

Moments later, Jason was transfixed by large, flat-screen televisions at each end of the long room.

"Take a look around," Skip said, gesturing. "The team provides food here before and after games. There're drinks over there. We've got gum here... You chew gum?"

Jason nodded sharply and silently as he took in his new surroundings. It smelled like a recently cleaned barn and rain-soaked horse tack.

"Good. The video rooms are over there," Skip continued with a wave. "Someone can help you with that. Over there are the tables for the trainers and the physical therapists. The weight room is through there." He gestured again to a door on the other end of the room. "Rookies are expected to lift weights before the veterans." He considered Jason's physique. "Do you even work out?"

Jason shrugged his square shoulders. "I work on the farm. I do not know 'work out.'"

"Yeah, I bet you don't." Skip grabbed a bag of chewing tobacco from a box on a counter. "I guess you don't need this." He dropped it back into the box. "And finally..." With a flourish, Skip pulled down a white cloth to uncover a door with Jason's name on it. "Your own locker room. "Coach Pate told me you needed it. And..." Skip reached into the small closet and pulled out a uniform shirt emblazoned with YODER.

"Congratulations," he said, handing Jason the uniform. "Welcome to the Chicago Cubs."

Jason smiled and looked around, dumbfounded.

"Well, this is it," Skip said. "The rest of the team will be along in a while. Make yourself comfortable. My office is back over there, down the hall. That's where I'll be."

"So, what do you think about Jackson?" Dave asked.

Skip and Dave had just finished several long hours of planning when he brought up the subject of a troubled shortstop prone to errors.

"If he managed to lose thirty pounds in the offseason, he may make a decent ballplayer," Skip replied.

"What about the kid?" Dave asked. "What do you plan to do with him?"

"Oh man, Jason," Skip said, leaping from his chair and racing for the door. "I forgot about him."

He rushed into the locker room to find Jason sitting on a bench alone, hat in hand, a group of well-dressed players silently standing around him.

The players looked to Skip, and he cringed at the awkward situation.

"So you men are getting to know one another, good, good," he said, assuming his coaching bravado.

"Is Halloween early this year, Skip?"

"Who's the kid?"

"What gives, Skip?"

"Yeah, Skip, what's going on?"

"I don't have to explain anything to any of you," Skip responded to the onslaught, "because I'm the manager. Jason, get changed."

Skip pointed, and Jason closed the door behind him as several players murmured at the newly constructed room.

"But because I'm also a nice guy," Skip continued as he pointed to a handful of players near the door, "Kyle, Drew, and Evan, if you gentlemen will join the others and have a seat, I'll tell you what's going on."

He shared with them as little information as necessary to satisfy their concerns, before concluding, "...and he's one of the best players I've ever seen."

"I don't know, Skip, it seems awfully far-fetched," Art Stone said, shaking his head.

"Yeah, Skip," Jennings said.

Just as others began to question his story, Kinnick and Cody wandered into the clubhouse together.

"Hold it," Skip said, raising his hands to the late-comers, "You two saw Jason in person. What did you think?"

Kinnick looked at the other players. "The Amish kid? He's amazing."

"He's better," Cody added, crossing toward his locker. "He's the real deal."

"Enough of this," Skip said. "Get changed and get out onto the field, and you'll all see for yourselves."

ALONE AND ALREADY IN UNIFORM, Jason thoughtfully turned a baseball in his hands. The colors of his uniform were more intense than anything he'd ever seen. They were like drugstore cotton, the ripest strawberry, and an Iowa sky bluer than he could ever imagine. He was here. It was happening, but he was more uncomfortable than he thought possible.

"You about ready, Sport?" Skip asked through the closed door, with a gentle knock.

Jason stood up, startled. "Yes, sir."

"You OK?" Skip asked.

"Yes, sir," Jason said, stepping from his small room.

"That's the attitude," Skip said, smiling. "Let's go show 'em what you're made of."

"Yes, sir."

They were walking out when Henry rushed in.

"There you are," Henry said, exasperated. "Let's go."

Jason looked questioningly at Skip.

"Go where?" Skip asked, equally confused.

"This way..." Henry led them out a door and down a hallway.

"But where are we going?" Skip demanded.

They turned the corner.

"I sent you the memo."

"I didn't see a memo."

"I'm not surprised," Henry said. "I don't think you read any of my memos." He led them through another room and down another hallway. "Here we are—" Henry gestured, and they walked past him through parted curtains—

—Into a huge news conference. Cameras flashed as Jason looked around like a trapped, six-foot-six-inch-tall bunny. Large imposing cameras were scattered among the dozens of people in the room.

Hope stood near a table of microphones, several men in suits beside her. A man on her left had the same excited expression as the others, but his glasses made his eyes even more pronounced.

Skip turned angrily to Henry.

"What is this, Henry?"

Henry made brief eye contact with Skip before shrugging and stepping to the microphones.

"Thank you all for coming," Henry said graciously to the crowd of television cameras, photographers, and reporters. "You all know Manager Stephen Anderson..." Skip glared at the crowd. "Let me introduce the reason you're all here," Henry continued. "All the way from Kalona, Iowa, seventeen-year-old Jason Yoder."

Cameras flashed as people applauded politely, and reporters started shouting questions. Henry clapped as he moved aside and gestured for Jason to step forward.

Jason's face looked as though he were witnessing a murder. Glancing around desperately, trapped and frightened, his voice was barely above a whisper. "No photographs." He turned away.

Henry motioned Jason forward and exaggerated applause.

While Jason remained frozen, Henry stepped to the microphones. "Please ask your questions one at a time." He gestured at Jason. "Let's make this shy Iowa farm boy feel welcome," he said as he stepped back to make room for Jason.

Turning his body away from the photographers, Jason studied the floor for a way out until he managed to catch Skip's eye. "Coach?" he pleaded softly.

Skip moved to Jason's side, putting his arm around his shoulder.

"What's wrong?"

"I cannot do this."

"Why? What is it?"

"The Ordnung—" Jason whispered.

"What?"

"The Ordnung—"

Henry blustered over and demanded in a loud whisper, "What's going on here, Coach?"

"I don't know, Henry," Skip replied, annoyed. He turned to Jason, "What about the Ordnung?"

"It prohibits graven images," Jason explained through clenched teeth. "I must not pose to allow my photograph to be taken— it is Hochmut. It is wrong."

"What's he talking about?" Henry asked.

"We're leaving," Skip said, stepping forward as he pushed Jason behind him.

"What is this? Some sort of joke?"

"It's OK, sport," Skip said to Jason in a comforting tone he never used at the ballpark.

Skip stepped to the microphones, holding his hands up for silence as Jason turned his back and studied the floor, a hand covering the side of his face.

"If I could have your attention," Skip said to the assembled throng. "Jason won't be talking to members of the media here or in the clubhouse or on the field."

The reporters started yelling questions at once. "What's going on here?"

"Who's the new player, Coach?"

"Who is this kid?"

"Tell us who he is, Skip."

"I'd appreciate it if you'd all give him a chance to get used to the major league," Skip said simply. "He's only seventeen, and he needs time to adjust. So, please give him that time."

"You can't stop us from talking to him," blurted out a reporter. Skip hated the guy.

"Yes, I can," Skip said. "Anyone— anyone who speaks to Jason Yoder will be banned from the locker room for the rest of the season." Skip put a hand on Jason's shoulder, and they began to walk away.

"When's he going to play, Coach?" a reporter called out.

Skip answered over his shoulder but kept walking, "He'll be on the mound opening day."

Reporters shouted more questions as Henry grabbed Skip. "I don't understand this," Henry spit angrily.

"I'm not surprised," Skip snapped, turning away. "Let's go." He took Jason's arm and guided him through the maze of people.

"Wait," Henry called out, "what about the news conference?"

"Tell them whatever you want," Skip said, walking away. "Jason will be on the field."

As they walked, Skip considered the dozens of times a week his players were photographed. This was getting more complicated with each passing hour.

JASON USED his thumbnail to trace the words burned into the barrel of the bat.

"No pictures, eh?"

Jason looked up to see Dave speaking to Skip.

"Nope," Skip replied.

"Gonna make his cards pretty valuable. I'll have to remember to save me a few," Dave said.

Skip didn't respond and Jason returned his attention to the bat.

After a moment, Dave said, "Think I'll go see how he's doing."

"Nervous?" he asked Jason as he approached.

"A little."

"Don't be," Dave said casually. "It's just BP."

Jason didn't respond, so Dave clarified, "Batting practice." When Jason still made no reply, Dave turned and scanned the field. "As a matter of fact," he continued, nonchalantly, "I suspect you can pretty much hit everybody in our bullpen. For you, everyone is throwing batting practice."

Jason smiled at the compliment.

"Of course, our rotation has the depth of a cereal bowl, so your teammates back in Iowa could probably hit them, too." Dave winked. "So don't worry, you'll do just fine. OK?"

"Yes, sir," Jason said slowly, not entirely convinced.

Dave gave him another wink, then turned to the man in the batting cage, clapping his hands.

"OK, Greenie, last pitch, let's give Yoder a shot."

Jason looked at the batter when he heard the name, staring like the seventeen-year-old fan he was. He watched Mark Green take his last hit and step out of the cage.

"Get you some good swings, kid," Green said, as Jason walked slowly toward the plate, swinging the bat tentatively.

At the same time, Stone lumbered out to the mound and muttered something to the puzzled assistant throwing batting practice, who shrugged and walked away.

Jason watched Dave look to Skip for approval, and the manager acquiesced with a sharp, silent nod.

Jason got comfortable and nodded to Stone, who pitched at nearly full speed.

Jason hit the ball softly into the infield.

Stone threw a few more, and Jason hit each one with authority.

With each pitch, more players began to gather around the batting cage. Finally comfortable for the first time in weeks, Jason saw only the ball and heard only the sound of the bat making contact.

"He's playing with ya', Artie!" Green yelled.

"Number one, Stone! Give him the heat!" a sunburned Jeff Vance called out.

Clearly agitated, Stone started throwing harder.

"The kid's got light tower power!"

Jason stroked every pitch solidly, farther and farther. With each hit, the other players cheered Jason and jeered Stone.

Stone grunted with exertion, throwing as hard as he could.

Jason swung effortlessly, and the ball cleared the fence by ten feet and rattled around the empty seats.

"Fastball, Artie!" Frank yelled. "Try throwing a fastball!"

Jason knew the other players were teasing Stone, but he wasn't sure why.

Stone leaned over and stared intently at Jason, who returned his gaze with an impassive expression. Stone stood up and pitched.

The ball hit Jason in the helmet and bounced high into the air. Jason dropped to the ground, instantly unconscious.

Jason's head swam with buzzing darkness and the aroma of his mother's fresh-baked bread. As massive bees buzzed and pounded on the inside of his skull, trying to get out, he opened his eyes and saw nothing. He was blind. Darkness.

He imagined life on the farm as a blind man. He thought of Faith —it would not be fair to marry her now that he could no longer see. He thought of the blind man they brought to Jesus, and the Lord's willingness to heal his blindness. Perhaps if my faith is strong, the Lord will heal me as well, he thought. And then he remembered how helpful everyone was to Daughty Schupp when his vision faded.

He thought of his future, sitting on the front porch rocking chair, feeling the sun and wind on his sightless eyes, as the days and years passed. Even now, he could feel the sun on his face. It was pleasant, but the buzzing bees made it impossible for him to fully relax, to enjoy the warmth of the sun, and accept his new condition.

"¿Puedes oírme, amigo? o contigo c?? ¿Estás bien? La fuerza de la tira fue tan fuerte que no puede levantarse."

Jason opened his eyes. The world was dark shadows and bright lights. Men looked like trees, walking. The bees in his head raged at the light and buzzed louder. He closed his eyes again.

He was an old, blind grandpa, regaling the children with stories from his past and the time he went to the city, where the Lord struck him blind. He told the children that life in the city was much, much worse than they could possibly imagine. Seventy-five years later, he opened his eyes again.

"Vamos, muchacho. Haz tu cabeza juntos."

The sky was yellow, and the sun was blue. A black mask babbled words Jason did not understand.

"¿Está bien?"

Jason blinked, and many of the bees flew out his ear and into the sky, where they became clouds and flowers. He knew the bees were happier in the sky rather than in his head. Why was he lying in brown flour?

"Ich feelt net goot," he mumbled with a mouth that tasted of pennies. He knew if he moved his head, it would fall off. He didn't want to sit up and leave his skull behind. A bee settled into the side of his brain and began to make honey. "Ich hop n kupvay."

"Hombre, usted no parece buena," the mask said.

"OK, give him some room," a voice Jason vaguely recognized said to the men gathered around his prone body. "This isn't the United Nations."

Someone knelt by Jason's side, as the man in the mask took it off and backed away.

"Can you bear the choice?" the man asked.

Jason blinked. "Its dess day Daughty haus?"

"I said, can you hear my voice?" the man asked more forcefully. He looked deeply at Jason. Jason was frightened by the concern in the man's eyes.

"Ich brrosht tzu gaya heim."

The man gently helped Jason's helmet off.

"I do not feel so good," Jason whispered to the bee in his head. "I better go home."

"Boy, he really got his clock cleaned," said another familiar voice.

"Yeah," the first voice agreed. Jason recognized it as Skip.

"Help me get him up," the man said to the others, putting an arm under Jason and slowly lifting him to his feet.

The man walked him away as the players called out encouragements.

"Tough it out, Jason," Dave called.

Seemingly intending to apologize, Stone leaned toward Jason's still ringing head and whispered, "Welcome to the Show, rookie."

ON HIS COUCH, arms behind his head, Skip was unsuccessfully trying to relax when Annie entered, looking worried.

"You're sure he can take a Tylenol?"

"Yes."

"I just feel so badly for him," she said, sadness shrouding her face.

"He had a hard day," Skip conceded. "The other players greeted him like he was a freak. Henry and that press conference. Then he gets beaned. A trip to the hospital. All before noon."

Annie shook her head, gloomily. "Welcome to the major league."

"Some welcome," Skip said. "I don't know what's up with Stone. He took an instant dislike to the kid. Unbelievable."

"The other players?"

"They seemed to like him," Skip said quickly. He considered for a moment. "At least I hope so." He kept thinking about the day. "I don't know. This isn't going like I thought it would."

She took a sip of wine. "What are you going to do?"

"Keep going," he replied. "What choice do I have?"

"What about Jason?" Annie quietly asked. "Can he keep going?"

"He'll be OK," Skip said. Was he trying to convince her or himself? He didn't know. "Sure. He'll be OK."

On the other side of the house, homesick and alone in the guest room, Jason lay in bed, the covers pulled up to his chin, his face wet with tears.

Slowly, softly, he sought solace and comfort in the familiar as he began to sing a prayerful hymn. Written by an ancestral martyr, Jason had heard the hymn his whole life, but his day gave the words new meaning.

"O Gott, Vater, wir loben dich und deine Güte preisen wir," he intoned, slowly singing the hymn that began his district's worship service.

Sounding like a monk's chant, the tune had been sung without instruments for hundreds of years, getting slower with the passage of time.

"Eternal Uncle in heaven, I call to you from my innermost being. Do not let me turn away from you, but keep me in your truth until the end. Oh, God, keep my heart and my mouth. Watch over me every hour. Do not let me turn away from you because of anxiety, fear, or distress. Keep me steadfast in your joy... I lie here in chains, waiting on you, God, with a very great longing for the time when you will set me free."

Jason continued humming the tune as he drifted into restless sleep haunted by bees and the smell of his mother's fresh-baked bread.

"THE ORGANIZATION still needs your Social Security number to pay you," Skip said when he stopped by Jason's room the next morning.

"I don't have one."

"What?"

"I don't have one. I don't have a Social Security number."

"How do you get a job without a Social Security number?" Skip asked, more curious than concerned. He crossed his arms and leaned casually against the door frame to await the answer.

"I have never had a job that paid money," Jason said with a dismissive shrug. "Not one off a farm. I've got lots of jobs on farms," he said with a wide smile.

"You've never had a paying job where you collected a paycheck from a boss, an employer?"

"I have done work for people—carpentry, farm work, things like that. But that's usually cash or in trade. We grow vegetables that we pick and sell. Maam sells relish, jams, and jellies at different places. Sometimes she will also sell bread and rolls and pies at the farmers' market in Iowa City. But no, I have never been paid by a company or anything."

Now Skip was really interested. "How did you get a driver's license without a Social Security number? They have special ones for the Amish?" he asked with a smile.

"I don't have a driver's license."

Standing up straight, Skip's mind raced. "What do you mean you don't have a driver's license? You helped drive when we were in Missouri."

"You didn't ask if I had a driver's license," Jason said. "You asked if I could drive."

Skip remembered the conversation south of Nowhere, Iowa. Suddenly overtaken with fatigue, he had looked at Jason and asked, "Do you mind driving for a while? I'm really tired."

Obligingly, Jason nodded and took the wheel as Skip asked, "you can drive, can't you?"

Jason drove for several uneventful hours while Skip dozed in the passenger seat. Jason didn't even turn on the radio. Skip remembered thinking at the time how quietly the time passed.

"So why did you drive if you don't have a driver's license?"

Jason shrugged. "Because you asked me to."

Skip blanched. "That wasn't your first time driving a car, was it?"

"Yes..."

Skip's stomach dropped, like riding the first dip of a very tall rollercoaster.

"I have driven pick-up trucks before, around town and on farms," Jason continued. "Helping the families of some of my teammates. Neighbors. Most of the trucks had a clutch and standard transmission."

The rollercoaster had another hill. Skip had to sit down.

"The second baseman on our team, Dan Schumacher, his truck was an automatic, so driving your car was a little like that."

Skip nodded blankly, his face the color of a baseball, as he plunged down another hill.

"Anytime I drove was just around town or on other people's farms. I have never driven on an interstate, of course," Jason said.

"Of course," Skip repeated in a dull tone, ready for the rollercoaster ride to be over.

"Or even a highway, for that matter," Jason said, scratching his head thoughtfully.

"You seemed awfully good at it for never having done it before," Skip said.

Jason smiled. "It was fun. I can see why kids like it," he said, growing more animated with the memory. "I hadn't ever gone that fast before until I was riding in the car with you. Of course, I was a little worried about slowing down—"

"Of course," Skip repeated, struggling to remain calm as the rollercoaster careened down another hill.

"So when I was driving, I was worried about stopping the car, because I had never done that before from a fast speed. But I had seen you do it a few times."

Skip nodded, suddenly dizzy. He looked for a place to lay down.

"I enjoyed driving. I will do it again if you would like me to," Jason volunteered.

"Thanks for the offer, Jason," Skip replied. "Hopefully, that won't be necessary."

"Yes, sir."

"So you don't have a driver's license, or Social Security card, or Social Security number," Skip said, summing up the situation. "I don't suppose you have a checking account or savings account?" he asked, afraid of the answer.

"No, sir."

"Of course you don't. That would be too easy. If you've never had a job that gave you a check, then you never needed any place to put the check."

Jason smiled sheepishly. "The savings and loan in Kalona will cash checks for the Amish when we need it," Jason offered helpfully.

"I'm not sure they want to cash a check for one million," Skip replied.

They silently considered the situation.

"It would help if there were some way I could give the check to my mother," Jason wondered aloud.

"You're giving the money to her, anyway, right?" Skip asked.

Yes," Jason nodded. "And then she would put the money into her checking account."

"Her... checking... account?" Skip repeated slowly.

"Yes, sir, her checking account for house and farm expenses," Jason explained.

Skip spoke slowly. "You can just endorse the check over to her, and she can deposit it."

"That is allowed?" Jason said in the tone that betrayed his amazement with the ways of the English.

"Yes, Jason, that's allowed," Skip answered wearily. "Why didn't you say your mother has a checking account?"

"You asked if I had a Social Security number. And then you asked if I had a checking account," Jason explained. "You didn't ask about my mother."

"No, Jason, I didn't," Skip agreed as he struggled to exit Jason's room.

⚾⚾⚾ ⚾⚾⚾

JASON DRAGGED his cleat around third base while Skip and Dave looked on with Henry and Hope.

The dirt smelled dead.

He raked at the ground closer to the shortstop. It smelled worse than dead. Death was natural. His first time on the infield and he couldn't place the smell of it. When plows or shovel blades cut into Iowa soil, the rich aroma of minerals filled the air like the dust in a corn silo. A person could get nourishment just by breathing in the dark dirt.

Freshly raked, the dirt looked like his mother's garden after a rain, the earth made smooth by the raindrops. He missed his mother. He dragged his cleats through the dirt, marking out patterns like the rows of her garden. The new shoes had been waiting for him in his changing room. Like minor miracles on his massive feet, they fit better than anything he'd ever worn, perfect in every way. He knew he would run faster because of the shoes.

But the soil underfoot wasn't soil. It was different. He glanced at the pitcher's mound. He didn't have time to notice that soil. It looked different. Was it different dirt?

This dirt was like so much in the English world: it looked real, but it wasn't. It was fake.

They have fake flowers and plants inside, to remind them of what they're missing outside, Jason thought. Fake lighting to replace the sunlight they block out with curtains. So much of their world was safe and clean. So many of them removed from life. Far from natural things. The field, the stadium, looked beautiful, like a photograph. But it was all artificial, not authentic. Like the fake quilts that looked

Amish but weren't. Someone probably painted the grass green at night. He kicked the ground again. Maybe it wasn't dirt at all. Maybe it kept the color and felt as it did because it was ground brick and not soil.

The lush grass, thick like the brushes in a boot cleaner or a horse brush, reminded him of his yard at home. Home. He wondered what his Maam was doing. Every day of his life, he could simply go inside and see her whenever he wanted. Now, he couldn't.

Now, he was here, standing on dead dirt.

Over at the dugout, Skip was watching Jason closely while Dave, Henry, and Hope looked on.

"You're not worried about him getting hurt?" Dave asked Skip.

"I'm more worried about him not in the lineup," Skip replied. "He should pitch every five games, but he'll miss some days in the rotation because of travel. He won't go to West Coast games; it would take too long to get there and back. He'll miss a couple of East Coast trips, too. He can get his rest at home on the couch, watching the games on TV rather than sitting in the bullpen eating sunflower seeds like the rest of the rotation.

"We're limiting his pitch count during spring training to fifty. During the first half of the season, ninety-five a game. But we don't expect him to throw that many in most starts."

"What do you mean?" asked Hope.

"He has electric stuff. His control is the best on the team. His slider moves like he's dropping it off a table from a foot away. His cutter changes lanes like a car on the interstate. As a pitcher, we're working to refine him, but he doesn't need spring training. The entire staff agrees he's ready to start right now. So this gives us more time to prepare him to play third."

They watched as Jason continued to drag his feet through the dirt.

"What's he doing? What's he looking at?" Henry asked, glancing around the infield.

"He's getting used to the position. This isn't his high school field.

Cut him some slack." Skip clapped his hands loudly. "You ready to field a few, Jason?"

Jason nodded in response, kicked at the dirt a final time, slapped a fist into his glove, and peered at Dave, who was standing ready to bat at home plate.

The ball came off the barrel slowly, and Jason fielded it cleanly and whipped it to first. He got into position, and Dave hit another ground ball. He retrieved the ball and fired it across the field with the delicate force of shoeing a horse.

"See how he keeps his feet moving, and his hands soft? Hard to believe he's a pitcher, isn't it?" Skip said to Henry and Hope.

Hit after hit, Jason gathered the ball with the smooth, flowing motion of a creek in summertime, but after a final throw to first, he gestured to Dave at home plate to stop and beckoned him over.

"What's going on?" Skip called.

"Dunno," Dave replied, jogging toward Jason. "I'll find out."

As Jason spoke, Dave listened intently, turning several times to survey the infield when Jason gestured. Seemingly convinced, Dave finally nodded at Jason and jogged over to the pitching machine near the baseline.

"What's he doing?" Henry asked as Dave rolled the machine onto the infield grass and pointed it between second and third bases.

"I have no idea," Skip said.

Dave got the machine in position and, after exchanging nods with Jason, turned it on. A ball shot out and bounced sharply on the ground in front of Jason, who fielded cleanly and threw the ball to first. The next ball shot at Jason hard. Unconcerned, he calmly fielded and fired to first.

"His range is so good he can nearly play shortstop, too," Hope said.

The machine fired another ball at the ground in front of Jason, who gathered it up effortlessly.

"Having Yoder at third should lower Jackson's errors on the year," Skip said.

"One more man on the team to count his blessings that Jason's here," Hope said.

Skip agreed.

After practice, Jennings was standing near the batting cage when he called out to Skip, who was making his way across the field with Dave.

"Hey, Skip, could you help me here?"

"What's up?"

"I'm pulling everything," Jennings continued. "Could you give me a couple of pointers?" His fingers worked the grip of a bat, the barrel resting on his shoulder.

"Sure," Skip said, nodding. "Go man the monster," he said to Dave. Dave jogged to the pitching machine as Skip watched Jason disappear inside.

Chapter 9

"Hey, rookie," Cory said, knocking on the door of Jason's dressing room.

His jersey un-tucked and unsnapped, Jason opened the door to find several players gathered in various stages of undress. He searched the laughing and snickering faces of his teammates for a clue of the situation. Two players led in a blonde woman carrying a medical bag. Her nurse uniform appeared too short and very tight. She wore blue eyeshadow, red lipstick, and high heels. She was exceptionally attractive.

Jason hastily pulled his shirt closed. "Excuse me," he said.

The players all spoke quickly. "Don't bother buttoning that."

"This is Doctor Kelli."

"It's time for your physical."

"What?" Jason asked, bewildered. "I do not understand."

"Your physical."

"You've got to have your physical, rookie," Whitehall said. "Didn't you know that?"

"I have already had a physical," Jason protested.

"This is your second physical. Everyone gets a second physical," Rico assured him.

"Everyone?" Jason questioned, his eyes scanning the men around him.

"Oh, yeah, man," Cody nodded solemnly. "We all got them twice."

Jason's face clouded with worry as he lowered his head and studied the floor. "Coach Anderson said nothing about a second physical," he said to the carpet. "The first one was bad enough with the shots."

"Skip ain't gonna bother you with every little detail," another player added. "There's no shots this time."

"Now you don't worry about us, you just go ahead and get your physical," Cody said, pushing the woman forward. She stumbled on her high heels but quickly recovered and struck a pose.

"I do not think this is right," Jason said in a worried tone.

"Just relax, baby," said Doctor Kelli.

"But a woman doctor?" Jason said. "This is not proper."

"This is who the team sent over," Vance said.

"We all got our physicals from women doctors," Cory added. "Didn't we, men?"

The guys nodded.

"It's what you gotta do if you wanna play big-league ball."

Jason looked at the woman and then looked sadly at Cory, who nodded sincerely.

"Go ahead," Cory said.

"If I must," Jason surrendered.

"That's the attitude!" Kinnick boomed.

The men cheered as Doctor Kelli led Jason by the hand into his dressing room, closing the door behind them.

In moments the door exploded open as Jason stumbled to the floor.

"What... what she did..." he said, his shirt unbuttoned, his belt and pants open. "That was nothing like the other physical."

The players erupted into laughter.

THE DAYS GREW LONGER as the boys of summer slowly shook off the doldrums of winter and looked toward the new season.

Skip wouldn't have thought it possible, but Jason improved with each passing day. Despite his inexperience, Jason quickly made adjustments and separated himself from his teammates.

"He's moving in a higher gear than the others," Dave said. "And at a different speed. He's astonishing."

With major league coaching, Jason refined and polished every aspect of his game. His pitching achieved new levels as he learned the intricacies of the position. He walked onto the field, knowing how to make the ball dance around the plate and cut away from batters, but the coaching staff taught him how a major league game is played. His extraordinary prowess with the bat took on legendary status while the stands filled with eager fans and opposing players who turned out just to watch him take batting practice.

With every practice, the crowds grew larger and more enthusiastic. The outfield swelled beyond capacity to become a packed swarm of humanity struggling to catch a ball.

Maybe Jason really did have a gift from God?

ON THE FIRST pitch of his first at-bat in the first game of spring training, Jason muscled a flair over the shortstop's head that dropped in shallow left field.

"Gimmie the ball," first base coach Johnny Church called to the infielder, clapping his hands. "First base hit."

In one motion, Johnny slipped the ball into his back pocket and then shook Jason's hand.

"You get to the show, I'll take care of your first hit ball. For now, this'll do, rookie," Johnny said, slapping Jason on the back pockets.

Like the sound of a popcorn machine, Johnny spoke in short explosive bursts, punctuated by clapping his hands, as Jason stepped from the bag.

"One out. You saw Jack's sign at third?"

Jason was bent nearly in half, intently studying the pitcher. "Yes, sir."

"Attaboy. Don't go on the crack of the bat; listen to me. Pick up Jack at third. Make sure you see him before you make the turn at second."

"BACK!"

Jason lunged at the base, his outstretched arm grabbing the bag, well ahead of the pickoff throw.

"Safe!" the umpire called.

"Attaboy."

Jason sprang to his feet, brushing the dead dust from his chest.

"Did you see his move?" Johnny asked, holding Jason by the shoulders and whispering in the earhole of his helmet.

"Yes, sir," Jason nodded as he stepped away from the bag and resumed swaying.

"A ground ball; don't get tagged out. But break-up the double play if you can."

"BACK!"

Jason easily stepped on the bag ahead of the throw. Preoccupied with Jason dancing around first, the pitcher had yet to pitch a strike.

"You saw it again?"

"Yes, sir. Someone ought to tell him about that."

"Ha, funny, rook, funny. OK, rook—"

They both saw the second baseman move two steps to his left, and with the third step, Jason took off. There was no play at second as Jason slid in, his eyes turning to third base coach Jack Crabtree.

Jason's head swiveled as he looked from Jack to Johnny, to the positions of the shortstop and second baseman. Jason moved from the bag toward third. In the next two pitches, the pitcher walked Murphy, distracted by Jason's constant motion behind him.

Mark Green's sharply hit ground ball was smothered by the shortstop, who shoveled it to third just as Jason slid into the bag.

The umpire called him safe on the close play as Jason got up, brushing himself off. He quickly stepped from the bag and jogged across the field as the umpire and opposing players looked on in shocked and silent amazement.

"Are you alright?" Johnny called. "Are you hurt?"

"I'm fine, Coach, thanks," Jason said as he jogged past.

The stands buzzed like an aggravated hive.

"What are you doing?!" Dave yelled to Jason before unleashing a stream of obscenities Jason had never heard before.

"Dave," Skip spoke sharply.

Jason wasn't sure why Dave was angry, but he didn't want to make the mistake again.

Amid murmurs of disbelief, the third baseman quickly threw the ball to the first baseman, who, in turn, tagged Jason with the ball as he jogged past on his way to the dugout. The umpire called him out with a silent gesture and then shook his head.

Skip and Dave met Jason as he approached the top of the dugout.

"What's this all about?" Skip demanded.

"I was out," Jason said.

"What are you talking about?"

Most of the team gathering around Jason reacted with a mixture of laughs and curses.

"What is this," Dave asked, "some kind of joke?"

"I've been hearing that a lot lately," Skip said.

"No, sir," Jason answered Dave. "The throw beat me by half a step. I was out."

"This isn't the honor system," Skip said.

"But I can't lie about it, I was out."

Skip ran his hand through his hair, struggling to find the words. "Umpires make mistakes against you, right?"

"Yes, sir."

"Then let 'em make a few for you, it's only fair," Skip said before he slapped Jason on the seat of his uniform and walked away.

⚾⚾⚾⚾

"WHAT MAKES HIM SPECIAL?" Stone demanded, his words dripping with contempt.

Jason stood behind his special door, hearing the angry words from his teammate.

"His own locker room. Special privileges. It ain't fair," Stone continued.

"Skip explained it—it's his religion," Murphy said simply.

"He can explain it," Stone spat, "but it don't make it right. And what the hell was that today? That 'I was out,' crap? He's an embarrassment to the team."

"Man, lay off him," Hab interjected. "Haven't you been paying attention? Haven't you watched him? The writers are talking about us going all the way. You're just jealous." Hab laughed.

Jason wished he had someone to talk to. To give him advice. He missed his community.

"I ain't jealous of that freak," Stone responded.

Jason took a breath and stepped into the room. Stone sat at his locker, shirtless, and a handful of other players in various stages of undress stood nearby. Jason was unsure of how to address Stone's complaints.

"There he is," Stone said, gesturing as he stood and moved toward Jason. "The superstar. The superstar screw-up."

"I do not understand." Jason glanced at the other men, trying to read their faces.

"Of course you don't," Stone said scornfully. "You don't understand anything."

He pushed Jason hard, slamming him against the wall like a discarded towel. Jason didn't raise a hand.

"Back away, Artie," Hab warned, placing his hands on Stone's shoulders.

"Come on, rook," Stone taunted, "let's see your brush-back pitch."

He pushed Jason again, harder, as Skip and Dave walked in.

Dave stepped between them, shoving Stone backward into Hab's arms. "What is this?"

"We were just talking, Dave," Stone replied, shaking off Hab's grip.

"Jason?" Skip arched a questioning eyebrow.

Jason studied the floor.

"Okaaaay," Skip said slowly. "I don't want to see you two talking like this again." He glared at Stone. "You hear me?"

"Yeah, Skip, I hear you," he said. He looked at Jason menacingly before finally walking away.

"I'm sorry, Skip," Coach Pate laughed. "You gotta admit, it's funny."

"It was the screwiest thing you've ever seen," Skip said, laughing, too. "I thought Dave was gonna have a coronary. Our boy just wandered off the bag like he was in the cereal aisle at the grocery store."

"At least it happened during spring training rather than the regular season."

"Yeah, but then what happened later in the locker room wasn't funny at all," Skip said, his tone growing serious as he explained what had occurred in the locker room between Stone and Jason. "I just don't know what to do. The guy's got it in for him, and Jason won't stand up to him."

"And he won't ever," Coach Pate responded. "An Amish person would rather move away than fight someone."

"What do you mean, 'move away'?" Skip asked, a tone of alarm rising in his voice. "He'll just back away from the confrontation?"

"No, Coach, he'll move," Coach Pate explained patiently. "He'll pack up and move. Amish families have been known to sell an entire farm and move to another state when they have a serious disagreement with a neighbor— especially if it's an English neighbor. The Amish moved to the United States in the first place to avoid conflict with their fellow countrymen."

"He won't stand up for himself at all?" Skip asked.

"He'll take a lot of abuse, for a lot longer than you or I would," Coach Pate said. "He'll never stand up for himself. Ever. But at some point, he'll simply walk away. You're going to have to handle this for him, or he will leave."

The next morning, after meeting with Art Stone, Skip looked on as Stone angrily shoved his things into a bag, packing to leave.

JASON STARTED WALKING around the subdivision with Annie after dinner. After just a few walks, he began to go by himself, leaving the concrete street and large houses on landscaped lots and traveling into the desert.

He walked nearly every night, usually after excusing himself for bed. Each time he ventured further into the desert, escaping across the sand like the lengthening shadows of the evening. His nights reminded him of Jesus in the wilderness, far from others, but still tempted by things of this world.

He had never experienced sand like this, and he enjoyed it. Eventually, he began to run as fast as he could, each step sinking into the sand. His breath pounding in his ears drowned out his throbbing heart. He found the faster he ran, the more he skimmed across the surface, like a stone skipping across water.

He ran until the lights of the subdivision behind him were little more than small dots on the horizon. He came to recognize the Anderson porch light from a half-mile away.

The stars sparkled and shined like the sand beneath him. The sky looked like fine soot on a black wool coat. It was more magnificent than the stars back home, and he hardly believed it possible. He marveled at the immenseness of it.

The vast expanse reminded Jason that God's creation existed beneath, beyond, and above the man-made world.

Once, he stayed out all night and watched with wonder as the sky slowly shifted from black to dark blue, then to pink, red, and orange as the sun rose and filled the sky with light. He never saw such amazing colors back home. God's colors were amazing. Creation was amazing. He felt connected to the infinite— as insignificant as the sand and the stars, but as unique as the rising sun.

These were the moments he felt truly free.

⚾⚾⚾⚾ ⚾⚾⚾⚾

"I APPRECIATE you taking the time to do this," Annie said.

"I have lots of time," Jason replied, watching the traffic.

"You don't have to work out?"

"Tom, one of the trainers? He said that he wished all the

players had my...conditioning," he said the word slowly and smiled. "Tom asked what he needed to do to have all the guys look like me." He retrieved a banana from the grocery bag on his lap. "I said they can all go work on a farm. Five hours checking and hammering the nails in a wire fence builds wrist strength. Even I know that."

"What'd he say to that?"

"He said maybe they'd be hitting .525, too." He finished the banana in two bites and then watched the traffic in silence.

They pulled up to the hospital, and Annie led the way to the children's wing, where they met Mark Green, Danny Murphy, and his wife, Stacie.

"Jase," Danny said, offering his hand.

"Murph," Jason responded, shaking hands, shocked by how easily he slipped into using and accepting nicknames.

Clearly unsure of what was expected of him or what he was to do, Jason followed Green and Murphy down the sterile hall. The veterans introduced themselves to nurses and doctors while signing autographs. Jason thought it silly that people would want his signature, but he carefully wrote it out for those who asked.

The commotion drew a little girl from a nearby room who walked in holding hands with her mother. No taller than Adam, her sick eyes gazed out from deep within dark circles.

"Vi bisht doo, glay maedel," Jason said, kneeling to speak to her. "Voss iss day noma?" He took her hand in his. "Eekk been Jason. Doo bisht gonz shay."

Her eyes grew wide and bright as he spoke.

"How are you, little girl?" he repeated, gazing steadily into her eyes. "What is your name? My name is Jason. You are very pretty. Doo bisht gonz shay." He smiled and winked.

"Her name's Caitlin," said the mother, who was standing above them.

"Vi bisht doo, Caitlin. Would you like this?" He slowly produced a baseball from his paper bag. The girl's complexion matched the dull rawhide of the ball. She gave him a tight hug with frail little arms and rushed back to her room.

Jason followed Murph into a room where a child lay connected with wires and tubes to beeping medical equipment, his ashen complexion the color of the hospital floor.

"Vi bisht doo, bu," he said, handing the boy a ball. "Shamas doe rriva?" he said, his hand outstretched. "Shamas doe rriva. Throw it here."

Weakly, the child tossed the ball a few inches into the air. Jason's hand shot out and snatched the ball. "Sell iss goot!" The boy's eyes grew wide as Jason handed him the ball.

When a group of children gathered around Jason in the hallway, he flopped onto the floor to look them in the eyes. Amid shrill peals of laughter, he put his hat on each of them, their faces reflecting all the joy and happiness that pours unbidden out of a child's heart.

A nurse slowly rolled a small girl in a wheelchair over to Jason, her mother and a doctor at her side. Her thin frame, sunken eyes, and the small oxygen mask over her mouth and nose made her appear older than her six years.

Jason slowly rose to his feet and moved toward her, his heart throbbing with concern.

"Voss iss lets mit da maedel?" He shook his head, frustrated with himself for slipping into his native tongue. "What is wrong with her?" He asked the adults, his voice just above a whisper.

"Acute lymphocytic leukemia," said the woman doctor who looked older than Jason's mother. He smiled weakly and shook his head.

"A type of childhood cancer," the nurse explained.

Jason winced. "Is she dying?"

"She's getting better very slowly," the doctor explained. "The illness and treatment are very difficult."

"It's hard on everyone," the nurse said. "The child, the family, the staff, even the doctors. It's curable, but this is one of the worst illnesses a child can experience and still survive."

Jason spoke quietly to the mother before he knelt and handed his hat to the little girl. A hand on the mother's forearm and the child's shoulder, he closed his eyes in prayer as the child fell asleep holding his hat.

Jason wore a ball cap off the field for several days before a new straw hat arrived in the mail.

Chapter 10

S kip had to look again.

Surely that wasn't his Amish star pitcher— the phenomenon the reporters called the Bashful Basher—walking up the loading ramp of a beer truck. Surely he was mistaken.

He waited until the figure emerged from the back of the truck, a full keg in each hand, the Mjollnir logo painted on the sides.

The weariness of a thousand sleepless nights settling on his shoulders made Skip close his eyes. He opened them to see Jason glowing in the early morning sunlight. As Jason hurried to the concession stand, Skip had to admit that he did look a little like some sort of mythological god, the sun shining on his golden hair and reflecting off the silver metal kegs in his hands.

"Jason, what are you doing?"

The boy carried an empty keg under each arm and two in each hand.

"Halllooo, Coach Anderson," Jason called cheerfully.

"What are you doing?" Skip repeated.

"Helping out," he beamed, his face dripping sweat.

"So I see. Why?"

"I get here early, and there's no one to throw with, so I help out," he said, loading kegs into the truck. "Yesterday, I helped Tino."

"Who's Tino?"

Jason cocked his head sideways, surprised at Skip's ignorance.

"He's a groundskeeper. I raked the mound before the game."

"You started yesterday."

"Yes, sir."

Skip's mind flashed to Mark Fidrych, the Detroit Tiger who manicured the mound by fixing cleat marks and moving dirt during games.

"You were raking the infield before you pitched?"

"Just the mound, yes, sir," he said, passing his fingers through his sweaty hair. "And around first base. And second." He smiled. "Ya, I guess I did rake the infield," he laughed.

"Shouldn't you rest up before your next start?" Skip asked. Jason had thrown seven shutout innings in eighty pitches.

"We say the best rest comes after working hard."

"Yeah, son, in baseball, players generally rest before they play, so they're at their best when they take the field."

Jason laughed. "I'm at my best all the time."

Skip believed him. Jason's last pitch yesterday was his fastest of the game. He didn't get tired or show signs of losing his control, no matter how long he pitched.

"What if you'd gotten hurt?"

"Hurt raking?" Jason laughed with abandon. "I've been raking my whole life. I might get hurt in all that big city traffic out there"—he gestured at the empty parking lot—"but I'm not gonna get hurt raking or carrying stuff. Back home, I do more work than this before breakfast." He glanced over to see another man struggling with a single keg, his arms extended with effort. "Sorry, Alex."

"No problem," Alex puffed as he passed by.

Jason smiled. "Besides, I like helping out. Being useful."

"OK." Skip knew it wasn't a good idea to have his young prospect performing manual labor, especially at the ballpark, but he didn't have a compelling argument against it. "OK," he repeated. "Just be careful."

COACH PATE RECOGNIZED Skip's anxiety. He was half Skip's age and had a fraction of his experience, but he completely understood Skip's turmoil.

"I have no idea what I'm doing with him," Skip said during one of his increasingly regular phone calls.

"Yeah, I know that feeling," Coach Pate replied. "I spent the entire season like that. And then we won the state championship for the first time in school history."

"What do I do?"

"Understand that he'll have trouble making choices."

"Why? He's free to do anything you wants."

"And that's the problem," Coach Pate said. "His life hasn't been about freedom, and so making choices can throw him into turmoil."

"What are you saying?"

"When an Amish person joins the church, they make a choice. Most important choice of their lives. But when they make that choice, it relieves them of making other choices. Understand?"

"Not really. It feels like the more I learn, the less I understand."

"Think of it this way. The Ordnung is the way they live their lives. It's like joining the military or a club— a club you've spent your whole life growing up in, and then you decide to stay. But once you make that decision, your other choices disappear. This is all about the rules he lives by. The rules of the Ordnung limit the choices he can make. So if he sees something familiar to him, like unloading a truck, then that's a choice he'll make, almost without thinking."

"Would you be interested in coming out here to Mesa? A part-time job?"

"I'd love to help coach, but I'm still in school. I teach history, and I'm a guidance counselor. I couldn't leave if I wanted to."

"Sure, I understand. Listen. Thanks for all of your help."

"No problem," Coach Pate said. "Talk with you in a few days."

Coach Pate hung up the phone and sat in the silent room. He imagined the experiences Jason was having, both good and bad. Jason was living a life that countless boys had dreamed of for more than a hundred years.

As he thought of Jason walking through a big-league locker room or shagging balls on a manicured field, he remembered having his own dreams, and the exact moment he let them go.

It had been years since he thought of that sunny, Sunday afternoon and that last summer in the minor leagues. His mind wandered back to that season, the other players, the coach, the buses, and travel. He had stood on second after a clean double to right and realized he would never be as good a player as he was that day, on that field. And it wasn't enough. He remembered his feelings when he had to acknowledge that he had fallen short and would never be good enough to be a daily major leaguer. He wasn't bitter— he'd given the game his best, and then it was time to tip his hat and walk away. He was pleased to have had the opportunity. But that feeling of almost making it never went away. It haunted his memories like fog on an early morning field. The feeling lingered, disappeared, and then returned another day.

He smiled ruefully. Jason was better than all the men he faced in his career. Jason would never have to make the tough choice he had to make that afternoon. Jason was living an opportunity that few men had, but he was so far out of his element that it must have been nearly impossible for him to fully enjoy it. What a shame.

"No church this week, so let's play ball," said James Yoder, waking his six-year-old son.

They trudged across the grass of the high school field, James carrying the bushel basket of baseballs, two gloves balanced on top, while Jason lugged a battered wooden bat. Most Sundays in the summer, they could play for hours on the high school field before ever seeing another soul.

"You remember the pitcher's pickoff move at the game last week?" James asked while they were throwing the ball back and forth. "Do you remember his heel and how it slid before he moved? Ya? Someone should tell him about that." James winked.

Later, as Jason took relaxed practice swings, James stood in front of the pitcher's mound.

"You're getting really good," he said. "I will toss it in there a little harder."

Jason nodded, and his father threw the ball at three-quarter speed. Jason sent the ball soaring into shallow left field.

"You learn to hit my fastball, you can hit anything," James said before throwing again at nearly full speed.

Jason drove the pitch straight back at the mound, and with lightning speed, James snatched the ball from the air with his bare hand.

"Good one, son," James exclaimed happily. "That's High Clinton, that is. Now let's hit some curveballs." Batting practice continued until the bushel basket was empty, baseballs scattered across the green outfield like biscuit crumbs on a tablecloth.

Jason smiled at the memory.

"Yoder! On deck!"

Rising from the bench, Jason pulled his helmet on and made his way up the dugout steps. Humming Das Loblied, he wondered how many more Sundays would pass before he found himself in a worship service.

⚾⚾⚾⚾

"Hope, this is Skip. I need your help."

"What's going on?" He heard the smile she gave over the phone.

"I need help with the kid. It's hard enough managing this crew under ordinary circumstances, but he's distracting a lot of the other players."

"I can understand that."

"It's not fair to the kid that he's stuck with me all the time."

"You want him stuck with me?" she said with a light laugh. "The team will love that."

"I just don't have the time to babysit him every second of the day," Skip continued. "And it's not fair to him to be stuck with the manager. None of the other players are willing to talk to him. Half of them think he's some sort of spy, and the other half think he's a joke."

"Well, his curveball isn't a joke," she said. "And that should be all that matters to them."

"You know how a club house can be," he said. "Will you help me?"

"You want me to spend all my time hanging around that muscular, beautiful farm boy?" she gushed. "Gazing into those blue eyes, holding those strong muscular arms, running my fingers through that beautiful blond hair? Is that what you want, Coach?"

"Ahhh," Skip stammered. Aware of her overt flirting and double entendres, he had never experienced it firsthand.

"Because I would be happy to."

HOPE STOOD in the center of Skip's small office, wearing the same blue skirt she wore to Iowa. Her muscular legs strained against the material, clinging to her body like it was painted on.

She was interested in the farm boy on many levels.

"You wanted to see me, Coach? I—" Jason froze.

Hope smiled. She would never tire of seeing that reaction.

Like it was with most men, Jason's eyes followed the thin gold chain around her neck as it disappeared into her white silk shirt where the buttons strained against her chest.

He's like the model for Michelangelo's David, she thought.

"This is Hope Chambers," Skip said.

"Close your mouth, farm boy," she said. "You're staring."

"Hope's going to...help you out," Skip said.

She winked lasciviously at Skip. She enjoyed it when men blushed.

"What do you mean, help me out?" Jason asked.

"She'll drive you on any errands you need, to the bank, or shopping. Take you to and from the ballpark."

"I do not understand. Why can't I keep riding with you?"

"I don't have the time to help with everything you need," Skip said. "When we get to Chicago, I'll be working longer hours, and it just won't be practical. You don't have to be here if it's not necessary. There are plenty of people to rake the field and unload trucks. You need to get used to resting and letting your body heal and recover."

"I—"

"Don't argue, Superman," Hope interrupted. "You and Skip may be buddies, but you've got to get used to doing what you're told. You may feel fine today, and even tomorrow, but the schedule is grueling. It takes more out of you than you know."

She ran her tongue across her teeth. She could see a drop of sweat appear at his temple.

"...take you out for meals," Skip was saying. "Help you set up a bank account, help you find an apartment in Chicago. Teach you how to pay bills, to get along. You'll need to get an agent. Talk to your teammates, they'll give you some ideas of names. But she'll help set up the meeting." Skip cut his eyes at Hope. "Imagine her as your own personal assistant."

Hope sharpened her gaze at Skip before softening her expression to Jason. "I'm here to help you transition."

"I just want to play baseball," Jason said, "I don't know about that other stuff."

"That's right, you focus on baseball, and I'll help you with everything else."

"Now you sound like Doctor Kelli," Jason said.

Hope turned a questioning gaze to Skip.

"Yeah," Skip exhaled in disgusted frustration. "I heard about that. Hope, you don't want to know. Jason, I'm sorry it happened. Dave's had a talk with the guys responsible. It won't happen again."

Jason nodded.

"So what do you say, sport? Instead of having to wait hours for me, every day, Hope will take you home whenever you're ready."

"Whatever you say, Coach. I'll do whatever you say."

"That's the attitude."

"I'll take you back to Skip's house today, farm boy, when you're ready," Hope said. "If you want, we can stop for something to eat."

"I can always eat."

"You know, maybe you should slow down, you might actually taste the food," Hope said, reaching for her frozen drink, the bright green of not-yet-ripe tomatoes. "Or at least try eating less. You ordered a lot of food."

He had ordered the steak fajitas, an entrée of tacos, shredded beef chimichangas, carne asada, and appetizers of cheese dip, guacamole, bean dip, and pulled pork taquitos with chipotle ranch dipping sauce.

"It's OK," he said between bites of fajitas, "I have my..." he struggled for the word, "my per diem?"

"That's only a hundred dollars a day. A couple more platters of steak, and you'll reach it."

"A hundred dollars and fifty cents. Fifty cents. All those quarters," he said, shaking his head and sopping up grease with a tortilla. He had taken to giving the quarters to the children as he left the ballpark and pretended their parents weren't taking photos. "I haven't spent much of it."

He took a final bite of grease-soaked tortilla, licked his fingertips clean, and wiped them on a handful of paper napkins. He retrieved a wad of money from his pocket that unfolded to display several hundred-dollar bills.

"How much is that?"

He shrugged. "Nearly all of it."

"All of your per diem? Since when?"

"Since they started giving it to me. I don't have anything to spend it on. Except food. I buy food. I don't even have to buy a newspaper; there is always one in the locker room. I will give the rest to my mother when I see her."

"When is that?"

"I'll go home for a few days before the regular season starts." He demolished a taco in two bites.

"How are you going?" she asked. "The train?"

He dipped his head. "I don't know. I'll do what Coach Anderson says."

"More or less," she added with a teasing wink.

"Yes," he admitted. "There are some things I won't do. Can't do. But he says I'll leave Mesa before the rest of the team, I'll be home for a few days, and then I'll be in Chicago when the season starts."

"I'm curious about the length...of that 'won't do' list," she said slowly.

He was sure he misunderstood, so he turned his attention to the arrival of the crispy chicken flautas and devoured them in two bites each.

⚾⚾⚾⚾ ⚾⚾⚾⚾

FILING into the clubhouse after the game, the team's excited chatter centered around Jason's performance on the mound.

"Yoder handing out golden sombreros all afternoon."

"And a platinum sombrero," someone yelled. "Did you see that?"

"They were swinging wild like Saturday night at the club."

"Tony Two-Bags today!"

Jason had no idea what they were talking about. He heard Hab's loud voice booming through the commotion.

"I still can't believe I'm platooned," he said. "A year from free agency, and I get platooned."

Jason knew what that meant.

"I'm not the only Muslim in professional sports," Hab Samkhalifa had told Jason when they first met, "but I'm the only one in baseball. My father is Egyptian. I was born and raised in Arizona."

Hab had skin the color of unstained mahogany. His teeth were white like milk, and he showed them whenever he threw his head back and laughed, which was often. Immediately, Jason liked him very much.

"I only play on days Jason pitches. The rest of the time I ride the bench," he was saying.

It hadn't occurred to Jason he was taking two positions on the roster. He was stricken by Hab's complaints.

"I am sorry, Hab," Jason said. "I am taking your job, costing you your pay."

Hab grabbed Jason's neck and laughed. "You're so funny, rook. I get paid either way. Do not worry, my Christian brother."

Jason had pitched six scoreless innings and went three-for-three with two doubles and a stolen base.

"Come here, my Christian brother," Hab said, wrapping an arm around Jason and grasping Jason's massive forearm with his other hand. "Our God has blessed his arms. He has made him big and strong and powerful. Jason is our prophet," he said in his booming voice, loud enough for the entire team to hear. "We must all follow him. Like Abraham, he will lead us. Lead us all to the World Series." And then he laughed a loud laugh that echoed through the locker room.

Jason was relieved.

"Playing part-time in the big leagues is better than playing full-time in the minor leagues," Hab laughed. "I would spend the entire season sitting on the bench if it meant we get to the postseason." He tousled Jason's golden hair with his dark fingers. "I would hold your water cup nine innings, every game if that would win us the World Series."

"You don't have to do that," Jason said with an embarrassed, crooked smile, pulling away.

Hab laughed. "Whatever you say, Jase. Whatever you say."

Chapter 11

Down one run, with runners on second and third, Jason was in the hole as he made his way to the dugout steps.

"We don't need a tater, Jase, we just need two ribbies. Throw a gork down the right-field line, and let's go home."

In the process of putting on his helmet, his index fingers in the earholes, Jason froze. He stood statue-still, his bat under his arm, as he tried and failed to process the words.

He remembered the first time he heard an English person speak — how strange the words sounded. Even words he recognized sounded so different.

These words were so strange, he couldn't distinguish the voice. Someone said something about the right-field line, he repeated to himself. He blinked and surveyed the field. Tater? Ribbies? Gork? This wasn't Rico speaking his Spanish. They sounded like English words, but not really.

Was someone mocking him? He looked at the faces of the teammates on the bench and standing nearby— no one seemed to be sharing a private joke. On the contrary, his teammates looked at him with expressions of excitement and expectation. Everyone seemed as though they wanted him to do well. Several smiled and nodded in return to his gaze.

Gork?

How long had they been calling him Jase?

Hab grounded out to shortstop.

With a backward glance at the dugout, Jason moved to the on-deck circle.

Gork?

He looked at the crowded stands and was reminded of his uncle Amos' dairy farm. All different, each unique, but all the same.

Cows and people, he thought with a smile, taking a half-speed warm-up swing. I really am changing if I compare cows to people.

Scanning the faces in the crowd, he reminded himself that they were all made in God's image. The beasts of the field, like cows and horses, were provided by God to help men in their labor. He noticed a small beer seller struggling with the box of ice and bottles hanging from his neck, the weight of it bending him over. Beasts of the field, he thought again with a smile.

Gork?

When Murphy flied out to shallow left field, the runners were unable to advance. Suddenly the game was on the line, and he was thinking about cows and horses.

Jason scolded himself for becoming distracted.

Someone asked for a gork, he thought as he marched intently toward the batter's box, so I must do my best.

The celebration following his home run seemed louder than when they won the state championship, but even hours later, he wasn't sure why.

"How'd you like to be a special consultant for the Chicago Cubs this summer?"

"What—?" Coach Pate had just answered the phone when Skip made his proposition.

"Sure. Share an office cubicle with Ryne Sandberg. Get paid to come to games. Keep an eye on our boy. Help him make the transition. Keep him out of trouble—"

"Is he getting into trouble?"

"Well, no, not exactly, just a figure of speech. He's...he's...just having trouble fitting in."

"He won't fit in, Skip—"

"Hope Chambers is trying, but maybe things will go better if you were here, helping."

"Skip, listen to me, he may never fit in. It's not going to happen, at least not like you want him to. Think of him like he's a Japanese player, a completely different culture, language, all things you don't understand. Only instead of loving the American culture and wanting to be part of it, he doesn't like the culture and wants nothing to do with it. Except baseball."

"OK."

"I keep telling you, this isn't going to be easy. For any of you. Not you, not him, not the other players. Of course, I could be wrong. We know his plan is to play just a year, maybe a couple years, then come back home."

"I know."

"Folks around here think he'll change so much that he won't want to come back. If that happens, once he decides to stay in Chicago, be a professional ballplayer, and everything that comes with it, then he'll start to change enough that he may fit in a little bit better. But he won't ever fit in the way most guys would. People who leave the Amish leave behind a community. They leave looking for something else, but in the looking, they give up more than they expect or realize. You're asking him to fit in with things he doesn't understand or like, and leave behind everything he knows. He's gonna have to love baseball an awful lot to do that."

Skip realized that Jason was far from the simple farm boy he appeared to be.

"Listen, I'm sorry for going on and on," Coach Pate said. "Remember, just as you don't understand his ways, he has no comprehension of yours. I'll think about the offer. Sounds like more fun than teaching summer school."

⚾⚾⚾

"I— I HAVE A—" Jason hesitated, "—a problem."

"Problem?" Skip repeated. Jason had stopped him after the game, and he felt the increasingly familiar surge of panic as his rollercoaster stomach began rumbling. He wondered when the anxiety would subside. After they win the series, he decided. "What do you mean, 'problem'?"

Jason looked around. "The dugout is so..." He struggled for an English word. "Not tidy."

Skip considered the filth that was a professional dugout as they stood inside it. The layer of garbage covering the concrete. Sunflower seeds, gum wrappers, paper cups, spit. He remembered the immaculate condition of the high school dugout—because the boys had to clean the dugout themselves afterward, they kept the area well-policed during the game.

He thought about the rite of passage from college to professional when players bought their first real suits, picked up the first check, and stopped caring about the appearance of the dugout. He toed a banana peel inches from a half-empty garbage can. Maybe the kid had a point.

"What would you have me do?" Skip asked. "I don't want you distracted."

"I do not know," Jason said, staring at the ground, mesmerized by the mess. "Maybe I can try cleaning up between innings. "Eekk conn bootsa tzu halt ess swova," he murmured, as he raked his cleats through a pile of crushed paper cups. He looked up and smiled. "I can clean to keep it clean." He glanced around him. "Of course, it would help if I had a shovel—"

"Stop right there, Jason," Skip interrupted, holding up his hand. "I'll not have you cleaning up the dugout during the game. I might as well have you raking the mound between innings—"

"I don't need the warm-up pitches," Jason said quickly. "I would be happy to rake—"

"Stop. Just stop," Skip said. "I don't need you thinking about raking or cleaning or anything other than pitching and hitting."

"I can do both. It's been pretty easy to think about other things while I'm playing. I don't think about the pitching or hitting at all, really. I just do it."

As Skip shook his head in wonder, he wondered how many times Jason would make him wonder.

DAVE WONDERED what Jason was doing in the maintenance area by left field. The game long since won, Jason was still in uniform and talking to... What was his name? Tony? Geno? Tino?

Dave's clipboard slipped from his hands and clattered to the concrete of the dugout when Jason and Tino slowly dropped to their knees, heads bowed, hands clasped in prayer.

Dave looked around for someone, anyone, to corroborate what he was witnessing. They wouldn't believe him when he told the story later.

He was instantly ashamed of his thoughts. Watching the intimate moment, he realized he was invading their privacy.

At that instant, Jason and Tino rose and walked away talking.

What was it about the kid, Dave wondered, that people reacted the way they did? A few seemed to loathe him, while so many others clamored to be near him. Jason was a natural born leader, and he had no idea, Dave realized. This kid could do anything he wants, at anytime, anywhere, and he wants to grow vegetables and shovel horse manure? Skip's right, we have to do everything we can to keep him on this team.

IN THE BATTING CAGE, with fluid, casual swings, Jason crushed the ball, sending it over the wall. Watching from his dugout, the visiting coach grew visibly angrier with every pitch.

"Hey, Anderson," the visiting coach yelled, walking onto the field. "What's this kid doing taking batting practice with a corked bat? What is this, a joke?"

"It's a regulation bat," Skip yelled back.

"I was born yesterday? Look at the ball. The bat's corked."

The impact of the bat on the ball echoed like gunshots across the desert.

Skip purposefully strode to the opposing dugout.

"Gimme a bat," he grunted, passing the other man.

"What?" the coach said, taken aback, as Skip stepped into the visitor dugout. Pulling a bat from the rack, Skip repeated, "Give me a bat."

Bat in hand, Skip calmly walked to the cage. "Here, kid, use this," he said, shoving the barrel of the bat into Jason's ribs.

Jason glanced around as he tossed his bat aside and took the other from Skip.

Skip gestured with his hands. "Go, go, get back in there."

Stepping to the plate, Jason took a tentative swing with the new bat and nodded to the pitcher. He stroked the next pitch to the left field wall. With just another pitch, he got back into a groove and was driving balls deep into the stands.

Skip grinned happily as the other coach looked on, his mouth agape.

DAVE AND SKIP were finishing paperwork when Dave muttered under his breath.

"What?" Skip asked.

"I said the kid's a real Dick Smith," Dave said.

"I haven't heard that name in forever. You really think so?"

"Has the kid even been to a restaurant with a teammate, much less picked up a check? I like him well enough, and I know what he's doing to this team, but he's as green as a pool table. He's a Dick Smith."

"That's a little harsh, don't you think? He'll learn," Skip replied. "He's learning."

Dave stroked his bottom lip pensively. "Talking to him sometimes feels like delivering mail to the wrong address," he said. "Dick Smith, I'm telling you. The kid's a loner. God knows we need him, but he's making some of the guys uncomfortable."

"They'll get used to him."

"Maybe if you let him out from under your wing, mother hen, and keep Hope's claws off him for a couple of days. Let me see if we can get someone to room with him. Maybe a road roommate will help him fit in. Let him room with..." Dave glanced down at his roster, "Jennings."

"Skip, gotta minute?"

As the players got off the bus, collecting bags and heading to cars, Jennings stopped to talk with Skip.

"What's up?"

"The kid—" Jennings started, clearly uncomfortable. "What is he, some kind of—"

"What's wrong with him?"

"Last night, he was really creeping me out."

"What are you talking about?" Skip demanded.

"You don't know? You gotta see for yourself. The kid's strange."

At eight-thirty that night, after a quick knock at Jason's bedroom door, Skip entered. "Hey, sport—"

"Yes, sir," Jason responded as he came out of the bathroom. Skip's mouth fell open at the sight of Jason in an old-fashioned nightshirt, his strong, muscular legs bare from the knees down. He didn't dress like this on the train. Now he understood Jennings' comment.

"You wanted to talk with me?" Jason asked as he stepped past and turned back the bed covers.

"What?" Skip answered, rattled. "No. Never mind."

"I was about to go to bed."

Skip looked at his watch. "Yeah, sure, look at the time. Go ahead," he mumbled.

Jason dropped to his knees, bent his head, and clasped his hands in prayer.

Skip was shocked anew. He looked around self-consciously. It wasn't a trick.

Slowly, he sat down. As if moving on their own, his hands came together, and he bowed his head and closed his eyes. After a moment, an eye winked open to sneak a look at Jason. The differences between their two cultures were never more stark than at this instant. A massive teenager in an anachronistic nightshirt praying on his knees at eight-thirty in the evening in the twenty-first century.

Jennings and Rico were warming up on the field the next morning when Skip walked by.

"Hey Skip, careful you don't wear out the knees of your pants," Jennings said with a smirk.

"You're looking a little slow getting to second," Skip responded. "You better take an extra ten laps around the field."

"You gotta be kidding?"

"Fifteen. Why don't you get started now?"

Jennings shook his head bitterly before throwing his glove down and slowly jogging away.

Skip looked at Rico. "You got anything to say?"

"No, sir," Rico snapped.

"That's the attitude."

Moments later, Skip stormed past Dave, who was watching practice. "Road trips—Jason wants a roommate? He rooms with you or me," he said, not waiting for a response.

Chapter 12

Jason stood in the on-deck circle, casually swinging the bat and watching Luke Giolita on the mound.

He had faced Giolita before, who was as easy to read as the lineup card. He knew from the sports pages and the radio that Giolita, a league leader in strikeouts, gave guys a lot of trouble. He couldn't understand why.

He knew pitchers were supposed to have the same delivery for every pitch. That's what he tried to do. Was it really so difficult for others?

He knew the pitch was a curve before the ball left Giolita's hand. He could tell by the direction the stitches spun which way it would break. Otherwise, he expected a fastball.

Besides, when Giolita threw a fastball, he relaxed the shoulder of his glove hand just a bit before each pitch. Giolita relaxed the way a horse does when the tack comes off. Jason had watched Biscuit relax that way nearly every day of his life, and Giolita moved his shoulders the same way. It was so obvious that he wasn't sure he saw it the first time. But after watching the pitches to the three batters before him, he saw it as clear as spring water. Everyone was so impressed with his first-pitch home run, but he knew it was a fastball before Giolita started his windup. The distance did surprise him, he thought, looking to the outfield. The parking lot outside the stadium seemed a long way away, but deep into the cornfield back home felt further.

Home. With each new day, home felt further away.

Facing Giolita wasn't like the time he faced the major league's only knuckleballer. He had been excited to challenge himself against Dickey. A long-time veteran, Dickey had worked with all of the living knuckleballers of the past to perfect his pitches.

When Jason finally faced him, he took two called strikes on three pitches, standing with his mouth open and the bat on his shoulder.

The ball had no spin, just as they said, but it did dance on the currents of air. But the speed wasn't any faster than a mouse across the barn floor. Jason had no trouble tracking the ball— without a spin, the ball just floated in, and he could clearly read the words printed on the rawhide. He was astonished to distraction by his ability to read the ball. When he read the commissioner's signature, he wondered if he would ever meet the man.

Ahead in the count, Dickey wasted the next pitch low and outside. As he watched the ball go into the catcher's glove, Jason gathered his thoughts enough to realize the next pitch might be a strike, and he ought to be ready to hit it.

The ball floated in like a big, fluffy cloud stitched together with red thread. He crushed it harder than any pitch before or since. Jason heard that the home run was the first highlight on Sports Center for all of spring training. He didn't know what a highlight on Sports Center was, but the guys were excited about it.

He went three-for-three with two home runs and a triple before he knocked the legend out of the game.

He enjoyed watching Dickey pitch but couldn't understand how the knuckleball made his teammates so verrickt.

He had practiced a knuckleball in the barn that was nearly as good as his curveball, but Coach Anderson hadn't asked about a knuckleball, so Jason hadn't shown it to him.

As Murphy grinded, fouling off pitch after pitch, Jason glanced at the packed stands and thought of the crowds of people back home who had come to watch him play.

Home.

A young mother and baby caught his eye, and he imagined himself as a father. He thought of the midwife coming to their home to deliver Faith's baby. As an only child, he always wanted a large family. When would he be ready to start a family? How would he know?

He looked around the stands again and realized for the first time how many children there were at the ballpark. It was fitting so many children would watch a children's game.

Amish children were always nearby when parents worked. His children couldn't spend their days at the ballpark, and he'd be traveling for portions of the season, anyway. He couldn't have children and play baseball. Besides, Faith wouldn't marry him until after he was done with baseball and returned home.

Home. Such a short word, and so far away.

JASON CONTINUED his home-run trot across home plate and toward the dugout. As he made his way down the steps, he was greeted with high fives and slaps to the back.

"That ball still hasn't come down," Hab said.

"Did you get that?" someone asked.

"What do you mean...that?" Jason questioned, smiling weakly, searching their faces for a clue.

"Did you get all of it?" Murph asked, the teammates in earshot exchanging glances as they teased Jason about the blast that cleared the left-field fence by twenty feet.

"Ah," Jason nodded with understanding. The smiles around him melted like April snow as he responded seriously. "No, I didn't. As I made contact, I saw I was hitting the ball on the stitches, not clean on the leather. And I was under it, just a hair. I tried to turn the bat over more, to make up for hitting the stitches, but I didn't have time." He looked out at the field. "So, no, I didn't get all of it. But I remember him, and I'll get a little more next time." He winked as he smiled.

CONDENSATION CLOUDED the windows of the Yoder kitchen as Faith and Grace listened to Jason's radio and cheered for the man in their lives when he hit his home run.

"Thank you for all your help," Grace said as Faith moved another completed case of relish. These batches of relish, using store-bought vegetables, were destined to be sold at the first farmers' markets of the season. Faith had been working with Grace for much of the day. "Jason has taken care of me since his Daa went home to be with the Lord," Grace continued as she topped off the water in a boiling pan. "Did you know, his Daa was very good at baseball when he was a teenager, too?"

"I didn't know."

"He was so strong," Grace said, smiling at the memory. "His son is so much like him."

She turned her attention to a new set of jars. "I had the same fear you've probably had, that he would leave and not come back." She glanced over to see Faith looking on silently. "It was hard. Of course, for you, he's actually left, and James stayed." She nodded to herself. "Maybe it's for the best. Jason can get the baseball out of his system once and for all. James always loved baseball.

"You probably don't remember, but James organized several trips each summer to baseball games in Cedar Rapids. He took your father and uncles, and a few other men. Jason went too, of course."

"I didn't know that, either."

"And then, after we lost him, his friends lost interest in going. Jason's not been to a game since." She paused, a drop of food coloring poised over the jar. "At least that's what I thought."

Faith inclined her head.

Grace hesitated and consider her words. "Has he told you about the accident?"

"He's never spoken of it."

Grace nodded. "I don't remember much. Doctors said the memories were damaged by the crash." She touched her head gently and smiled sadly. She spooned relish into waiting jars.

"We were coming back from town, out on 22, and were hit from behind, by a young man...texting? I'm still not sure what that means," she said, shaking her head. "He hit us at full speed, didn't even slow down. The buggy was destroyed, smashed to splinters. I was injured, the horse was killed, and James was taken from us."

Faith nodded as she began moving cooked jars of relish out of the hot water and onto the cooling rack.

"They said Jason must have been thrown clear. They found him holding his Daa's hat in the wreckage." Grace placed tops on full jars. "He was not quite seven. He says he has no memories of it. But I sometimes wonder if he remembers more than he says."

"Don't we all?" Faith said.

Grace nodded in agreement. "It's good to think more than we speak. But sometimes I wonder what he remembers. We got Biscuit after the accident, and of course, we had the field horses. With no Daa, or brothers or sisters, or even me to help, he's spent more time with the horses than most boys his age."

They worked in silence as Grace prepared to boil the next set of jars, and Faith carried in another new case.

"You know, he's never been spanked?" Grace said into the sound of boiling water. "He's always been such a good boy. He probably won't think of doing it with his own children. Keep that in mind, yes?"

Faith nodded again.

"Of course, you're both so good, you'll have doubly good children, right?"

Faith smiled demurely.

"No need for you to spank your children if they grow up to be as upright as you two. And he's such a good boy. A good son. Now, a good man." She spooned relish into the recently sterilized jars. "But I don't need to tell you that." They grinned at each other. "You have been writing each other?"

Faith bobbed her head.

"It's not been easy for him."

"No, it hasn't."

"It's not been easy for any of us. But Jason was right about one thing," Grace said.

"Yes?"

"Oh, Faith, the money," Grace said, breathlessly. "His pay is deposited directly into the checking account. There's so much, so much money. I'm afraid to spend it."

"What do you mean?"

"Mr. Landis at the bank said it wasn't a mistake. He checked for me. The baseball men said it's the right amount. Jason and Mr. Anderson both wrote and said it was the right amount, but Faith, it's just so much."

"Has it helped with expenses, as Jason intended?"

"Faith," Grace said softly, as though afraid an elder might hear. "They have deposited nearly twice the amount of all of our debts and annual expenses for years."

Faith blanched. "Surely there was some mistake?"

"That's why I asked Mr. Landis. He said no. We took Jason's contract to the Mennonite lawyer that Mr. Landis recommended. He says the money is Jason's. He called it 'guaranteed.' Everyone tells me to spend it, but I'm afraid to."

"If you have bills that must be paid, that's what the money is for. That's why Jason has gone from us to earn this money."

"I still don't understand what he's doing to earn so much."

"The man on the radio said today he has the most home runs," Faith said.

"Yes, and he leads in stolen bases—"

"That's not as bad as it sounds," Faith said quickly.

"I know," Grace smiled. "You're so sweet to be worried. He wrote and explained." She began moving jars from the boiling water onto the cooling rack. "He leads in these areas. He must be very good."

"Remember, I saw him play with the high school."

"Yes," Grace nodded. "Yes, you did."

"Jason was always the best player on the field, so I'm not surprised he's the best there. Do they pay him to be the best, maybe?"

"Our Jason," Grace said with a smile. "Let me share with you some of the letters he's written? I'll read out loud while you work."

The Iowa snow drifted into deep piles along fence lines and against buildings, while Grace read about the warm weather of Arizona.

A single news van idled in the road beside the Yoder farm.

WHEN JASON STEPPED to the plate or toed the rubber, sounds faded away like misty morning fog. He heard only the pulse of his own heart, beating steady like the rhythmic clomping of hooves on asphalt.

In the minutes before, though, the on-deck area was like walking the street of an exotic foreign city. His senses hyper-alert, he noticed everything.

The bright colors of the stands and the shining, happy faces of different tones and ages, from the darkest to the lightest, the youngest to the oldest, reminded him of a massive pasture filled with wildflowers on a sunny afternoon.

He still wasn't used to the echo of the announcer calling out names, positions, and batting order or the snippets of songs echoing through the stadium to introduce each player walking to the plate. He had no idea what the songs were, but they were loud.

He looked at the thousands of cheering people. Why are so many of them happy watching me, he thought to himself. I'm just a simple man playing a game, and yet they seem so overjoyed.

The wind carried familiar smells. He knew somewhere in the stadium they were cooking sausages and onions. Once he could smell a fresh orange, the zesty aroma so enticing it made his mouth water. He saw the child ten rows up, dismantling the piece of fruit.

Despite all the new and different things he witnessed, he was still surprised to notice a child holding a big, pink, fuzzy ball. The little boy, half the size of Adam, was in the front row, just to the right of the dugout roof.

It looked like insulation, but he knew it wasn't because the boy and his dad were eating it, peeling off pieces.

Dismissing the pitcher—Jason was two for two, had seen all his pitches, and knew what the man would throw before he did— Jason walked over to the stands.

"Hello," he said in a friendly tone as though addressing a familiar face at the farmers' market. "What are you eating?"

The man looked like he couldn't remember the color blue. "Why, why, wha—"

"It's cotton candy!" The boy shouted with pink-stained lips.

"What are you doing?" the father asked, surprised into lucidity.

"I'm waiting to bat," Jason said to the father before turning his attention to the child. "What's cotton candy?"

"You've never had cotton candy?" the boy asked, perplexed. "Like at the fair or the circus?"

"I've never seen it."

"Seriously?" the father asked.

"Seriously."

"It's great," the boy yelled proudly. "Have some!" He held it out ,and Jason peeled off a piece. The touch of sweet heat dissolved on his tongue.

"It's spun sugar," the father said.

"Excuse me," Jason said when his name was announced. "I have to go."

Jason smacked a double but was stranded on second at the end of the inning. He returned the little boy's joyful wave as he waited for Jackson to bring him his glove.

At the end of the next inning, as Jason made his way toward the dugout, the boy gestured wildly, beckoning Jason over. As though bestowing a great prize, the father and son proudly presented Jason with a fresh bag of cotton candy.

Jason's heart twinged, remembering the lost years without his own father.

"Thank you," he said.

On the bench, Jason shoved another sticky bite into his mouth.

"What are you doing?" Hab asked.

"I'm eating cotton candy," Jason replied. "It's spun sugar. It just looks like insulation."

Hab's baritone laugh echoed through the dugout.

"What are you doing?" Hope asked as they got into her car.

"Eating cotton candy," Jason said. "It's spun sugar. It just looks like insulation. Would you like some?"

"I'm fine, thanks," Hope said, starting the car. "Why do you have four bags?"

Jason just smiled as Hope drove them away.

⚾⚾⚾ ⚾⚾

His DESERT NIGHTS were a break from the heat of the day.

Sometimes he felt like Moses and the Israelites: lost and alone, wandering in the desert. Perhaps they walked at night and rested under tents during the heat of the day. He couldn't remember what scripture said. He read his Bible every day, but each time, it felt as though he was reading less and less.

He hadn't bothered bringing his Bible to the desert. He looked up at the billions of stars spread across the sky like the breath of God. Bishop Lapp would disagree, but the Bible was unnecessary in the living light of the Lord.

Like Moses, he felt he needed to remove his shoes in the Lord's presence. He smiled. But he wasn't wearing sandals, and this night he brought his new cleats to run.

Memories of the day faded like the colors of the sunrise.

So he ran.

He ran past the 270 feet in a triple. He was gaining speed as he passed the 400 feet of an outfield fence. Wind blowing in his ears, arms pumping, breath panting, his problems, concerns, and decisions faded like the city lights in the distance.

ON THE TEAM bus to Phoenix, Jack King sat down next to Jason, who was always in the first seat, looking out the windshield as well as the windows on either side.

"Got a minute, rookie?"

Jason nodded silently. He had recognized King's name when they were first introduced. King was a legendary player, so it was easy for Jason to remember games the previous year when King was so bad he didn't last to the third inning.

"You're having a pretty good spring training." King paused as though awaiting a response.

Jason didn't know what he was supposed to say. "Yes, sir," he agreed. Judging his expression, he couldn't tell if that was what King expected.

"You're not a big talker, are you, rook?"

"Listen and silent have the same letters."

King was quiet for a moment. "Yeah, you're having a career-making spring training," he finally said. "You're on Sports Center every damn night," he said, seemingly to himself. "Oh, sorry," he added as an afterthought. Jason had no idea what King was talking about. He concentrated on the words and King's expression.

"I'm getting to the age where heat won't cut it anymore," King continued. "I've got to learn better ball control, and I've got to learn it fast. I'm getting beat up out there. I've got the worst spring training ERA of my career..."

He manipulated a baseball in his hands as he spoke. Jason noticed his fingers struggled to find a place on the ball.

"Listen, Jase, can I ask you, how did you develop your accuracy? You remind me of Greg Maddox, with your precision. Maddox when he played for Atlanta, not us. You're like a surgeon out there. How do you do it?"

Jason considered the question. He thought of a day in the schoolyard. His Daa had been gone for almost two summers. While walking to school, near the tree line, nearly one hundred yards from the building, he had noticed an unusual commotion.

As the panic unfolded, everything slowed down for Jason. It felt like a folk tale from the Old Country or the Old Testament. He heard high-pitched, otherworldly screams from a group of children gathered near the side of the school. The wind whipped hair and scarves. The vivid, colorful clothes flashed like laundry on the line as his classmates bunched closer together. The budding trees were flecked with hues of green and yellow; a cloud of pollen hung in the air, a silent witness.

Their young teacher was afraid. Little more than a teenager herself, her fear frightened him, while the children's screaming confused him. As if responding to a silent command, his schoolmates bunched closer together near the schoolyard fence, climbing on top of each other like a litter of blind, newborn puppies.

Then he saw it, between the door of the building and the children—a fox jerking erratically, obviously sick with rabies.

The teacher and the children were trapped with nowhere to go.

He thought about getting help, but he knew help was too far away—the fox could bite or scratch someone at any moment.

Instinctively, Jason picked up a rock and heaved it at the fox. Despite the distance, he was absolutely certain he wouldn't miss. The stone struck the fox in the head, killing it instantly.

"I guess I've always been good at throwing." He shrugged.

"On my best day, I was never as good as you are on your worst," King said, leaning forward earnestly. Jason could see the worry on the man's face and genuinely wanted to help him.

"I heard your high school coach hardly coached you at all?"

"Oh, no, I wouldn't say that," Jason quickly answered. "Coach Pate taught me a lot."

"What did he teach you to make you so good?"

"He's very patient and kind. And supportive. I wouldn't be here without Coach Pate."

"Patient, kind, and supportive. OK. He sounds more like your mom than a coach."

"He helped me with my stance at the plate," Jason said.

"I don't need to raise my batting average, kid."

"He also gave me pointers concerning my curveball."

King leaned forward again. "Now we're talking." He handed Jason the ball.

"I can show you my dipsy-doo pitch."

"Is that your slider?"

"Sort of. I learned it when I was a boy."

He burst out laughing. "Last week?"

Jason smiled. "It was a long time ago."

"Yeah, I'd like to see that dipsy-doo pitch."

Jason pulled a black Sharpie from his shirt pocket and gave the ball back to King.

"Put your fingers here," Jason said, moving the older man's massive digits. "And here, along the seam, like that." He pulled the cap off the pen and traced along King's fingers. "You forget how to hold it, you can check it with this. Throw it just like a slider, but hold it like this."

"It will have that movement?" King asked, flexing his wrist.

"Slicker than the butter side of the toast," Jason said with a smile.

"BETTER LATE THAN NEVER," Hope said, pulling into her reserved parking space at Sloan Park, the rising sun already warming the morning air.

"Better never late," Jason smiled as he finished his tenth Dunkin' doughnut.

She scrunched her nose and stuck out her tongue.

"There's someone I want you to meet before practice today," she said as they made their way inside. "I don't know why we didn't think of this before."

Walking through the cramped complex, she explained that another Christian was working in the organization. Hope offered introductions and then disappeared.

"Have a seat," Anthony invited, gesturing to the only other chair in the small, windowless room.

"Hope said we should meet face to face because I'm Christian, too. Although it's not as obvious for me as it is for you," Anthony said.

Jason looked around the office. There was nothing to indicate Anthony's faith. Perhaps in his Chicago office, he thought. Other than clothes, Jason wondered how someone would know a Christian just by looking at them. Would he recognize Christians who weren't

Amish? Perhaps there were other Christians on the team? I don't think I should ask them, he decided. I'll wait for them to come to me.

Anthony seemed familiar, but Jason wasn't sure why.

"I've been reading about the Amish since you signed," Anthony said quietly. "I write news releases about the team and also blog posts that try to explain to the fans about you and your ways."

Jason wasn't sure what a blog post was, but he didn't like the sound of it. It made him feel exposed, like standing outside on a frosty February morning. He hadn't considered that the thousands of people in the stands might read about him or know anything more than his name and the number on his back. When he listened to the games in the barn at home, he didn't think about the players and their personal lives; he only thought of the game. He knew very little about the players. He assumed the fans were as ignorant of him as he was of them.

He thought of the thousands of people who watched him play, the tens of thousands more listening on the radio. He rebuked himself for not realizing it sooner.

Most of them were probably like Anthony. They knew nothing about the Amish before they heard the name Jason Yoder. He might be the first and only Amish person many of them would ever see. The responsibility dawned on him like an early sunrise splitting the darkness.

He represented his family and his community; he knew that from the beginning. But he was also representing all Amish. Iowa, Ohio, Pennsylvania, Indiana, Wisconsin, New York, Illinois—nearly half the states had Amish people, and he was the most prominent of all of them. Ever.

More than two hundred thousand Amish in the country, and he was their face? Jason Yoder. That's not demut, he thought. Not at all.

God put him in this position, he reminded himself. Perhaps it was God's will that he serve as a good example of a Godly person. But he wasn't a good example. He was a sinner, just like everyone else. And away from home, he was afraid he was sinning even more.

When the public looked at him, would they see God's gifts on display, or would they see a sinner?

Perhaps playing baseball would allow him to let people know more about the Amish Mission Fund. He could speak about the evangelical outreach of the Plain People. He thought of the people who heard or watched him play, and the possibility that just a fraction of them might support the Fund. The Fund could do so much with donations he would help bring in. Perhaps Anthony could help him spread the word and tell others about the Fund.

Anthony had stopped talking and was staring with a bemused smile.

"Have we met before?" Jason asked, trying to collect his thoughts and recollect the man's mildly familiar face. Was it his glasses?

"I was near you during your press conference—"

"That," Jason said with a tone used to describe dog vomit.

"Yeah, that. I helped organize it. I knew it might be a problem, but the higher-ups insisted. I'm really sorry it happened."

Jason shrugged and looked at an autographed baseball on the desk.

"Listen, since I have you here, can I ask you a few things?"

Jason nodded and relaxed, his curiosity piqued.

"I've read about your church services. There are no buildings? The service is held in people's homes?"

"Or in barns. When the service is held at our house, it's in our barn, to make it easier for my mother. There are a few other barn services in our district—there's one at the Fisher's every third month and Ruby and Mark Zook host every eight weeks. Different homes on different Sundays, so everyone shares."

"I know services are every other Sunday, not every week. Why is that?"

"That's right, every other Sunday. The reason's pretty simple." Jason smiled. "Every district has a bishop they share with another district. When Bishop Lapp isn't with us, he's in the other district. Every other Sunday."

"What are the districts?"

Jason hesitated, considering his response. "An important part of being Amish is being in community," he explained. "When a church district gets too big, it's hard for everyone to know everyone, so lines get redrawn, and a new district is created. We have three ministers and Deacon Kline and Bishop Lapp in our district."

"The ministers preach, just like other churches?"

"I've never been to another church, but I've been told our ministers are like other ministers—they preach on Sunday, they do funerals, they baptize, they do communion. Just like other Christians." He smiled dismissively.

"Not just like other Christians."

"Well, we don't have stained glass windows or choirs or buildings, but we still have preaching and singing and the Bible. You should come to an Amish church service. Someone will translate for you."

"Seriously?"

"Seriously."

"I could just come to a service?"

"Yes." Jason smiled. "We're Amish. It's not a secret."

"I want to ask about the way you dress," Anthony said. "That's one way you're not like other Christians at all."

Jason cocked his head and waited.

"I understand wanting to wear plain, simple clothes, but why old-fashioned clothes? Why not something that doesn't call attention to you?"

Jason took a long minute to ponder his answer. "When my ancestors left Switzerland in the early 1700s, they were dressed similar to how I dress," he said, gesturing to his shirt. "Our clothes are wool or cotton, not mixed materials like the Bible says. We've kept most of our rules about clothes, just like we've kept our rules about everything else for hundreds of years."

"Like the beards and haircuts. I understand the beards," Anthony said, "but why no mustaches?"

"Amish are peaceful people. Military officers in the 1700s had big, bushy mustaches. Our beards and shaving were the way we quietly let people know we were different. We remain different. If we start changing rules for clothes or shaving, where do we stop changing rules? I still sing the same hymns written by the first Amish, should we stop singing those?

"Where do we draw the line? If we move the line every year, then pretty soon, there is no line. We let electricity into our homes, and then radios? And then television? Then the internets? Then we let into our minds and hearts all the things on the TV and the internets. Why? How does it bring us closer to God?"

"What about educational shows that teach things?" Anthony asked.

"What am I going to learn watching the television programs that I can't learn from my uncle or mother or cousins or any one of a dozen members of our community? What will I learn watching television or on the internets, how to drive a car or fly an airplane? How to operate on someone like a doctor? That's not for us. Our jobs are simple. The simple life keeps us connected to each other and connected to God and God's earth. Farming, carpentry, even baseball. Simple, honest work, where we earn our daily bread by the sweat of our brow."

Anthony made a note on a random piece of paper.

"You mentioned ministers doing baptisms before," Anthony said. "You've not been baptized yet, right?"

"That's right."

Anthony had done a lot of research, Jason realized, impressed with Anthony's dedication.

Jason remembered watching Faith's baptism. Deacon Kline had scooped out a cup of water from a wooden bucket. He poured the water into Bishop Lapp's hands and onto Faith's head.

The process was repeated twice more. Faith seemed transformed. After the service, she spoke and moved differently, as though her teenage self was gone, a grown, mature woman left in her place. She was born again, of water. Jason remembered wanting that feeling, too.

Instead of being baptized, he was here. Talking with a baseball man. Watched by thousands of people. Playing on dead dirt made of brick. Eating Chinese food and spun sugar.

"I was baptized in a river when I was fourteen, full immersion. So does that make me more Christian than you?" Anthony teased.

Jason smiled, but the question gave him pause. How much of a Christian was he, he wondered.

"Of course you're Christian, I don't doubt it," Anthony said into the silence.

"I'm Amish."

"Are you? Here? Playing baseball?"

"Even playing baseball, I'm still Amish."

"If you're here, playing ball, out of your community, and not even baptized yet, what makes you Amish?"

Jason didn't respond.

"I'm not criticizing, I'm just trying to understand," Anthony said quickly, "so I can help others understand. I know you're still following the Amish rules." He gestured at Jason's clothes. "I heard about your train ride here. But being Amish is more than rules, isn't it?"

Jason was still thinking about community. He hadn't truly realized the importance of community until it was beyond his reach. Like spending too long in the barn on an autumn afternoon to emerge into darkness, the day gone forever.

Had his journey to this moment really been as bad as it now seemed? Each day he was surrounded by thousands, and yet he still felt isolated and alone.

Community was at the heart of being Amish. It was at the heart of being a Christian. Wherever two or more gathered in my name, he thought. Jason considered the redeeming grace of God. He reminded himself that Christ was with him everywhere he went. The community helped him remember, and while he felt alone outside the community, he knew God was always near. Walking in the desert helped him connect with God, but it wasn't the same as plowing Yoder farmland.

He thought of fellowship and scripture. He considered the importance of inviting the Lord into his life and into daily activities. He tried to do that, but it was difficult alone, without the community he was used to. There would be no friends or family dropping by to help with the chores. No visiting in the kitchen over coffee and cake. No shared history, no common culture. He hadn't realized how deeply he was falling into the English lifestyle. It was worse than too long in the barn on an autumn afternoon. He wasn't emerging into evening without a flashlight, he was leaving the barn for the dangers of a city street in the dark of night, blindfolded.

"Let me know what I can do to help," Anthony was saying. "That's why Hope brought us together. She probably wouldn't describe it this way, but she's trying to help you with a sense of community, by introducing you to the only Christian she knows. You're welcome to come to my church on Sundays when you're not starting." He looked around. "We can study the Bible. I don't have a hardcopy of scripture in the office, but I do have access to every translation on my phone, including German. If it would help, I'd be happy to pray with you. Right now, if you want."

Jason felt a flood of relief to be in such a spiritual moment.

"Yes, sir, that would be fine with me."

They closed their eyes. Jason began the Lord's Prayer silently.

"Dear Lord," Anthony began. "I pray for my brother Jason, that he may walk through the valley and fear no evil. We ask that you comfort him, strengthen him, be with him, and guide him on his path."

Jason couldn't remember if he'd ever heard a prayer in English before. He was used to most prayers being silent.

"—that we more closely follow you, and be the people you call us to be."

When would he hear words spoken in German again? Six months? Nine months?

"We just want to thank you. Lord, for the gifts you've given us—"

After his quick trip home, it would be all spring and summer and into the fall before he'd be home on a Sunday again, before he heard another Amish person speaking. He wasn't sure how he was going to last that long.

"In Jesus' name, we pray. Amen."

Jason exhaled.

"If you need anything, let me know, alright?" Anthony stood and offered his hand.

"Yes, sir. Thank you."

Chapter 13

"There is a problem back home."

Skip felt the familiar jolt of terror that racked his body every time Jason mentioned a problem. He was getting used to it. As he fumbled in his pocket for the roll of TUMS, he thought of Jim Leyland smoking in the dugout. Maybe he should take up smoking.

He hadn't realized how precarious Jason's presence was. He was putting all of his hopes and dreams for the season and the World Series in one basket—a basket carried by a seventeen-year-old with a bad haircut and the most vicious slider professional baseball had ever seen.

"What's going on?"

"My mudder wrote me a letter," Jason replied. "English with cameras are bothering her."

"I remember seeing tourists with cameras in Iowa," Skip said, trying to minimize the issue.

"Dis is worse than tourists," Jason said, his accent thickened by frustration. "Large cameras, vans, television people." He ran his hand

204 | JIM MEISNER, JR.

through his hair. "They knock on her door all day, disrupting her and distracting from her work. She can't walk out to the garden without people coming into the yard wanting to talk to her."

"I'm sorry."

"She can't even sit on the porch without being bothered," he said, his voice rising. "They bother others who come to help her. They even bother my English teammates who are helping her when I'm not there."

Jason's tone was alarming.

"I'm not sure there's much we can do about it," Skip said slowly. "They have a right to do their jobs, too."

"They wouldn't be there," Jason said, his countenance clouded with frustration, "if I wasn't here. Maybe I need to go home."

Skip changed his attitude toward it faster than a called third strike. "I'll have someone call the police. We'll have them charged with trespassing or harassment."

"Police? The government? My people don't usually involve police."

"Don't involve the police? What do you do?"

"We talk to people and work things out. That's why I need to be there. I need to talk to them." He slapped his cap against his leg in frustration.

The gesture brought to Skip's mind a grainy black-and-white footage of Lou Gehrig kicking the dirt when he was robbed of a home run—a normally stoic man offering a rare display of emotion.

"I can't work things out here. I can't talk to them here. I can't help her when I'm here."

"You're helping her by earning a paycheck, remember? You can afford to hire a private security guard to stand in her front yard and keep back the curious. Let's let the novelty—"

Jason shook his head at the word as though rejecting the catcher's signal.

"—the newness of you, of the situation, let's let it play out for a week or two and see what happens. Once the season starts, reporters will have more to cover than your mother hanging out the laundry."

Skip sensed that Jason didn't like it, but they each had a job to do.

⚾

JASON HAD to look again as he stepped from the dugout.

Four Amish elders sat in the front row, just to the right of the dugout roof. Close enough to talk to. His heart was drawn to the familiar combination of straw hats, beards, and solid color shirts crisscrossed by suspenders.

His mind raced. Were there Amish in Arizona he had somehow overlooked? A community? Could he worship with them Sunday? Fellowship in some way? He considered the conversation and imagined explaining what he was doing there. Would they write Bishop Lapp? It didn't matter, because he wasn't alone. Wondering what to say to them, he longed to hear his native tongue. He didn't fully understand how alone he felt, until that moment, when there was the possibility of—

The hats were wrong. They were very young men wearing ridiculous-looking fake beards.

As he stepped closer, they jumped to their feet, chests puffed out at him, their thumbs looped through their suspenders.

"Shaynee hussa," he said to them, their eyes widening in surprise. "Doo sin unfwaushtendeekk." He pulled at his pants with his fingers as he shook his head. "Your pants are unbelievable."

The boys high-fived each other as Jason walked to the batter's box.

"Word's getting out that you talk to the people in those seats," Hope explained after the game. "Fans call them the 'speaking seats' because they figured out that you'll speak to them if they sit there."

"Is it that big a deal?"

"Yeah, it's a big deal," she said. "Most players don't talk to the fans."

"That doesn't make sense," he said, scrunching his forehead.

"Tell me about it."

"The fans are here to watch us play."

"I know."

"They are sitting right there talking to us. How do you not talk to someone sitting right there speaking to you?"

"I understand what you're saying," she said. "Most guys are thinking about getting ready to hit."

"It's rude not to say something."

"Yeah, but you can't respond to everyone who yells at you."

"We grow up getting stared at. We get used to it. People taking pictures." He frowned. "But I feel like I should say something when someone that close speaks to me."

"You do what you need to do," Hope said, smiling, "but a long season may get longer if you try to spread yourself too thin."

"HE CAN'T PLAY LIKE THAT," Henry commanded Skip.

During the game that afternoon, a crack of the bat had sent a frozen rope down the third base line. Jason left his feet and, as the ball scorched over the bag, instinctively snatched it from the air barehanded.

The move electrified the crowd and horrified both benches.

Dave had already cleared the dugout's top step, rushing to offer assistance, while the image of shattered bones in Jason's pitching hand overtook Skip's mind and dashed their hopes for the spring.

Before the dust settled on Jason's prone body, he shot to his knees, the ball held above his head in celebration, his filthy face split by a massive white smile. He whipped the ball to the shortstop from his knees. Laughing as he got to his feet, he playfully shook his hand and blew on it.

At the same time, Skip exhaled a breath of relief.

"He can't not play like that," Skip responded. "That's the only way he plays. He'll win us twenty-plus games on the mound and twenty-plus games at the plate and in the field. That catch today saved the game."

"But he could've gotten hurt and been out for six weeks," Henry said.

"I can keep him on the bench, and he'll never get hurt."

"That's not what I'm saying," Henry snapped. "Can't you tell him to take it easy? No point getting hurt during a preseason game."

"Tell a seventeen-year-old kid not to hustle in spring training, but hustle in two weeks?" Skip shook his head. "He plays like that, everyone on the field plays better. I've got veterans out there hustling harder because of him. The whole team is playing like winners. We have a winning spring training record. It's all because of him. And you want me to bench him?"

"How's it going?" Skip said to Hope.

"He's eating his way through Arizona," Hope responded through the line.

"Oh, yeah, I should have warned you."

"I've never seen anyone eat like that," she replied breathlessly. "He eats the way he pitches. With such...intensity."

"Imagine him working his way through the Brennaman filet mignon at Precinct."

"In Cincinnati?"

"Yeah," Skip said. "It's a healthy slab of meat, but I can picture him polishing off two of them."

"One after another, or even at the same time, one on top of the other. With sautéed mushrooms in-between. He can pick it all up and eat it like a sandwich."

"The kid has an appetite."

"He's ravenous."

"Imagine his metabolism? It's like keeping a steam engine stoked all day."

"We've had Mexican and Chinese several times," Hope said. "The new steak restaurant. More ice cream than I thought humanly possible. The food trucks were an adventure. Yesterday, I watched him eat an entire large pizza. And the fruit. I don't know how he puts away so much fruit. I bought him a fruit basket as a joke, and he demolished half of it in the car before we got to the park."

"Other than that, how's it going?"

"He really is odd, but he's an amazing specimen. I could get used to this special assignment," she said. "Have you looked at his forearms? Or spent any time feeling his muscles?"

"Not as much as you, I'm sure. Be careful, Hope, you two are co-workers. Also, he's seventeen, and when you accompany him home, you'll be traveling across state lines."

"So?"

"They amended the Mann Act to apply to teenage boys as well."

"I'm sure I have no idea what you're talking about."

"I'm sure you don't. Talk to you in a couple of days."

"It's fun to see a guy hit for the cycle," Dave said as the team lined up to shake hands after another win.

Skip nodded.

"Looked a little like he slowed down to get that double, didn't it?"

"Yep, that's how it looked to me," Skip agreed.

"I've never seen a guy hit the cycle so...so...effortlessly. Have you?"

"Nope. Can't say that I have."

"A three-bagger, a dinger, a single, then jog into second for a double and stop, rather than another standup triple. It's like he hit the cycle on purpose. I've never seen anything like it."

"Me neither."

"Do you want me to say something to him about slowing down at second?"

"The kid hits the cycle, goes four for four, and you're seriously offering to tell him to run faster and get the extra base?" Skip shook him off.

"'Speed plus confidence equals success' is the saying, but this is just crazy. I wouldn't believe it if somebody told me. I stand here watching every day, and I don't believe what I'm seeing."

Skip nodded silently.

"He's gonna lead the league in walks this year," Dave said. "Pitchers are terrified of him."

"That reminds me—about his home run trot, tell him to slow down. He runs like he's being chased. It's not a race. Tell him to watch how Greenie does it."

Dave nodded.

Skip scratched his sideburn. "Have you noticed how he inches toward the plate when catchers slide over for outside pitches?"

"Yes!" Dave nearly shouted.

"I asked him about it the first time I saw it. I worried he was somehow sneaking a look at the catcher, and I warned him he can't."

Dave nodded.

"He said he could feel the catcher move."

"What are you talking about?" Dave asked.

"That's what he said. He says the pitcher telegraphs an outside pitch— don't ask me how; he can't explain it —and then he feels the catcher move. Then, as if that's not crazy enough, he moves too, gets reset, and hits with authority."

"He's making adjustments at the plate that it takes some guys weeks to learn," Dave said, "only he's doing it between pitches."

"During pitches. He's making adjustments during pitches. Between the set and delivery."

"And then hitting for the cycle."

"I don't even know what to make of that."

"It's gonna be an amazing year. It's too bad Steve Goodman never had the chance to see him play."

They turned their attention to Jason shaking hands with his teammates.

"Yep, an amazing year," Skip said.

He looked into the stands, where Henry was clapping enthusiastically. He smiled approvingly at Skip, who nodded in return before turning to watch his team.

"WHAT ABOUT THE ARIZONA SERIES?" Dave asked, his eyes scanning the page. Dave and Skip were deep into scheduling paperwork, open beers in front of them.

"Oh, man," Skip said, leaning back in his chair. He locked his hands behind his head, considering the question. He combed his fingers through his hair as he spoke. "We can try to get him out here. He'll have to miss the first game while somebody drives him. He'll play third the second game or pinch-hit, and he'll start the third game. Hab will have to play more often than he expects."

Just then, Henry stuck his head in the door. "Hey, Coach, I wanted to let you know, the opening home stand is completely sold out."

"Home stand?" Skip asked. "You mean opening day?"

Henry exploded into the room with excitement.

"The entire home stand. Opening day, and the five games after that. Sold out. And the next two home stands. All of them. Already sold out."

Skip and Dave exchanged shocked expressions.

"I've never seen anything like it," Henry continued. "This was the best spring training the Cubs have had in years. World Series here we come. And the Yoder boy, I'm not too big a man to admit it, I'm glad I agreed to pay him the signing bonus. On to Chicago!" Henry disappeared out the door.

"Glad to see him finally coming around," Dave said, before raising his bottle. "On to Chicago!"

Skip raised his beer. "Chicago!"

JASON COULDN'T SLEEP. His run in the desert did nothing to dispel the conflict in his heart. He'd been sitting at the kitchen table for more than an hour, a half-empty glass of milk in front of him, when Annie came in rubbing her eyes.

"Are you all right?" she asked.

"Yes, ma'am," he replied, his words empty of emotion.

"Are you looking forward to visiting your family on the way to Chicago?"

"Yes, ma'am."

"Are you worried about Chicago?"

His expression softened. "Yes, ma'am," he nodded. "A little."

"You don't have anything to worry about," she said. "The other players respect you. The fans love you. You're the best thing to happen to Chicago baseball since Shoeless Joe Jackson. You'll be fine."

"Their hearts should be full of love for God, not me," Jason said with a sad shake of his head. "I am distracting them from God."

"Trust me," Annie explained, "anything that fills their hearts with love of anything is a good thing."

"I am Hochmut," Jason said despondently. "Feeling too proud."

"You have reason to be proud."

"'Pride goes before destruction, and a haughty spirit before a fall.'"

"What?" She shook her head. "I don't understand."

"Pride is wrong," he said, struggling to describe his complex feelings. "Very wrong. '"God opposes the proud, but gives grace to the humble.' I should show Demut." He saw the puzzled look on her face. "Humbleness," he explained.

"Jason," she started, placing her hand tenderly on his strong shoulder. "It's alright to be who you are. You should respect and honor your religion, but it doesn't have to control your whole life."

"My religion is my life."

Annie couldn't respond.

"I thank you for all you have done for me," he said, changing the subject. "You have been very kind."

"Are you sure you're all right?"

"Yes, ma'am," he said, rising. "I will go to bed now. Again, thank you for everything."

"I'm happy to do it. Good night. See you in the morning."

In his bedroom, Jason noticed his water glass from the night before. He looked at the air bubbles clinging to the sides. His life was becoming like the glass, on display and public, the air slowly seeping out.

Chapter 14

He thought about his visit with the sick children in the hospital as he sat on a large stone, his bare toes buried in the familiar sand of the desert. He was happy to have given the children a few moments of joy and distraction from their illnesses. He couldn't believe it had only been ten days ago. He'd seen and done so many things in the week and a half that had followed that it felt like ten months, ten years.

Remembering how much was packed into each day made him tired. All the things he did and the constant line of people Hope introduced him to. It was like trying to de-tassel a forty-acre field alone. With one hand. He smiled. In the rain. At night.

His time was consumed like ten-year-old kindling in a hot wood stove. He missed the smell of wood stoves. He was here to play baseball, and it felt like he did everything but play ball. Most of the other guys talked to reporters and got their pictures made. He'd have to do that too, eventually. He couldn't hide forever in concession stands and maintenance sheds—but he was willing to try. He smiled at the idea.

Jason rolled a baseball in his hands and dug his fingernails into the red stitching. He thought of the empty barn he used to play in and heard his Daa's words carried on the wind.

"Lemme show you how to throw the dipsy-doo pitch," James had said. "You remember how to hold the ball to make it move?"

Jason bobbed his head sharply.

"Dipsy-doo is almost the same. Put your fingers here like this," he said, moving Jason's small fingers to the right spot on the ball. "Watch." With a pen, James drew an outline around Jason's fingers. "You forget how to hold it, you can check it with this." He dropped the ball into Jason's coat hanging on the hook. "Now throw this one."

James quickly hurried into position and gestured to Jason. The ball snapped into the glove.

"That's how you do it!" James said, standing up. "Move your arm like this," he demonstrated. "That will save it from getting tired later."

Jason acknowledged the advice. He stepped back and launched the ball. It popped loudly into the glove.

"That's right," James said, whipping the ball back from his knees. "Just like that. You feel the difference? Now do it again."

They had passed the ball back and forth for hours— Jason throwing with all his might, the ball dancing at the edges of the plate like a mouse in a grain elevator.

"You did really good," James said as they put away the equipment. "You're getting stronger and better every day. I got lots of other pitches to show you next time."

Next time.

"We will work on them all when you get bigger," James said as they left the barn. "Look at that, it has gotten dark." James cast his gaze skyward and pointed at the stars.

"God made each of those stars, just for us to look at," he said. "As pretty as a flower in summertime."

"It is pretty," Jason said, patting the ball in his coat pocket.

"'The Lord determines the number of the stars; he gives to all of them their names,'" James said. "'They display the Lord's handiwork,' but I do not know any of them. Maybe one day, you can learn them and teach me?"

"All those stars?" Jason asked, his voice full of awe.

"Maybe you will start with the brightest ones?" James had said, tousling his son's hair.

The desert breeze that reminded Jason so much of home had slowed to little more than a warm puff, carrying the memory away. Jason dropped the ball into his hat and looked up at the countless points of light piercing the blackness. Like the need for a lantern by the dark of the moon, Jason had somehow slipped beyond the familiar into a struggle with the darkness of the unknown. This wasn't supposed to happen.

It frightened him to imagine what Chicago would be like. He was glad Hope would be there with him.

He glanced at his new astronomy book and compass propped against his rolled socks. He squinted an eye to look through the telescope before him.

Would Chicago have as many people as there were stars in the sky? Probably not. Yet the Lord knew each of them, stars and people alike. The Lord heard the prayers of everyone and searched their souls.

Search my soul, O Lord, and judge me worthy, he prayed.

"How ARE you so attuned to pitchers?" Hope asked while they drove back from Peoria.

"Attuned," he said with a furrowed brow. "I do not know what that means." He thought about the game. Despite going into extra innings, he had gone six-for-six. Everyone was surprised they kept pitching to him.

"Maybe they were thinking he was due to get out," Greenie had said.

"Maybe they need to think again," Hab had laughed. "Our boy never gets out."

Jason finished the bag of cotton candy while Hope explained.

"Attuned. Plugged in. You know," she said, in a tone he didn't recognize. "In-sync. You seem to know what a pitcher will do before he does it. Are you guessing?"

He shrugged.

"And stealing, you've never been picked off. You're ten-for-ten in stolen bases. What's your secret, farm boy?" She asked with a smile. "How do you do what you do?"

"I just do it," he said, retrieving a banana from his bag.

"Aaah, no," she said. "You have some secret. What is it?"

He chewed slowly, thinking, remembering.

"Pitchers are like horses and horses are like people," James had told his son, harnessing the standardbred. He leaned forward to whisper, "But don't tell the horses; they may not like it." Horses were an extension of James' body, as they were for all Amish men.

He smiled before he continued. "Horses are strong and powerful but also very delicate. They are all different, but also all the same. Just like people. A horse will show you what he is thinking if you pay close attention. Horses can tell you when they are hungry or tired or well-rested. A mare more than a filly, and geldings, not as much," he said, working the strap through the buckle. "Gotta keep your eyes on geldings," he winked. "They still have a lot of vinegar in them. Like your maam's relish sometimes. A horse will show you what it is thinking," he repeated. "So will a pitcher, you just have to look close enough. Come on, Shadow."

As James had led Shadow through the barn, the horse paused at the buggy out of habit. Clicking his tongue, James led him past the stalls of the draft horses and out of the barnyard.

"Remember the pitchers in Cedar Rapids?"

Jason nodded.

"Each of them showed us what he was thinking, right?"

Jason nodded again. He looked on as James harnessed Shadow to the manure spreader.

"Alright, boy," James said, lifting Jason from his feet and swinging him onto the equipment. "Up you go."

With Jason standing alone in the front of the spreader, the reins loose in his young hands, James clicked his tongue, slapped the horse's haunches, and sent the horse on his way.

Jason must have ridden the spreader with his Daa before, although he couldn't remember doing it. He couldn't imagine his Daa just loading him onto the equipment and sending him into the field alone. That's why the memory was so special to him. More than any other, it represented the love and confidence his Daa had in him.

"Watch him close," the elder Yoder yelled, "Shadow knows the way, let him show you what he's thinking."

The horse's brown haunches seemed massive, larger than ever before or since. The spreader rolled smartly across the frozen ground. The sound and smell of steaming manure flinging out behind him was still etched in his memory.

Shadow seemed to move faster as he made his way further across the field. The fence at the edge of the field loomed larger, and Jason's panic grew with every step. He imagined Shadow walking through the fence and proceeding into the next field. And then he saw it. Ever so subtly, Shadow was snapping his head to the right, anticipating a turn. Jason dipped one knee and pulled the reins with all his weight. Miraculously, the massive power responded, and the horse turned in the direction he pulled. Daa knew he could manage the horse.

"That's how you do it, son," James called as they passed him. Had he been in the field the whole time, walking alongside the spreader? "Next time, we will hook up the team."

Jason reflected upon the responsibility of guiding a team. A team. Late the following year, Jason finally realized that his Daa harnessed Shadow, rather than a draft horse, for Jason's first try on the equipment alone. James instinctively knew what Jason needed. He always knew.

Emotions piled cold against his heart like drifting snow.

Jason swallowed the banana. "Dunno," he shrugged. "I just know."

"I have to swing by my apartment, do you mind?" Hope asked casually.

"It's late."

"I know, but just a few minutes."

"OK."

"Seriously, how do you do it?"

"A pitcher will tell you what he's thinking if you look close enough."

"What's that mean?"

"I pay attention to a pitcher the same way I pay attention to a horse."

"You pay attention?"

"Eekk been ookk is what we say. "I have to be open to what they will do at any moment."

"OK, open."

"The word we use is gelassenheit. It means...calmness. Being calm as often as we can."

"If you were any more calm, you'd be asleep half the time."

He smiled. "That's what I try to do on the ball field, gelassenheit. I try to be calm and open, and see as much as I can, just like working with a horse."

"Give me an example."

"Well, when Scott Tillman, with the Dodgers, is about to throw to first, his pickoff move? He leans more to his left than his right before he goes into his windup. And of course, his eye moves."

Jason opened a bag of kettle corn.

"Moves?"

"The corner of his left eye, he sorta twitches it, like a horse's rump, before he throws to first." Jason pointed to his own eye to illustrate. "He does it every time. I noticed when I watched him from the dugout before I ever got on base."

"You can see that?"

"You can't?"

She pulled into her parking lot and turned to look at him.

"Farm boy, I don't think anyone can see what you're seeing. I'm still not sure what you're talking about." She gestured with her keys. "Do you want to come up? It won't take a minute."

"It's late."

"Come on, it won't take five minutes."

"OK," he said. He followed her up the stairs, but he was hardly listening. His mind was on baseball.

Now it made sense. If other guys couldn't see what he saw, then of course they'd get fooled into swinging wildly. They had no idea what pitch was coming next. Of course they'd get thrown out stealing if they didn't know what the pitcher would do. Was he really seeing the game differently than everyone else?

"I said, do you want anything?"

Jason gestured at a basket of fruit on the counter. "May I have some?"

"Sure, sure, help yourself," she said, pushing the basket toward him. "I'll be right back."

He was growing very fond of her. She was making the English life much easier, and more attractive. Attractive. He thought of her lips. Not for the first time, he imagined life in Chicago. The city and all the people. Suddenly, she was standing beside him again. How long had she been gone? He was really dizzy in her apartment.

"Listen, I have to take care of a few emails and make a few phone calls. Would you be willing to stay here tonight?"

He looked around, lightheaded. "You don't have a couch. Do you have a guest room?"

"I was thinking we could sleep...together." She smiled and ran her tongue across her teeth, which were the bright white of his uniform, not the dull white of milk. He remembered her doing that with her tongue before, but he couldn't remember her wearing lipstick like that.

"In the same bed..." she continued. "Together."

He thought of the moment in Iowa when he first saw her. Her heeled shoes and the shape of her legs. He remembered the way her buttons strained against her shirt in the office. Her whole apartment smelled like her. He tried to remember something, but the smile in her eyes distracted him. He studied the floor as he considered his answer. "We aren't courting, but I guess we can bundle."

"Bundle?" she repeated slowly.

"We don't do it much in Iowa, but I've heard rumors about it being popular back east. Back in the past."

"Okaaaay. What is it?"

"It's from the Bible. Unmarried couples lie on the bed together."

"Now, you have my attention."

"In our tradition, the women get under the covers—"

"Go on," she said. He noticed the look on her face. He hadn't seen it before and didn't know what it meant.

"—and the men stay on top of the covers."

"Well, that's anticlimactic," she pouted, her bottom lip out.

He realized she did that with her lip often, but he had never seen another woman do it. She wasn't like any other woman.

"Bundling is in the Old Testament," he continued, looking at her lips. When had she changed clothes?

"Why don't you stay here and finish off my fruit basket, and I'll get the bed ready for bundling?"

He wondered what her apartment in Chicago looked like. He couldn't begin to imagine all the restaurants they could visit. If he had to be in a city like Chicago, he was glad she would be there for him. Did her Chicago apartment have a guest bed, or would they bundle there, too? Did she wear any shoes that weren't heels?

He looked down to see that he had absentmindedly eaten most of her fruit. He searched the kitchen for a place to dispose of the peels and cores and retrieved another apple from the bowl.

Shuffling down the hall, apple in hand, he heard her muffled words.

"...I know. I miss you, too. Not much longer, now. I'll see you in a week. Yes... Love you, too."

The words echoed like a shout in an empty stadium.

Leeba deekk, tzu? He repeated to himself.

What? Who was she talking to? Not her maam.

Love you, too.

Heat flooded his chest, neck, back, ears.

"Leeba deekk?"

His heart pounded in his ears as he silently stumbled backward.

Feeling as he did when Miller hit him on the head, the walls pitched from side to side like saplings in a violent summer storm.

It was all wrong. All of it. Being there, at her apartment. Being in Arizona, away from home. From his maam. From Faith.

Emotions churned together like the ingredients in a jar of relish. He was sad, angry, humiliated, used, betrayed. Alone.

He had to be home, right then.

OPENING the front door of the air-conditioned apartment was like opening a wood stove—a blast of heat hit Jason's face. Knees weak, he stumbled across the sidewalk toward the street.

His hand was wet. He'd crushed the apple like a marshmallow, the pulp oozing between his fingers. He slung the waste away and began to run.

He suddenly remembered the sea bird that was lost at the edge of the field. It hadn't made its way home. He found it days later, on the far side of the pasture. Dead. Dirty feathers wet and matted.

Blindly, he ran toward the highway, away from Hope. Away from it all.

The bird died lost and alone. Afraid.

He had lied to himself about the bird, just as he lied to himself today. Lied to himself every day, about everything. All lies. Everything.

He ran. Until his lungs burned and threatened to explode, he ran. The muscles of his legs screamed with the pain his heart felt, and he ran.

He was that dying bird, alone.

"Jason?"

Gulping air like a drowning man, he slowed to a walk. Soaked in sweat, he stopped to catch his breath, doubled over, his hands on his knees, his entire body burning.

"Jason!"

Slowly, he turned toward the strange voice.

A face smiled at him from the open window of a car.

"Jason Yoder, right?" the voice asked.

Jason nodded, gasping breath, still unable to speak.

"You need a ride?"

Stepping closer, Jason saw that the driver of the yellow cab was not much older than himself. His skin was the light brown of desert sand in the early evening.

"How do you know me?" Jason gasped.

The young man laughed. "Everyone in Mesa knows you, man. Everyone in Chicago knows you. Hell, everyone in the world knows who you are."

Jason shuddered.

"Where are you going? Lemme give you a ride."

"I am going to the ballpark," Jason said, gesturing vaguely toward the east.

"Now?"

"Do you know it?" He began walking, and the car rolled along beside him.

"Sloan Park? Of course I know it. Everyone knows it." He gestured at the back door. "Get in, I'll take you there, slugger."

"I will walk," Jason said, staring straight ahead, plodding mechanically.

"Man, it's seven miles! Half of that is Rio Salado Parkway. There ain't no sidewalks for you to walk on. Hop in, I'll give you a ride, free of charge!"

Jason stopped, looking toward the road.

"Get in," he repeated. "No charge."

His eyes burning, Jason relented and climbed into the backseat.

"My name's Eddy," the young man said as the car pulled away. "It's a pleasure having you in my cab. Man, for you, I'll even turn on the AC." The blast of cold air made Jason lightheaded.

"Thank you for the ride," Jason said, nodding, resting his head against the seat, his eyes closed.

"Man, you can kill the ball," Eddy gushed, speaking faster than he drove. "I've seen you three times, and you just crush it. Man, that triple against Spinoza, it's like he tossed it in underhand."

Jason remembered the triple. He'd recognized the pitch before Spinoza began his windup. The ball was exactly where the catcher wanted it and where Jason knew it would be. His only surprise was the ball catching the top of the wall, rather than sailing out for a home run.

He opened eyes to see a crucifix and religious medallion hanging from the mirror.

Eddy met his eyes in the rearview mirror.

"You admiring my Saint Fiacre medal?"

Jason nodded.

"He's the patron saint of taxi drivers. Most drivers like Saint Christopher, but I like Saint Fiacre. He's also the patron saint for people with VD," he snickered.

"VD?"

"Venereal disease," Eddy said.

"What?" Jason shook his head.

"The saint for people with venereal disease," Eddy said. "You know, VD. The drip. The clap. STDs."

"Ah, ok," Jason said. He realized he wasn't really listening and didn't want to hear, anyway.

"He's also the patron saint for gardeners," Eddy said. "You'd like that, being Amish, and all."

"How do you know I am Amish?"

"Man, you just like they say," Eddy said, laughing and shaking his head. "Everybody knows who you are, and what you are, and what you can do with a baseball. Man, you already legendary."

Jason looked out the window.

Eddy glanced in the mirror. "You alright, my man?"

"Ya, I'm ok," Jason replied, and then fell silent.

As he pulled into the stadium parking lot, Eddy looked at Jason again. "Listen, there's something wrong, I can tell," he said. "You don't want to talk, that's fine by me. None of my business, and I ain't askin'."

He pulled to the sidewalk and put the car in park. As Jason moved to get out of the cab, Eddy retrieved the Saint Fiacre medallion.

"But I'm a big fan, and I want to help." He handed Jason the metal circle. "You take this. A French saint, born in Ireland, looking out for a cab driver from Arizona and an Amish ballplayer from Iowa."

Jason shifted his gaze from the medal to Eddy's eyes.

"Ain't that the way God works?" Eddy asked. "You pray to Saint Fiacre, he'll look out for you, put in a word with God, right? You know as well as I do, when we pray, God hears us. We're not praying to ourselves. God hears. No matter what happens, no matter how bad things might get, God hears us. Right? Jesus will comfort us. We call on him, and he'll hear us, right? No matter how dark the night, the sun will come up in the morning. We pray to Jesus, and he'll hear." He closed Jason's hand over the medallion. "I'll tell you what. I'll pray for you, you pray for me, OK?"

"OK," Jason replied without thinking.

"So, we'll pray for each other. It's a tough world out here, amigo, take care and walk with God."

⚾⚾⚾⚾

"Jason," Anthony said, flipping on his office light and juggling his coffee cup and the bag containing his breakfast bagel. "Are you alright? What are you doing here?"

"Anthony," Jason gasped, relieved to see the familiar face.

"What's going on?"

"Everyone lies," Jason said, staring at the floor.

"What are you talking about?" Anthony looked at the floor, at Jason's feet.

"Da English... The English. No one is true. It is all fake."

"Tell me what's going on," Anthony said, closing his door behind him.

After a few moments of conversation, Anthony picked up the phone and Jason wandered down the hall in search of a restroom.

"Coach Anderson? Anthony Buchanan down in the media relations office."

"Yeah, Anthony," Skip said, more distant than an upper deck. "Listen, I can't talk now, I've got a problem I'm trying to deal with."

"Jason's with me."

"Thank you," Skip exhaled.

"He spent the night here at the ballpark," Anthony said. "He's really upset."

"What happened?"

"I get the impression it has to do with Hope Chambers, but he's not saying what."

"OK, you'll keep track of him until I can get down there?"

"He asked me to take him home," Anthony said, "right now. He's insistent."

"Annie and I are both at the house. Can you bring him here?"

"No, Coach. He means Iowa home."

Skip's stomach dropped, and the rollercoaster started moving faster.

"What's the plan supposed to be?" Anthony asked. "I know he was leaving spring training early to spend time with his mother."

"Hope was supposed to take him on the train. Can you help him get home?"

"To Iowa? Skip, I hardly know him," Anthony protested.

"He obviously trusts you, and that's what matters."

"Iowa. I don't even have a winter coat; it's in my apartment in Chicago."

"I'll cover any expenses the organization doesn't," Skip said. "You know how important he is to the future of the club. I'll consider it a personal favor if you help out on this."

"Yeah, I'll do it," Anthony said after several long seconds. "You need to call my boss, tell him what's going on. I'll call Hannah in the travel office. But I'll take care of him."

"For his sake, I'd like to keep this as quiet as we can."

Jason entered the office and returned to his seat.

"I agree. From a PR perspective, we need to try to keep this tamped down. He was leaving spring training early anyway, so let's not make a deal about this. He's gone home, according to plan. He'll be the starting pitcher on opening day, according to plan."

"Sounds like a plan," Skip said. "Thanks, Anthony. Is he there? Let me talk with him and I'll explain it to him."

JASON HAD OFFERED nothing but wordless shrugs and nods for more than half a day. They had been reading for hours as the train rolled eastward, Jason poring over the Psalms, and Anthony a novel that grappled with the issues of self-defense, violence, and faith in a post-apocalyptic United States.

Jason broke the silence when he asked, "Do you believe you can lose your salvation?"

"If you think you can lose it, did you really have it to begin with?"

Jason shrugged.

"Look at it like this. People are drowning in the ocean. Some don't even know it. Jesus is on the beach, pulling people to safety like a lifeguard."

Jason had never seen an ocean.

"Once Jesus saves you, and you know you're saved, you're not able to get back in the ocean."

"I don't know. That's not what my people believe. Sin can pull you back in. Scripture says you must work out your salvation with fear and trembling."

"Yeah, Philippians. Other translations say faith, not salvation. 'Work out your faith, with fear and trembling.' Gives it a different meaning, doesn't it?"

Jason shrugged.

"What does Paul say? If you confess with your mouth that Jesus is Lord and believe in your heart that God raised him from the dead, you will be saved. Right?"

As Jason shrugged his response, Anthony mimicked the motion. Jason grinned.

"I suppose in the context of that scripture, you can reject Jesus, deny he pulled you from the ocean, embrace a life of sin, and then lose your salvation. But then that goes back to what I was asking: Did you have it in the first place if this is how you lose it?" Anthony pointed. "I swear on that Bible if you shrug your shoulders at me one more time, one of us is going out that window."

Jason smiled. "I'm not sure what I believe about sin or salvation anymore."

"I'm no theologian, and I'm not a preacher," Anthony said. "I'm just a guy who couldn't hit a curveball, so I got a degree in sports information. Don't worry about what I think, or what other people say, or even what the Ordnung says. Read it for yourself, pray on it, and God will give you an answer, right? God always gives us answers if we're willing to actually hear the answer. Even answers we don't like."

⚾⚾⚾ ⚾⚾

THE RENTAL CAR had barely pulled into the driveway before Jason leaped out. Grace met him on the porch, where they embraced warmly.

Isaac emerged from the barn, pulling on his coat. Anthony carried Jason's bag and followed them into the warm, welcoming kitchen.

"Maam, Onkel, this is Anthony Buchanan. He is a baseball man," Jason said. "He is my friend."

Grace crossed her arms as Isaac turned his attention to the Englishman among them.

"What has been going on?" Isaac demanded in the tone he used when a barn was on fire.

"I'm sorry?" Anthony asked, taken aback. The gas lights hissed like snakes.

"My boy was attacked by another baseball man. Struck in the head— the head— with the baseball," Grace said, striking her hand against her temple. "Taking photographs? And a woman doctor gave him a physical?"

"I'm sorry, I don't know anything about this," Anthony confessed. "I'm not involved in the daily operations of the organization."

"Coach Anderson told us he would protect him," Isaac said.

"I understand your concern, Mr. Yoder," Anthony responded calmly. "But accidents happen in baseball."

"He would not be assaulted here at home, on the farm," Isaac said.

"Assaulted?" Anthony turned a shocked expression to Jason.

"He is seventeen years old, and no one is taking care of him," Grace said, months of frustration pouring out.

"Where was Mr. Anderson?" Isaac said. "We trusted him, and we were wrong. Just as we feared, horrible things happened."

"I'm sorry, Mrs. Yoder, Mr. Yoder," Anthony replied emphatically. "I wasn't aware of any of these incidents. I'm sorry they happened. The fact is, Jason was the finest player on the team during spring training. He is the best pitcher in all of major league baseball. He led spring training in home runs and stolen bases. Despite everything that happened on the field, he is the greatest player in the game."

"Haufa mischt," Isaac muttered as he turned and walked away.

Anthony turned a questioning look to Jason.

"Horse manure."

"...AND there are long stretches, acres and acres of sand where no crops can grow, just the cactuses and weeds."

"Why do they live there?" Faith asked.

They had been talking on her front porch for more than an hour. Across the yard, Adam used a baseball bat to swat the dirt out of a rug hanging on the clothesline.

"I do not know," Jason replied. "I have wondered, but I don't understand. There are many things I don't understand. So much of what they do is unnecessary, like lawns in the desert, like a candle at noon."

They fell quiet.

"Levi Oberholtzer has called on me," Faith said, shattering the silence.

Shock, anger, and jealously flushed red across Jason's neck and ears. "Levi?" Like Faith, Jason had known Levi since childhood. Jason thought him weak—physically and spiritually.

"My Daa likes him," she said, with a flick of her chin. "And he is here. You are not. What am I to do?"

"Tell him to go away," Jason nearly shouted. "We are to be married."

Faith said nothing and looked away. "You will leave for Chicago soon?"

"The day after tomorrow."

"You will do what you must do," she said. He remained silent. "And I will do what I must do."

He studied her with searching eyes, trying to understand, but her expression revealed nothing.

Chapter 15

"Some neighbors have brought your mother newspaper stories," Isaac said in his native tongue, stopping to wipe the perspiration from his hatband. "Stories with photographs of you."

Jason nodded. Dave would be horrified to see him working with his hands, removing and sharpening the plow blades.

"What about being too hochmut?"

Jason nodded thoughtfully. "I have prayed about that a lot. I think of the people watching me, taking pictures. The newspaper people taking pictures. The other cameras. But that's about them, right? What they do, it's got nothing to do with me. It's like the English who take our pictures, at the farmers' market, or even here in the yard. I'm not leading them to sin. Not causing them to stumble. I am just playing a game." He smiled. "A children's game."

Isaac nodded and considered Jason's words. "Yes," he finally said, stroking his long beard pensively. "You are not causing others to stumble, but are others leading you to sin? Perhaps they are, and you do not even realize it, maybe?"

Jason shook his head slowly. "I don't know."

Isaac nodded. "I do not know, either." He looked at the machinery. "I have been thinking about that trip I took to Missouri. When my boys and I went to help rebuild after the tornadoes, remember?"

"Yes, sir."

"I enjoyed that time. Meeting new people, helping others. Being useful."

Jason nodded.

"I met a man. I believe he was from around St. Louis. I do not remember now what he called his faith, but he agreed with us about not posing for photos." Jason nodded again. "I remember, he said something curious. He said, 'Photographs should only be taken of God's natural creations.' Like I say, he shares our beliefs about posing. But I didn't agree with him about that. Isn't man one of God's natural creations?"

"Yes, sir."

"I'd say that man is God's greatest creation, wouldn't you?"

"Yes, sir."

"That is what I thought, talking with that man in Missouri. If it is acceptable to take photos of God's natural creations, then, is it permissible to take photographs of us, because we were created by God in His image? His greatest creation?"

"I don't know. Maybe."

Isaac nodded. "I don't know, either. Maybe. Maybe not."

Jason considered Isaac's words.

SOMEONE WAS LIVING A LIFE.

He was in a strange dining room in a stranger's house inside a train station, eating at a table he didn't recognize.

He saw himself, but he wasn't himself. He was living the life of his teammates and talking to the souls of people he knew, but they were in the bodies of strangers.

The real Jason Yoder was the illusion of a shadow.

There were marble columns in the corners, and the marble floors were covered with large rugs. Thick, rich tapestries hung over the windows. Potted plants held baseball bat branches and leaves of green money.

His suit and tie were made from Italian silk spun by worms that were fed nothing but truffles and mineral water.

He didn't recognize the three children at the table. One of them sported a long white beard. They ate off fine bone China from an ancient dynasty using utensils handmade by indigenous Indians in a Peruvian village. A seabird stood on a chair, blinking in confusion.

A strange woman spoke of private schools and vacations in Ireland and Jamaica. The mother of the children needed her check. All of them needed to get more plastic surgery. She said it was desperately important they hire an interior decorator. And buy a larger jet, because the current plane was too small to carry the children's dogs.

He glanced over to see the dogs at their own table. They were expensive breeds, wearing expensive clothes. The maid served the dogs meat that had been ground and then hand-formed into the shape of steaks. The woman talked about the dog's private school, while the children complained about the size of the ice cubes in the soup.

Above the confusion in the museum dining room, he felt the sound of being loved. He loved her, and she loved him, but she wasn't in the room. She was in another life being lived by someone somewhere else.

Realizing he was still asleep, he tried to focus on the dream, so he'd remember it when he awoke. Was he Joseph, his dreams prophesying the future? Or did he need a Joseph to interpret his dream? But the next morning, all he remembered was the empty space where memories should have been.

⚾⚾

JASON WAS WAITING in the yard when Skip pulled up in his rental car. He watched Skip favor his sore knee as he stepped into the cold, leaving the door open, the engine running and the heat on.

Skip's expression changed like clouds covering the sun.

"You aren't coming." Skip said quietly. The unspoken truth was as clear as the morning's midwestern sky. "I can't say as I blame you. I don't understand, but I don't blame you."

"I will give back the money."

"No, you keep it. That's why it's called a signing bonus. Besides, you earned it."

"Thank you for the chance. I found out. I am good enough."

"You would have been the best there ever was." Skip offered his hand. "If you change your mind, you know where I'll be."

"I will not change my mind."

"I know." Skip smiled softly.

"If I leave, I would never return. So I can't leave."

For a moment, each was lost in his own thoughts and fears, considering what might have been, and thinking of what the future may be.

"It was an honor to know you, Jason Yoder," Skip said.

"And you, Stephen Anderson. Gott segen eich."

"Take care. Have a good life."

Jason watched the road where Skip drove away long after the car was out of sight.

He turned around and looked at his house and the well-worn path to the barn. Memories of his Daa poured over him. Taking slow, considered steps up the driveway, he studied the green yard, the garden, and the fields beyond. He was home.

This was his father's home. One day, this would be his child's home. And God willing, his grandchildren would play on the lawn where he had played as a child. Everything he could see in every direction would one day belong to his children. He could no more leave than he could forget the lifetime of memories here. If he had stepped over the line, he wouldn't have been able to come back. In the end, he really didn't have a choice. He couldn't leave his home.

"BASEBALL IN OCTOBER," the excited announcer gushed, "it can only mean one thing. The World Series. Something the Cubs haven't seen in quite a few years. But this year, the team had a date with destiny. On the first day of spring training, young Jason Yoder left his Iowa farm and turned baseball on its ear. His pitches were like lightning bolts from Norse mythology. At the plate, he was Thor swinging his mighty hammer like there was no tomorrow."

Half listening, Jason flicked invisible dust from his new black hat before carefully putting it on. He made final adjustments to his pressed, clean coat and shirt as a shadow filled the doorway. He fingered the metal circle in his pocket for reassurance.

"...And for Yoder, there was no tomorrow," the announcer continued. "Scheduled to start on opening day, instead Yoder walked away from baseball forever. God only knows where that kid is today, but the Chicago Cubs owe him a world of gratitude. He singlehandedly turned the team around—"

Jason turned off the radio. He removed the batteries from the back and put them, along with the radio, into a small wooden box, which he carefully placed high on a shelf.

"Are you ready?" Grace Yoder asked.

Jason straightened his coat. "Ya. I'm ready."

"It is time," she said. She looked at her son, grown now into a man. "You look fine."

"Thank you, Maam," Jason said, smiling his small smile.

"God has blessed me with a fine son," Grace said.

They looked at each other, warmth curling the edges of their eyes.

"Come," she said, "your wife-to-be is waiting."

Together they left the barn and walked the familiar path toward the house, the yard filled with buggies and horses. The midmorning shadows slowly stretched across the grass as the sun warmed the day.

Ever so slowly, the air began to stir. Fingers of wind brushed Jason's face. The soft prairie breeze rushed across the yard, through the field, and across the endless expanse.

Acknowledgments

This debut novel was 23 years in the making. I began the story as a screenplay when I was a reporter in Iowa. I picked it up and put it down many times over the years. When my daughter was born in 2014, I picked it up in earnest.

I have special thanks to:

Baseball blogger Jackie Howell.

Professional reader Gretchen Kraft, who edited an early draft.

Wes Yoder, who offered a page of notes and suggestions that I took seriously.

With her many suggestions, editor Lindsay Flanagan made the manuscript better and probably deserves a co-writing credit. Now I understand why writers always thank editors.

Samuel Stoltzfus, an Old Order Amish man who read and enjoyed my manuscript. All Amish errors are mine, not his.

The Richmond Flying Squirrels, who graciously allowed me access to the field to take publicity photos and photographer Jay Paul, who took the photos.

Johnny Grub, for his baseball insights. All baseball errors are mine, not his.

A special tip of the hat to the Chicago Cubs who won the World Series before I could finish the manuscript and to the Washington Nationals, who I watched win the World Series while I made final revisions.

"It's a beautiful day, let's play two."

About The Author

Jim Meisner, Jr. is the co-author of *American Revolutionaries and Founders of the Nation* and the author of *Soar to Success the Wright Way*. A former pastor, Jim holds a Master of Divinity degree and writes about faith on his blog www.faithonthefringe.com. This is his first novel. He is planning six more.

This has been an
Immortal Production

CPSIA information can be obtained
at www.ICGtesting.com
Printed in the USA
FSHW022224100720
71656FS